DARK VISIONS

A COLLECTION OF MODERN HORROR

VOLUME ONE

DARK VISIONS

A COLLECTION OF MODERN HORROR

VOLUME ONE

EDITED BY

ANTHONY RIVERA
SHARON LAWSON

GREY MATTER PRESS

DARK VISIONS
A COLLECTION OF MODERN HORROR - Volume One
ISBN 978-1-940658-09-4

First Grey Matter Press Trade Paperback Edition - September 2013

Grey Matter Press
greymatterpress.com

Grey Matter Press on Facebook
facebook.com/greymatterpress.com

Dark Visions Anthology
darkvisionsanthology.com

TO ALL THE SUGARPLUMS,
BUTTERFLIES AND UNICORNS...

TABLE OF CONTENTS

JONATHAN MABERRY

A *New York Times* bestselling author, multiple Bram Stoker Award winner and freelancer for Marvel Comics, Jonathan Maberry knows his horror. Maberry's body of work includes the novels *Extinction Machine*, *Flesh & Bone*, *Ghost Road Blues*, *Dust & Decay*, *Patient Zero*, *The Wolfman* and many others, including the upcoming new mystery-thriller Young Adult series, *Watch Over Me*. His award-winning teen novel, *Rot & Ruin*, is now in development for film, as is his adult zombie novel, *Dead of Night*.

Maberry is the editor and co-author of *V-Wars*, a series of vampire-themed anthologies, co-editor of the forthcoming *Out of Tune* dark fantasy anthology, and is developing other projects for both adults and teens. He was a featured expert on The History Channel special *Zombies: A Living History*.

Since 1978, Maberry has published more than 1200 magazine feature articles, 3000 columns, two plays, greeting cards, song lyrics and poetry. His comics include *Captain America: Hail Hydra*, *Doomwar*, *Marvel Zombies Return* and *Marvel Universe vs The Avengers*. In 2014 he will be launching two new original comics for Dark Horse and IDW.

Maberry teaches the Experimental Writing for Teens class, is the founder of the Writers Coffeehouse and is co-founder of The Liars Club.

He lives in San Diego with his wife, Sara Jo, and a fierce little dog named Rosie.

MISTER POCKETS
A PINE DEEP STORY
BY JONATHAN MABERRY

Author's Note: This story takes place several years after the events described in the Pine Deep Trilogy, of which Ghost Road Blues *is the first volume. You do not need to have read those books in order to read—and hopefully enjoy—this little tale set in rural Pennsylvania.*

* * *

There were towns like Pine Deep.
A few.
But not many.
Luckily, not many.

* * *

The kid's name was Lefty Horrigan.
Real name.
His father was a baseball fanatic and something of an asshole. Big Dave Horrigan thought that naming his only son Lefty would somehow turn the boy into a ballplayer, ideally a pitcher with a smoking fastball and a whole collection of curves and breakers. Big

Dave played in high school and might have made it to the minors if he hadn't screwed up his right shoulder in Afghanistan during the first year of the war. It wasn't shrapnel from an IED or enemy gunfire. Big Dave had tripped over a rock and fell shoulder-first onto a low stone wall, breaking a lot of important stuff. When he got home and got his wife pregnant, he transferred his burning love of the game to Lefty. Papered the kid's room in baseball images. Bought him a new cap and glove just about every year. Took him all the way to Philly to watch the Phils. Subscribed to every sports channel on the Net and had Lefty snugged up beside him from first pitch to last out.

Yeah, Lefty was going to go places. Lefty was going to be the ball-playing star of the Horrigan clan, by god so he was.

Lefty Horrigan hated baseball.

He wasn't entirely sure he'd have loathed baseball as much if his name had been Louis or Larry. Lefty was pretty damn sure, however, that being hung with a jackass name like that was not going to make him enjoy the sport. No way.

He was small for his age. A little chubby, not the best looking kid who ever pulled on a pair of too white, too tight gym shorts in the seventh grade. He had an ass and he had a bit of a gut and he had knocked knees. When he ran the hundred-yard dash the gym teacher threw away the stopwatch and pulled out a calendar. Or so he said. Often.

When the other kids lined up to climb the rope, Lefty just went over and sat down. His doctor's note got a lot more workout than he did, and had more calluses on it than his hands did. Nobody thought much of it. Fat kids didn't climb the rope. Fat kids sucked at gym class, and none of them went out for sports unless it was on a dare.

And it didn't much matter.

Nobody bullied Lefty about it. This was farm country, out beyond the suburban sprawl and infill of Bucks County, out where Pennsylvania looked like it did on holiday calendars. Not the gray stone towers of Philadelphia or the steel bridges of Pittsburgh, but the endless fields of wheat and corn. Out here, a fat kid could ride a tractor all day, or work the barns in a milking shed. Weight didn't mean much of anything out here.

So it didn't mean much in gym class.

Most that happened was people made certain assumptions if you were the fat kid. They knew you wouldn't volunteer for anything physical. They knew you were always a good person to tap for a candy bar. They knew you'd be funny, because if you weren't good looking you had to be funny to fit in.

Lefty was kind of funny. Not hilarious enough to hang with the coolest kids, but funnier than the spotty lumps that orbited the lowest cliques in the social order. Lefty could tell a joke, and sometimes he watched Comedy Central just to cram for the school days ahead. Stuff Jon Stewart or Stephen Colbert said was usually good for a pat on the back or a smile from one of the smarter pretty girls. If he made them laugh once in a while he was part of the group, and all judgment pretty much ended there.

But his dad was still on him about baseball.

Fucking baseball, Lefty thought. *What's the big deal with baseball?*

A bunch of millionaires standing around in a field, spitting tobacco and adjusting their cups as if their dicks were crowded for room. Once in a while one of them would have to run to catch a ball.

Shit.

Lefty worked harder than that pedaling his bike up Corn Hill. That was more of a workout than most of those guys saw in a whole game. And biking all the way across town or, worse, out to one of the farms, probably took more effort than playing a whole series. Lefty was sure of it. Just as he was sure that one of these days puberty would kick in so that he grew tall enough to stretch his ass and gut into a leaner hide. Just like Mom said would happen.

So far, though, he had hair on his balls, hair under his arms, pit-sweat stink that could drop an elk at forty paces and painful erections every time he saw either of the Mueller twins walk past. But he hadn't grown an inch.

At the same time, his Dad was hoping that the growth spurt would somehow unlock the baseball gene that must be sitting dormant in him. Big Dave usually hovered between hopeful expectation and active denial about his son's views on the American pastime.

* * *

He saw someone cut in front of him and head across the street. Old Mr. Pockets, the town's only homeless person. What grandpa called a 'hobo.'

Mr. Pockets looked like he was older than the big oaks that lined the street. Older than anything. Even through the thick gray dirt caked on his face, the hobo's face was covered in thousands of lines and creases. His brown eyes were so dark they looked black, deep-set as they were and half-hidden under bushy brows that looked like sickly caterpillars

Mr. Pockets wore so many layers of clothing that it was impossible to tell what was what. The only theme was that everything he wore—shirts, jackets, topcoats, aprons—seemed to have pockets. Dozens and dozens of pockets into which he stuffed whatever it was he found in the gutters and alleys around town.

Lefty smiled at Mr. Pockets, and the old man paused halfway across the street and stared at him in the blank way he does, then he smiled and waved. Mr. Pockets, for all of his personal filth, had the whitest teeth. Big and white and wet.

Then he turned away and trotted down a side street. Lefty rolled forward to watch him and saw that there was something going on half a block away. So he pushed down on the pedals and followed the hobo, curious about what the cops were doing.

There was an ambulance parked halfway onto the curb outside of Colleen's Knit-Witz yarn shop. And two patrol cars parked crookedly, half blocking the street and slowing traffic to a gawking crawl. Lefty pulled his bike as close as he could get, but all he saw was the chief and a deputy talking in the open doorway of the shop.

The chief of police was a weird little guy who walked with a limp. A long time ago, before The Trouble—and everything in Pine Deep was measured as being *before* The Trouble, or after it—Chief Crow had owned a store right here in town. A craft store, where Lefty's cousin Jimmy used to buy comics. Jimmy was dead now. He'd been badly burned in The Trouble and hung himself six years ago.

Lefty only barely remembered The Trouble. He'd been five at the time. For him it was a blurred overlap of images. People running, people screaming. The state forest on fire. Then all those helicopters the next day.

In school they all had to read about it. It was local history. A bunch of militia guys dumped some drugs into the town water supply. Drove everyone batshit. People thought that there were monsters. Vampires, werewolves and the like.

A lot of people went crazy.

A lot of people died.

Every Halloween the local TV ran the movie they made about it, *Hellnight*, in continuous rotation for twenty-four hours. Though, in the movie, there really *were* monsters, and the militia thing was a cover up.

Lefty'd seen the movie fifty times. Everyone in town had. It was stupid, but there were two scenes where you could see tits. And there was a lot of shooting and stuff. It was pretty cool.

Chief Crow wasn't in the movie—the sheriff back then had been a fat guy name Bernhardt who was played by John Goodman, who only ever played fat guys. But the guys in school said that the chief had gotten hurt in The Trouble and that was why he walked with a limp.

Now the chief stood with his deputy, a moose named Sweeney, who nobody in town liked. Sweeney always wore sunglasses, even at night. Weird.

A friend of Lefty's broke out of the crowd and came drifting over. Kyle Fowler, though everyone called him Forks. Even his parents. The origin of the nickname wasn't interesting, but the name stuck.

"Hey, Left," said Forks. He had a Phillies cap on and a sweat-shirt with the Pine Deep Scarecrows on it.

"S'up?"

They stood together, watching the cops do nothing but talk.

"This is pretty f'd up," said Forks. He was one of the last of their peer group to make the jump from almost cursing to actually curs-ing. Saying 'f'd up' was a big thing for him, though, and he lowered his voice when he said it.

"Yeah?" asked Lefty, interested. "I just got here. What's happen-ing?"

"She's dead."

"Who's dead?"

"Colleen," said Forks. "I mean Mrs. Grady. Lady who owns the store."

"She's *dead*?"

"Dead as a doornail."

"How? She was old. She have a heart attack or something?"

Forks shook his head. "They don't call the cops out for a heart attack."

That was true, at least as far as Lefty knew.

"So how'd she die?" asked Lefty.

"Don't know, but it must be bad. They have some guy in there taking pictures and I heard Sheriff Crow say something about wait-ing for a forensics team from Doylestown."

Lefty cut a look at him. "Forensics? For real?"

"Yeah."

"Wow."

"Yeah."

Forks started to say something, then stopped.

"What?" asked Lefty.

His friend chewed his lip for a minute, then he looked right and left as if checking that no one was close enough to hear him. Actually there were plenty of people around, but no one was paying attention to a couple of kids. Finally, Forks leaned close and asked, "Want to hear something really weird?"

"Sure."

Forks thought about it for another second and then leaned closer. "Before they pushed the crowd back, I heard them talking about it."

"About what?"

"About the way she died."

The way Forks said it made Lefty turn and study him. His friend's face was alight with some ghastly knowledge that he couldn't wait to share. That was how things were. This was Pine Deep and stuff happened. Telling your friends about it was what made everything okay. Saying it aloud gave you a little bit of power over it. So did hearing about it. It was only *knowing* about it, but not talking about it, that made the nights too dark and made things move in the shadows. Everyone knew that.

Forks licked his lips as if what he had to say was really delicious. "I heard Sheriff Crow and that big deputy, Mike Sweeney, talking about what happened."

"Yeah?" asked Lefty, interested.

"Then that doctor guy, the dead guy doctor…" Forks snapped his fingers a couple of times to try and conjure the word.

"The coroner."

"Right, then he showed up and started to go inside, but the sheriff stopped him and said that it was dark in there."

Lefty waited for more, then he frowned.

"Dark? So what?"

"No, look, all the lights are on, see?"

It was true, the Knit-Witz shop blazed with fluorescent lights. And, in anticipation of Halloween, the windows were trimmed with strings of dark brown and orange lights. All of the shadows seemed to be out here on the street. Underfoot, under cars, in sewer grates.

"Yeah, but the sheriff told the coroner guy that it was dark in there. And you know what the doctor did?"

"I don't know, get a flashlight?" suggested Lefty.

"No, dummy, he *crossed* himself," said Forks, eyes blazing.

"Crossed…?"

Forks quickly crossed himself to show what he meant. Lefty made a face. He knew what it was; it was just that it didn't seem to fit what was happening.

Then Forks grabbed Lefty's sleeve and pulled him closer. "And Deputy Sweeney said, 'I think it's *them*.' He leaned on the word 'them', like it really meant something."

They stared at each other for a long time. It was Lefty who said it, "You think it's happening again?"

Forks licked his lips again. "I don't know, man, but…"

He didn't say it, but it was there, hanging in the air between them, around them, all over the town.

Like an echo of last summer.

Nine people died in the space between June second and August tenth. A lot of bad car crashes and farm accidents. In every case the bodies were mangled, torn up.

It wasn't until the seventh death that the newspapers began speculating as to whether these were really accidents or not. That thought grew out of testimony and an inquest by the county coroner who said he was troubled by what he called a 'paucity of blood at the scene.' The papers provided an interpretation. For all of the physical damage, given every bit of torn flesh, there simply was not enough blood at the crime scenes to add up to what should be inside a human body.

In August, though, the deaths stopped. No explanation, and apparently no further speculation by the coroner. It just ended.

They turned and looked at the open door of Knit-Witz.

I think it's them.

Lefty swallowed dryness.

It's dark in there.

"You know what I think?" asked Forks in a hushed voice.

Lefty didn't want to know, because he was probably thinking the same thing.

"I think it's The Trouble again."

The Trouble.

Lefty looked away from the store, looked away from Forks. He studied the sky that was pulled like a blue tarp over the town. It was wrinkled with lines of white clouds and the long contrails of jets that had better places to be than here. A single crow stood on the roof of the hardware store across from Knit-Witz. It opened its mouth as if to let out a cry, but there was no sound.

Lefty felt very small and strange.

Movement to his left caught his eye, and he turned to see Mr. Pockets five feet away, bending to pick through a trash can.

Lefty touched his jacket pocket. He had a Snickers bar and he pulled it out.

"Here," he said, holding it out to the old hobo.

Mr. Pockets paused, one grimy hand thrust deep into the rubbish. Then he slowly turned his face toward Lefty. Dark eyes looked at the candy bar and then at Lefty's face.

The smile Mr. Pockets smiled was very slow in forming. But it grew and grew, and for a wild moment it seemed to grow too big. Too wide. Impossibly wide, and there appeared to be far too many of those big, white, wet teeth.

But then Lefty blinked, and in the same instant he blinked Mr. Pocket's closed his mouth. His smile was now nothing more than a curve of lips.

"May I?" he asked with the strange formality he had, and when Lefty nodded, the old hobo took the candy bar with a delicate pinch of thumb and forefinger. Mr. Pockets' fingernails were very long, and they plucked the bar away with only the faintest brush of nail on flattened palm.

The hobo held the candy up and slowly sniffed the wrapper from one end to the other with a single continuous inhalation of curiosity and pleasure.

"Peanuts," he said. "Mmm. And milk chocolate—sugar, cocoa butter, chocolate, skim milk, lactose, milkfat, soy lecithin, artificial flavor—peanuts, corn syrup, sugar, milkfat, skim milk, partially hydrogenated soybean oil, lactose, salt, egg whites, chocolate, artificial flavor. May contain almonds."

He rattled off the ingredients without ever looking at the wording printed on the label.

Forks was watching the cops and didn't seem to notice any of this happening. Which was kind of weird, thought Lefty.

Mr. Pockets began patting his clothing, a thing he did when he found something he wanted to keep. His hands were thin, with long, spidery fingers, and he went *pat-a-pat-pat-patty-pat-pat*, making a rhythm of it until finally stopping with one hand touching a certain pocket. "Yes," said Mr. Pockets, "this one has an empty belly. This one could use a bite."

And into that pocket he thrust the Snickers bar. It vanished without a trace, and Lefty was so mesmerized that he expected the pocket to belch like a satisfied diner.

Mr. Pockets smiled and asked, "Do you have another?"

"Um…no, sorry. That was all I had."

The smile on Mr. Pockets' mouth didn't match the humor in his eyes. They were on a totally different frequency. One was friendly and even a little sad, but there was something really off about the smile in the old man's eyes. It seemed to speak to Lefty, but in images instead of words. They flitted through his head in a flash, too many to capture, too strange to understand. Not shared thoughts. No more than looking at a crime scene was a shared experience.

"No," Lefty gasped, and he wasn't sure if he was repeating his answer or saying something else. "I don't have anything else."

Mr. Pockets nodded slowly. "I know. You gave me what you had. That was so nice, son. Soooo nice. That was generous. How rare a thing that is. I thank you, my little friend. I thank you most kindly."

It was the most Lefty had ever heard Mr. Pockets say at one time, and he realized that the old man had an accent. Or…a mix of accents. It was a little southern, like people on TV who come from Mississippi or Louisiana. And it was a little…something else. Foreign, maybe? European or maybe just… Yeah, he thought, *foreign*.

"You…," began Lefty but his voice broke. He cleared his throat and tried again. "You're welcome."

That earned him another wide, wide grin, and then Mr. Pockets did something that Lefty had only ever seen people do in old movies. He winked at him. A big, comical wink.

The hobo turned and walked away, lightly touching his pockets. *Pat-a-pat-pat.*

After a moment, Lefty realized that he was holding his breath, and he let it out with a gasp. "Jeez…"

Forks finally looked away from the crime scene. "What?"

"Man that was freaking *weird.*"

"What was?"

"That thing with Mr. Pockets."

"What thing?"

Lefty elbowed him. "You blind or something? That whole thing with me giving him my Snickers bar and all."

Forks frowned at him. "What are you babbling about?"

"Mr. Pockets…"

"Dude," said Forks pointing, "Mr. Pockets is over there."

Lefty looked where his friend was pointing. On the far side of the street, well behind the parked ambulance, Mr. Pockets was standing behind a knot of rubberneckers.

"But…how…?"

Forks said, "Look man, it's getting late. I need to get a new calculator at McIlveen's and get home. I got a ton of homework, and besides…"

Forks left it unfinished. Nobody in Pine Deep ever needed to finish that sentence.

It was already getting dark.

"See ya," said Lefty.

"Yeah," agreed Forks, and he was gone.

Lefty pulled his bike back, turned it under him, and placed his right foot on the pedal, but he paused as he saw something across the street. Mr. Pockets was standing by the open alleyway, but he wasn't looking into it; instead he was looking up. It was hard for Lefty to see anything over there because that side of the street was in deep shade now. But there was a flicker of movement on the second floor. A curtain fell back into place as someone up there dropped it. Lefty had the briefest afterimage of a pale face watching from the deep shadows of the unlighted window. Someone standing in darkness on the dark side of the street. Pale, with dark eyes.

A woman? A girl?

He couldn't be sure.

Mr. Pockets turned away and glanced across the street at Lefty. He smiled again and touched the pocket into which he'd placed the Snickers. He gave the pocket a little *pat-a-pat*, then he walked into the alley and disappeared entirely.

Lefty Horrigan see-sawed his foot indecisively on the pedal.

It was nothing, he decided. All nothing.

But he didn't like that pale face.

It's dark in there.

"Yeah," Lefty said to no one, and he pushed down on the pedal and rode away.

* * *

Lefty chewed on all of this as he huffed up the slope at the foot of Corn Hill, standing on the pedals to force them to turn against the pull of gravity. Aside from Lefty's own weight, his bike's basket was laden with bags of stuff he needed to deliver before dark. His after-school job was delivering stuff for Association members, and now he was behind schedule.

The sun was already sliding down behind the tops of the mountains. A tide of shadows was washing across the farmers' fields toward the shores of the town.

He rode on, fast as he could.

Pine Deep had a Merchants Association comprised of fifty-three stores. Most of the stores sold crafts and local goods to townsfolk and tourists. Lefty and two other kids earned a few bucks making deliveries for people who couldn't spare the calories to carry their own shit to their cars, their homes or, in some cases, to their motel units. On October afternoons like this Lefty enjoyed the job, except for that fucking Corn Hill. In the winter he called in sick a lot, and he never lost his job because people always assumed a fat kid got sick a lot.

Lefty pumped his way up Corn Hill until he reached Farmers Lane, turned and coasted a bit while he caught his breath. He had four deliveries to make today. The first was here in the center of town, and he made the stop to drop a bag of jewelry supplies—spools of wire and glue sticks—to Mrs. Howard at the Silver Mine. She tipped him a dollar.

A dollar.

Which bought exactly what? Comics were two-ninety-nine or a buck more. Even a Coke was a buck and a half. But he pasted on one of the many smiles he kept in reserve and made sure—upon her reminder—not to bang the door. She told him that every day.

Every single day.

Then Mrs. Howard went back to gossiping with two locals about what was happening down at Knit-Witz. It seemed that the town already knew.

The town, he supposed, always knew everything. It was that kind of town.

As he climbed onto his bike, Lefty heard someone mention The Trouble and the others cluck about it as if they were sure bad times were coming back. People threw out The Trouble for everything from a weak harvest to too many blowflies around a car-struck deer on Route A-32. Everything was The Trouble coming back.

It's dark in there.

Lefty wondered if there really was something, some connection. The town might know—or guess—but he didn't. And he didn't like the half-guesses that shambled around inside his head.

He turned around and found Corn Hill again and went three steep blocks up to the Scarecrow Inn to deliver some poster paint.

When he arrived, he saw that the inn was gearing up for Okto-berfest, and there were two waitresses making signs. The bartender told one of the waitresses to give him something. One of the girls, Katelyn, a seventeen-year-old who lived a few houses down from Lefty, gave the bartender's back a lethal stare and gave Lefty fifty cents.

Lefty stood, legs wide enough to straddle his bike, holding the handlebar with one tight fist and staring past the quarters on his open palm into the girl's face. He didn't say anything. Anyone with half a brain should understand. She did, too. She understood, and she didn't give a wet fart. She waited out his stare with a flat one of her own. No, not entirely flat. A little curl of smirk, daring him to say something.

Katelyn was pretty. She had a lot of red curls and big boobs, and she wore a look that told him that no matter what he said or did, this was going to end her way.

Hers. Never his.

Not now. Not ever.

Not just because he was a twelve-year-old fat kid.

Not just because she had the power in the moment.

She gave him the kind of look that said that this was small town America; he was fat and only moderately bright, living in a town that fed on fat and moderately bright people. They fueled the ma-chinery and they greased the wheels. Her look told him, in no un-certain terms, that when she was eighteen, she'd blow this town like a bullet leaving a gun.

She would. He wouldn't.

It was *always* going to be like this. She'd always be pretty. No matter what else he became. Even if he grew a foot and learned to throw a slider that could break the heart of a major league batter. She would always be pretty.

Here in Pine Deep, she had him by the nuts. And she fucking well knew it.

Lefty slowly closed his hand, feeling the coins against his skin. Strangely warm, oddly moist. He shoved his hand into his pocket but didn't immediately let go of the quarters.

Katelyn still stared at him.

They both knew that he would break eye contact first. It was the way it was supposed to work. The universe turned on such immutable realities.

Lefty wanted to tough it out, but…

He lowered his eyes and turned away.

Katelyn didn't laugh, didn't even give a victorious snort. It wasn't compassion or manners. He simply wasn't worth the effort, and they both knew it. In two minutes she would have forgotten the encounter entirely.

He knew he'd wear that moment when they put him in his coffin.

And that was the way these things worked, too.

He went on his way, holding his bike steady with one hand as he began to coast down Corn Hill. When he was far enough down he put his sneakers down and let the tread skid him to a slow stop. Then he took the coins out of his pocket, unfolded his hand and looked at two silver disks. Two quarters. A 1998—and didn't there always seem to be a 1998 coin in every handful of change?—and a 2013. Still new looking even though it was a few years old now.

The coins were still warm. Warmer now for having been in his pocket.

He raised them to his face and peered at them.

Sniffed them.

And licked them.

He had no idea at all he was going to do that.

He immediately pulled his head back, disgusted, wincing, wanting to spit.

Except...

Except all of those were fake emotions, fake reactions, and he knew it. He played out the drama, though. He even went so far as to raise his left hand to throw the coins away.

And yet, after he sat there on his bike for another two or three minutes, he could still feel the coins in his fist, and his fist was in his pocket.

The taste of the warm, damp silver was on his tongue.

He had an erection that he didn't know what to do with.

Not out here, right here on Corn Hill, right here in front of the world.

Lefty felt sick. On some level, he felt sick.

He knew he should feel sick.

He wasn't *like* that. He wasn't a fucking pervert.

Lefty threw the coins away.

Except that isn't what he did.

In his mind that's what he did, but the coins jingled in his pocket as he headed out of town to make his next delivery. With each pump of his legs he pretended that he couldn't hear them.

* * *

Lefty's last delivery was all the way out of town, way out on Route A-32. The Conner farm. The sun was fully behind the mountains now, and although the trees on the top looked like they were burning, the flat farmlands were painted with purple shadows.

"Shit, shit, shit," Lefty said aloud as he rode along.

The Conner's weren't home but there was a note on the door to leave the parcel on the porch swing-chair. He saw that they'd left him a tip.

An apple and a little Post-it that said, "Thanks!"

The note had a smiley face.

He picked up the apple and stared at it.

"Jesus Christ," he said and threw the apple as far as he could. It sailed all the way across the yard and hit the garden fence.

Dad would have approved. A fastball with a nice break down and to the left. A batter would break his heart swinging at that.

"Fuck," he said, annoyed that he'd thrown a good ball. Somehow it felt like an extra kick in the nuts.

He stomped down the steps and along the red brick walkway, then stopped when he realized he *was* stomping. He couldn't see himself, but the image of a disappointed fat kid stomping was disgusting. It disappointed him in his own eyes.

Lefty straightened, squared his shoulders and walked with great dignity to where his bike leaned against the garden gate. A pair of Japanese maples grew on either side, their pruned branches forming a leafy arch over the entrance. Lefty made himself stop and look at the trees for a moment because he was still pissed off.

His eyes burned as if he was going to cry, but Lefty cursed aloud at the thought of tears.

"You're so fucking stupid," he told himself.

He sniffed as he reached for his bike. And he glanced up at the sky and then along the road. There was no way he was going to get home before full dark.

His heart beat the wrong way in his chest as the truth of that hit home. It was like being punched in the sternum.

It's dark in there.

It's dark.

"Yes," said a voice behind him. "It's dark."

* * *

Lefty jumped and whirled. He lost his grip on the bike and it fell over with a clatter.

A woman stood behind him.

Tall.

Pretty.

Short red-gold hair snapping in the freshening breeze. Floral print housedress flapping around her thighs.

Mrs. Conner.

She smiled at him with ruby red lips.

"I...," he began but didn't know where to go with that.

"You didn't eat your apple," she said. "And it was so ripe."

He looked down at the apple. It had hit the fence hard and burst apart, the impact tearing the red skin to reveal the vulnerable white flesh.

But the apple was all wrong. The meat of the apple wasn't white—it was gray, and pale maggots writhed in it. Lefty recoiled from it, taking an involuntary step backward.

He bumped into the post and spun around.

It wasn't the fence post.

It was Mrs. Conner.

He yelped and spun around to where she should have been, to where she just was. But she wasn't there. She was here.

Right here.

So close.

Too close.

Much too close.

The top buttons of her housecoat were open. He could see the curves of her breasts, the pale yellow lace of her bra. The blue veins beneath her skin.

"It looks delicious," she said. "Doesn't it?"

He didn't know if she was talking about the apple or about...

No.

He did know.

Of course he knew.

It's just that it wasn't right. Not in any moral sense. It wasn't right because it didn't make sense. This didn't happen. Not even in his wet dreams. This never happened. Probably not even to the hunky guys on the football team in high school. Not to twelve-year-olds. Not to fat kids.

Not really.

Not ever.

Mrs. Conner moved a step closer, and he simply could not take his eyes off of her cleavage. The half-melon shapes of her breasts defined by shadows that curved down and out of sight behind the cups of her bra and the buttons that were still buttoned.

He stared at those breasts, looking at them, watching the rise and fall of her chest.

Except…

Except.

The breasts did not rise and fall.

Because the chest did not rise and fall.

Not until Mrs. Conner took a breath in order to speak.

"Ripe," she said. "Ripe for the picking."

Lefty slowly raised his eyes from those shadow-carved breasts, past that ruby-lipped mouth, all the way to the eyes of the woman who stood so close.

To eyes with pupils as large as a cat's.

Eyes that, he knew at once and for certain, could see in the dark. In any darkness.

He felt himself growing hard. Harder than before with Katelyn. Harder than in any of his dreams. Hard enough to hurt. To ache like a tumor, like a punch. There was no pleasure in it, no anticipation of release. It hurt, and he knew, on every level of his young mind, that hurt—that *pain*—was the point of this. Of all of this. Of everything in his life and in this odd day. Hurt was the destination at the end of this day. He knew that now even if he'd never even suspected it before.

It's dark in there.

And it was dark out here, too. And darkness called to him from the shadow beneath her breasts.

"So ripe," she said.

And he said, "Please…"

He was not asking for anything she had, not for anything she was. Not for those lips, or for those breasts. Or for any fulfillment of a fantasy that was too absurd even for his fevered midnight dreams.

"So, so ripe," said Mrs. Conner as she reached out and caressed his cheek with the backs of her pale fingers.

He shivered.

Her fingers were as white and as cold as marble.

"And juicy," she said as she bent to kiss him.

With those red, red lips.

Lefty wanted to shove her away. Wanted—*needed*—to run as fast as his stubby legs would go. Wanted to get onto his bike and ride faster than the wind, ride faster than the sunset. Ride fast enough to leave the darkness behind.

That's what he wanted.

But all he could do was stand there.

Her lips, when she kissed his cheek, were colder than her fingers. Her breath, colder still.

"Please," he whispered.

"Yes," she said.

Those were not parts of the same conversation, and they both knew it.

She kissed his cheeks, his slack lips. When he closed his eyes she kissed his eyelids and delicately licked the tears that slid from beneath his lashes. Then she kissed his jaw.

And his throat.

Her tongue traced a line along his flesh, and whenever his heart beat, she gasped.

"Please," he said again, and his breath was so faint, the word so thin, that he knew that it was his last breath. Or, maybe he could take one more. A deep one, so he could scream.

He felt her lips part. Felt the hard sharpness of something touch his skin.

Two points, like needles.

"No," said a voice.

Mrs. Conner was still so close when she turned her face that for a moment she and Lefty were cheek-to-cheek. Like lovers. Like people squeezing into a booth to take a photo. The coldness of her flesh was numbing.

But more numbing still was the figure that stood behind them. Not in the road, but on the red brick garden path, as if somehow he'd snuck over the fence so he could surprise everyone from behind.

A figure in tatters of greasy gray and the faded colors of countless garments.

A figure that smelled of earth and sewers and open landfills.

A figure whose lined and seamed face beamed a great smile.

Mr. Pockets.

* * *

Mrs. Conner said, "Go away."

Her voice was cold, sharp, without the sensual softness of a moment ago.

Mr. Pockets just stood there.

"This meat is mine," snarled Mrs. Conner. And with that she jerked Lefty nearly off his feet, pulling him in front of her. Not as a shield but to put him on display. Her property.

Her...

What?

She'd called him *meat*.

Tears burned channels down Lefty's face.

The old hobo kept smiling.

"Get away," said Mrs. Conner.

He stood his ground.

Mrs. Conner pointed at him with one of her slender, icy fingers. "Go on now," she said in a voice much more like her own, without sex in it but still with passion. "Go on, *git*."

The wind gusted and Mr. Pockets closed his eyes and leaned

into the wind like he enjoyed the cold and all of the smells the breeze carried with it. Lefty thought the wind smelled like dead grass and something else. A rotten egg smell. He wasn't sure if the wind already had that rotten egg smell, or if it came from the hobo.

Mrs. Conner tensed and took a single threatening step toward Mr. Pockets.

"Get your disgusting ass out of my yard, you filthy tramp," she growled. "Or I'll make you sorry."

"You'll make me sorry?" asked the hobo, phrasing it as if it was a matter of great complexity to him. His speech was still southern mixed with some foreign accent Lefty couldn't recognize. "What in the wide world could that mean?"

Mrs. Conner laughed. Such a strange laugh to come from so pretty a throat. It was how Lefty imagined a wolf might laugh. Sharp, harsh and ugly. "You don't know what kind of shit you stepped in, you old son of a bitch."

"Old?" echoed Mr. Pockets, and his smile faded. He sighed. "Old. Ah."

Lefty tried to pull away but the single hand that held him was like a shackle of pure ice. Cold, unbreakable. The fingers seemed to burn his skin the way metal will in the deep of winter.

"Let me go," he said, wanting to growl it, to howl it, but it came out as a whimper.

"Let him go," said Mr. Pockets.

"He's *mine*."

"No," said the hobo, "he's mine."

Mrs. Conner laughed her terrible bark of a laugh again. She shook Lefty like a doll. "You really don't get it, do you shit for brains?"

"What don't I get?" asked the old man.

"You don't know what's going on here, do you? Even now, you don't get it? You're either too stupid or you've pickled what little brains you ever had with whatever the fuck you drink, but you just don't get it. I'm telling you to leave. I'm giving you that chance. I don't want to dirty my mouth on you, so I'm letting you walk away. You should get down on your knees and kiss the ground where I'm standing. You should pray to God and thank Him for little mercies, 'cause I—."

"No," said Mr. Pockets, interrupting.

"What?"

"No, my dear," he said, and there was less of the southern and more of the foreign accent in his tone, "it's you—and anyone like you—who doesn't understand. You're too young, I expect. Too young."

She tried to laugh at that, but there was something in Mr. Pockets' voice that stalled the laugh. Lefty heard it, too, but he didn't know what was going on.

Or rather, he did know and could not imagine how any thought he had, any insight he possessed or any action he took could change this from being the end of him. The hardness in his pants had faded, and now he had to tighten up to keep from pissing down his legs.

The woman flung Lefty down, and he hit the gatepost, spun badly and fell far too hard. Pain exploded in his elbow and knee as he struck the red bricks, and as he toppled over he hit the back of his head. Red fireworks burst in his eyes.

Through the falling embers of sudden pain, he saw Mrs. Conner bend forward and sneer at Mr. Pockets. Her face contorted into a mask of pure hatred. The sensual mouth became a leer of disgust, the eyes blazed with threat.

"You're a fucking idiot for pushing this," she said, the words hissing out between gritted teeth.

Between very, very sharp teeth.

Teeth that were impossible.

Teeth that were so damned impossible.

"I will drink the life from you," said Mrs. Conner, and then she flung herself at Mr. Pockets, tearing at him with nails and with those dreadful teeth.

Lefty screamed in stark terror.

In fear for himself and for his soul.

But his fear became words as he screamed. A warning.

"*Mr. Pockets!*"

However, Mr. Pockets did not need his warning. As the woman pounced on him, he stepped forward and caught her around the throat with one gray and dirty hand.

And with that hand he held her.

She thrashed and spat and kicked at him. Her fingernails tore at his face, his clothes. Her feet struck him in the groin and stomach and chest.

He stood there and held her.

And held her.

Every blow that landed knocked dust from him. Lefty could feel the vibrating thuds as if they were landing on him, the echoes bouncing off the front wall of the Conner farmhouse.

And Mr. Pockets held her.

Inches above the ground.

Then, with infinite slowness, he pulled her toward him. Toward his smiling mouth.

He said to her, "Oh, you are so young. You and those like you. Even the ones you think are old. What are they anyway? Fifty years old? The oldest living in these mountains, the one who came from far away and settled here, the one who made you, he isn't even three centuries old. Such a child. A puppy. A maggot that will never become a fly." As he spoke, spit flecked her face.

Mrs. Conner squirmed and fought, no longer trying to fight. She tried to get away.

Mr. Pockets pulled her close and licked the side of her face, then made a face of mild disappointment.

"You taste like nothing," he said. "You don't even taste of the corruption you think defines you. You haven't been what you are long enough to lose the bland flavor of life. And you haven't acquired the savory taste of immortality. Not even the pungent piquancy of evil."

"You don't...know...what you're...doing..."

Mrs. Conner had to fight to gasp in little bits of air so she could talk. She didn't need to breathe, Lefty understood that now, but you had to breathe in order to speak, and the hand that held her was clamped so tight. He could hear the bones in her neck beginning to grind.

Mr. Pockets shook her. Once, almost gently. "You and yours hunt these hills. You are the boogeymen in the dark, and I suspect that you feed as much off of their fear of you as from the blood that runs through their veins. How feeble is that? How pathetic." He pulled her close, forcing her to look into his eyes. "You think you understand what it is to be old? You call yourselves immortal because some of you—a scant few—can count their lives in centuries. You think that's what immortality is?"

Mr. Pockets laughed now, and it was entirely different from the lupine laughter of Mrs. Conner. His was a laughter like distant thunder. A deep rumble that promised awful things.

Lefty curled into a ball and wrapped his arms around his head.

"If you could count millennia as the fleeting moments of your life, even then you would not be immortal. Then, all you would be is old. And there are things far older than that. Older than trees. Older than mountains."

His hand tightened even more, and the soft grinding of bone became sharper. A splintery sound.

"You delight in thinking that you're evil," whispered Mr. Pockets. "But evil itself is a newborn concept. It was born when a brother killed a brother with a rock. And that was minutes ago in the way real time is counted. Evil? It's a game that children play."

He pulled her closer still so that his lips brushed hers as he spoke.

"You think you're powerful because monsters are supposed to be powerful. But, oh, my little child, only now, I think, do you grasp what *power* really is."

"...please..." croaked Mrs. Conner.

Lefty's bladder went then. Heat spread beneath his clothes, but he didn't care.

"You think you understand hunger," murmured Mr. Pockets as gently as if he spoke to a lover. "No. Not with all of your aching red need do you understand hunger."

Then Mr. Pockets opened his mouth.

Lefty watched him do it.

He lay there and watched that mouth open.

And open.

And open.

So wide.

So many white, white teeth.

Row upon row of them, standing in curved lines that stretched back and back into a throat that did not end. A throat of teeth that was as long as forever. Mrs. Conner screamed a great, terrible, silent scream. Absolute terror galvanized her; her legs and arms flailed wildly as Mr. Pockets pulled her closer and closer toward those teeth.

As Lefty Horrigan lay there, weeping, choking on tears, pissing in his pants, he watched Mr. Pockets eat Mrs. Conner. He ate her whole. He ate her all up.

He swallowed her, house-coat and shoes and all.

The old man's throat bulged once, and then she was gone.

The world collapsed into silence. Even the crickets of night were too shocked to move.

Lefty squeezed his eyes shut and waited, for everything he was to die. To vanish, skin and bone, clothes and all, like Mrs. Conner.

He waited.

Waited.

The cold breeze ran past and across him.

And he waited to die.

* * *

When Lefty Horrigan opened his eyes, the yard was empty. Just him and his bike.

The rotten, shattered apple lay where it had fallen, visible only as a pale lump in the thickening darkness.

Mr. Pockets was gone.

Even so, Lefty lay there for a long time. He didn't know how long, but the moon was peering at him from above the mountains when he finally unwrapped his arms from around his head.

He got slowly to his feet. His knee and elbow hurt almost as much as the back of his head. The pee in his pants had turned cold.

He didn't care about any of that.

The wind blew and blew and Lefty let it scrub the tears off his cheeks.

He limped toward the gate and opened it and bent to pick up his bike.

Something white and brown fluttered down by his feet, caught under the edge of one pedal. It snapped like plastic.

Lefty bent and picked it up. Straightened it out. Turned it over in his hands.

Read the word printed in blue letters on a white background on a brown wrapper.

Snickers.

There was only the smallest smudge of milk chocolate left on the inside of the wrapper.

Lefty looked at it, then he looked sharply left and right. He turned in a full circle. Waiting for the worst, waiting for the trick.

But it was just him and the night wind and the bike.

He looked at the wrapper and almost—almost—opened his fingers to let it go.

He didn't though.

Instead he bent and licked off the chocolate smudge. Then he folded the wrapper very neatly and put it into his pocket.

He wasn't sure why he'd taken that taste. It was a weird, stupid thing to do.

Or maybe it was something else.

A way of saying something in a language he couldn't speak in words. And a way of expressing a feeling that he knew he would never be able to really understand.

He patted the pocket where he'd stored the wrapper.

A little *pat-a-pat*.

Then Lefty Horrigan stood his bike up, got onto it, and wet, cold, sore and dazed, he pedaled away.

Through the darkness.

All the way home.

.

JAY CASELBERG

Jay Caselberg is an Australian author based in Germany.

Caselberg's work covers a number of genres, has appeared in publications world-wide, and has been published in several languages. His long history of fiction writing has received a number of honorable mentions on many "Year's Best" lists.

Caselberg's fiction crosses the boundaries of science fiction, fantasy, mystery and the literary, but all generally contain a dark edge. He is the author of several novels, including his Jack Stein series and his latest, *Empties*, billed as a brutal tale of psychological dark fiction.

A selection of his latest short fiction will be appearing in several upcoming anthologies and magazines.

COLLAGE

BY JAY CASELBERG

It started with a phone call. A simple phone call. No visit. No long faces standing regretfully at the doorway mouthing *"Sorry for your loss"* or any other such platitude. Only a phone call.

The notion still made him furious when he thought back, and that happened often. They could have had the bloody decency to tell him face to face.

Sure, Jo and Marika were not yet husband and wife, they weren't yet living together, but they would have been soon. But he was merely her fiancé.

Sorry for your loss.

Marika had simply been in the wrong place at the wrong time. Or that's what they told him. Well, she was in the wrong place now — a place far away. Sometimes, Joseph thought he could feel her, but it was just the stiff brush of memory teasing his consciousness. Intellectually, he knew that, but emotionally…

Once again, the night was upon him. He stared into the mirror, in preparation, his thoughts on her, on the hollow inside that matched the shadowed wells that his eyes had become, the ever-present grim set of his jaw working with his thoughts. Nothing was fair about this existence. Nothing. But at least he could do something about it. Just as he'd been trying to since that evening, since the face-less voice on the end of the phone had told him what he had never expected to hear.

He sighed.

Already tired of the wordless conversation with his own reflection, he turned away and headed for the door, reaching for his coat, ready to perform his duty. The comfortable, cold weight resting in his deep pocket reassured him. He paused by the mantel, reached out with one hand and traced his finger along the edge of the silver-framed photograph. Her deep blue eyes, the thick red curls of her hair, her pale skin, the bridge of freckles across her nose, all of them looked out at him, gracing him with that little smile. But it was just an image. It wasn't her. He lowered his hand and turned away from the picture.

Jo Pereira had been adjudged reasonably good looking once, but now, with his shadowed look, the fixed jaw line, the brooding brow, he looked more haunted than anything else. And so he was. Haunted by the memory of what they had once had together, and ultimately, that which they might have had.

Some careless driver, over the limit, had taken all that away from him. The car had flipped as it rounded a corner too fast, and Marika, who was just about to cross the street, ended up underneath the wreckage.

There was nothing anyone could have done, and there had been no hope. No hope at all. *A freak accident. Wrong place at the wrong time.* That's what they had said, wasn't it?

He still had her photo by his bed, the small tokens and other things she had given him, including the framed photograph on the mantelpiece. These things were now his shrine. Her shrine. But as the days and weeks passed, he slowly came to the realization that it wasn't enough. Memory was fickle. There was only so much that could be kept alive through keepsakes and photographs.

In the daytime, he still appeared at his drudge of an office job that kept him in body, if not in soul. He had ignored the comments about how pale he had become, the queries about whether he really was okay, if there was anything they could do. When he first shared the news of what had happened, they tiptoed around him on eggshells. Eventually, when he showed little sign of changing, his co-workers accepted that it was the way he now was, and they let him be. It would pass with time. How little they knew... The caring turned to acceptance and eventually complacency, and that was that. Jo didn't care what happened in the daylight anymore anyway. It was in the night, and with the memory of Marika, that he now really belonged.

When they were together, when she was still with him, they'd talked about what they'd do if ever something was to happen to either of them. If there really was anything after this life. They'd make every effort to make sure that they were still together, both of them. *Together ever after.* They had promised. And in that promise, lay the irony.

It had never been a one-sided relationship. Well, at least Jo was still doing his bit to keep the dream alive. Perhaps, just perhaps, if he did enough, she would do her part too.

Jo took the steps from his place one by one, slowly, deliberately. He was in no rush. The night was still young. He opened the front door, stepped out and let it close by itself behind him with a click.

His block was set back from the street, the buildings in front shadowing the drive despite the lights set at ground level around the parking area. He paused for a moment, tasting the night before heading out into the street. It was a calm evening, the air warm. The murmur of the city drifted around him, undisturbed by the noise of wind. He could hear the sound of traffic a few blocks over, grumbling and protesting, marking his eventual destination.

He liked these still nights. They encouraged his resolve. Far better than if it had been teeming with rain or whipped with harsh-fingered gusts. He nodded to himself, and with head slightly down, his hands deep within the pockets of his coat, he walked slowly up the drive, through his murky portal to the night.

His was a small street, sparsely lit, with a number of trees spaced evenly along its length. Despite its proximity to the heart of things, it felt almost removed, and it was not until he emerged from its end that he felt truly a part of the city itself. A little piece of suburbia encapsulated within the depths of the city. He emerged now. As he walked—his steps deliberate but unhurried—he could not help reflecting.

It was after that moment of loss, when Marika had left him, that things became truly different. Nobody had seen her body following the accident. Nobody had been there with her. She had been on her own, and she had died alone, crushed between a weight of metal and the hard black surface of the road, the insensate driver pinned inside.

After the initial grief came something else. Call it obsession, call it anything, but he needed reason. He needed explanation. He had buried himself online, searching for some kind of answer. Joseph needed to truly understand that moment.

It did not take him long to come across the theory of the twenty-one grams that leave the body. That led him elsewhere. He sat transfixed as he processed the words about the *death flash*—that immeasurable surge of energy that passes from the dying to those living who were in attendance at the moment of death. He pictured Marika lying there, her energy lost, her actual being dissipating in that moment as she passed from life. The pain of it worked inside him, a hard ball of frustration and unfairness. He should have been there, been there for her.

He was determined to make amends.

He had a hunting ground now, a place of prospects that had grown over time. It lived within the throbbing depths of the city, a place of nightlife and parties, of rubbish and smells, glitter and neon slicking the dark surface of what truly lay beneath. He crossed the intersection, dashing through a gap in the traffic, just another indistinct figure in a long, dark coat.

He walked along the side of the big sandstone walls marking the edges of the barracks, lost in shadows, and down past the hospital.

As he neared, the sounds grew louder, the noise of the expressway more distinct. A pale light glowed above, full of the scent and hub-bub of life. All of it he noted and absorbed.

His hands shoved deeper into his pockets in readiness. A group of girls walked past, headed in the opposite direction, chattering and laughing amongst themselves. Out for a night on the town, apparently. He tracked them for a while, observing, but there was nothing there, no spark, so he moved on, ever closer to the center of the beating pulse. Almost midnight, and the place was starting to come alive.

Closer now, he passed a glitzy doorway, bright with red lights and stars, glittering. A bald thug stood at the entrance, black shirt, black trousers, arms crossed. A heavy beat, almost below sensation, throbbed from a stairway leading to darkness above. The bouncer gave him the eye as he neared, but Jo let his gaze slip away. There was nothing for him here.

He walked past and into the main strip proper, ignoring the gaze that tracked him. He didn't need the complication, and in this particular part of town, direct eye-contact meant only one of two things: an invitation to conduct business or to fight.

The place was crowded this evening. He crossed another inter-section and passed the kebab shop on the corner, a couple of bunched companions staring up at the white plastic menu board and other individuals leaning forward on the counter to shout their orders, the smell of meat and grease thick in the air. Groups of partiers, young men together, raucous and loud, couples come to see the sights, and women in groups, or pairs, or single and alone. Some of them stood in doorways, waiting, scanning the pedestrians, but he paid them no mind. They weren't what he was looking for. Not at all. He avoided their eyes wherever he could.

About halfway along the strip sat a coffee shop with tall wooden stools conveniently arrayed before the windows, all dark chocolate browns with a dim interior. A number of the locals frequented it, and occasionally, in the daytime, on weekends, Joseph too. But at night, he could take a cup of coffee, find a stool by the window and nurse his drink until it had long gone cold, observing the street and watching.

He ignored the other patrons, and they ignored him in turn. Nobody recognized anyone in a place like this unless you were part of a gathering, and that was good for him. Nobody questioned just what you were doing here. In a place like this it was not polite to ask.

He pulled back the door and entered, ordered a coffee and waited, scanning the outside street while his strong flat white was prepared. He nodded to the guy behind the counter as he took the cup and nursed it over to one of the window seats. He got nothing in return but a blank, passionless stare, nor had he expected anything else. Barely a word had passed between them.

It took half an hour before he saw what he was looking for. This particular evening, he was concentrating on her wrists. He could feel that memory fading, a certain turn, a certain carriage, a sense of pale fragility, and it was time. As the people passed, he scanned them, looking for the shape, the form, the match.

He almost started on his seat when he saw her. She was standing at the edge of the road, talking to another woman, waving her hands around. She had dark hair, tightly pulled back, heavily made-up face, large hoop earrings. It was not the hair or face that mattered tonight. It was merely her wrists.

With his first observation, he guessed she might be one of the local working girls, but she wasn't familiar. She was still deep in conversation, and he slowly lowered his cup and moved closer to the doorway to observe. A moment later, someone pushed past him on the way into the coffee shop. He mumbled an apology as he stepped aside and then out through the open door.

For an instant, he thought he'd lost her, but then noticed her a few paces further down. He sank back against the wall and waited. Her companion turned away and walked off rapidly down the street. Jo's heartbeat picked up a notch. Perhaps. She started up the street towards him and he held his breathing in check. The right direction. She passed, mere steps away from him, and he took a step forward in anticipation. But in an instant she had stepped onto the road and hailed a cab, that perfect wrist held aloft as she flagged it down. She slipped into the back, shut the door and was gone. Jo was left standing on the street staring at the back of the rapidly retreating vehicle, the disappointment turning his expression to a grimace. He turned, scanning, but he could not see anything more.

Two slow circuits of the strip yielded nothing. He was about to retire back to his perch and wait when he saw her on the other side of the street. She was standing, this new one, talking into her phone, her upraised arm holding the device in place, exposing her wrist to view. And on that wrist hung a bracelet. It was hard to make out from the distance, but it looked like it might contain silver charms. Just like Marika used to wear. Jo caught his breath.

With a disgusted look, she snapped her phone shut and shoved it into her bag, shaking her head. She gazed up and down the street and shook her head again. Then, with a heavy sigh, she turned against the flow of people and headed purposefully toward the end of the street.

Jo, giving a glance in either direction, was determined not to lose sight of her. Darting across the pavement between traffic, he barely missed a collision with a cab. He kept sight of the back of her head, long straight blonde hair swishing as she walked, a light cream jacket across her shoulders. Carefully, he narrowed the gap between them. After a couple minutes more, she turned down a side street, and he closed the space between them. As he neared, he could see the bracelet, the wrist. His pulse quickened. With one hand, he reached into his pocket, fingering the cold hardness that was there, touching the serrated edge like a caress.

She turned down another street, this one with less light, the buildings crowding one upon the other like dark witnesses. This was his moment. With half a dozen quick strides he was upon her.

He grabbed her by the shoulder and spun her around, slammed her back against the nearby wall with the flat of his hand. The breath left her lungs with the half spoken word, "What?"

Not hesitating, he pulled back the blade and drove it forward, hard and deep into her upper abdomen, angled. He looked into her eyes, watching as the shock registered and then something else as the understanding came. He could almost taste her breath. And then he felt it, that surge, that moment. He gasped.

Her eyes went wider and then relaxed. Slowly, he let her body slide down in front of him, freeing the blade. He looked at her on the sidewalk in the shadows. Her right arm had fallen across her body, exposed. The silver charms at her wrist seemed to glow in the streetlight from the corner, gleaming, beckoning. Just for a moment he was tempted. He peered down at the wrist that bore them. It was right. It was perfect. He committed it to memory like a snapshot. At the same time, he realized he had no necessity for trophies. He had everything he needed right then and there. It was enough.

Quickly he stooped, wiped both sides of the blade, and then slipped it back into his pocket. With a glance in both directions, he stood. One more fleeting look back down at the wrist and he turned away, striding quickly to the far end of the street.

It didn't take him long to get home through the small, dimly-lit backstreets. Of course there was blood, there was always blood, but there was the darkness of night to blanket him and the dark clothes that he had on to assist. No one really pays attention in the city anyway. He entered the stairwell, climbed the steps to his place and slipped inside. Closing the door behind him, he leaned back against it, his breath coming in short rapid gasps. After a while, he levered himself upright and headed towards the bathroom. Time to clean up.

Later he stood before the mantelpiece looking at her picture in the frame, at her slight, knowing smile, tasting the memories in his mind, affirming that they were right, that they were truly right. Her breasts, the subtle curve of her belly. Her hips, the pale strong muscle of her thigh. The fall of her hair. All that made her what she was. He cut the pieces in his memory, one by one, and shaped their edges to fit, supplanting the ones that had now gone or had faded. He didn't need a knife for that.

One by one, he pasted the pieces one atop the other. She continued to live, would continue to live. He had made sure of that. Death, after all, was only a relative thing.

It might be weeks, it could be months, before another piece would start to fade, become blurry and indistinct in his memory. He would be forced to find something in the night time to refresh it.

The real, sweet irony was that Joseph had ceased to realize that *his* Marika was no longer the same Marika that had departed on that night. There were subtle differences, shades of others, a collection of fragments that resembled, but were not necessarily the same in the end. But for Joseph, that did not matter anymore. He was oblivious. He was committed.

He would keep Marika alive.

His own Marika.

He had photographs to remind him, but that would never be quite the same, would it?

JEFF HEMENWAY

Working out of his home in Sacramento, California, Jeff Hemenway writes in a variety of genres that include both speculative and literary fiction. His short stories have appeared in *Big Pulp* and *Isotropic Fiction* magazines, the latter saying about his work: "Hemenway's writing possesses a rhythmic beauty that approaches music."

His most recent novel—a tale of supernatural intrigue set in an alternate present where Greek pantheism is the dominant religion—is almost complete.

Hemenway enjoys singing with the radio and likes to believe he's pretty good at it. He likes to believe a lot of things that are demonstrably false, which is probably why he started writing fiction in the first place. Also, his wife and kids would be sad if he didn't mention them. He thinks they are amazing, and he's lucky to have them in his life.

THE WEIGHT OF PARADISE

BY JEFF HEMENWAY

"A few things to know." The music was all beat and no melody. Alfred could feel it in his veins, pumping lightning-quick like a heartbeat. "First off, it hurts like crazy."

The girl smiled, little white teeth gleaming between lips the color of blood. Her eyes glinted from within twin caverns traced in smoke, thin slashes of pencil marking where her eyebrows used to be. She wore a white corsage on her wrist.

"I know it hurts," she said.

"Yeah. Second, if you've done any other drugs in the past week, it'll probably kill you."

"I haven't."

"No, look, you don't need to give me some spiel about how clean you are. I'm not your mom. I don't give a shit. But if I get you up there and it turns out you were lying, you die and I have to clean up the mess. I don't want to clean up your mess."

The teeth retreated. Her mouth was all lips now, and the spark in her eyes turned sharp.

"I'm clean. We good to go?"

"Almost. Last thing. It sucks. It's not worth it. Go home and forget about it and do something better with your life."

Another smile and she said: "The best things in life are borne of suffering."

"Uh huh. You've been talking to Xander, I guess?"

"Not actually to him, no. Why, you know him?"

"Never mind. You ready?"

The table was a winking circle in the strobing light of the club. Figures undulated through the gloom, all shadows and suggestions. Her hair was cropped short in places and long in others, with a shock of pink struck down the center that waggled like a sickly tongue when she nodded her head.

Alfred stood up with a wince and rubbed a hand across his bald dome.

"You okay?" she asked.

"Yeah, fine," he lied, massaging the place in the crook of his elbow with fingers bent into wizened claws. "C'mon. You have a car?"

"I took a bus."

"Then I guess we're taking mine."

"You got a name?"

"Alfred."

"Nice to meetcha. I'm—"

"I don't care. Throw down a twenty for the drinks and meet me out back."

"But I didn't drink anything."

"I did. And I tip well. See you out back."

Alfred walked through the club on legs full of acid as the girl reached into her pocket. She threw down a bird's nest of dirty bills and said something that died unheard in the blanket of noise and then followed him outside.

It wasn't raining, but it felt like it should be. Every time Alfred got his fix, he felt there should be some storm raging, something more portentous than clear skies and warm air. He saw the illumination of arc-sodiums and traffic signals and a thousand cars throwing streams of red and white.

She sat next to him in the Ford's threadbare interior looking out the window, silent. Eventually she asked, "Is it far?"

"No."

"How not-far is it?"

"Not very."

"You're awful talkative." She tried on a smile forged of ironic detachment, and the effect was lost in the gloom. "You ever met Sophie?"

"Yeah."

"Wait. Alfred? You're not... Oh shit, you're not Alfie?"

"You win a prize."

"Oh, goddamn!" She slapped her knee with one hand, and the black fingernails against her faded jeans looked like blood spatters. She shook her head and laughed. "Goddamn, you're Alfie! I got picked up by fucking Alfie!"

"Won the jackpot, I guess."

"Oh man, if I'da known I woulda sprung for a nicer corsage. I woulda brought a special needle."

"It's fine, really."

The corsages were Xander's idea, as well as the meeting in clubs. All the ritual, the pomp and circumstance, it was all Xander's doing.

"Will I get to meet Sophie?"

He looked at the girl in the seat next to him, the pink hair on her head, the white flower on her wrist and the schoolgirl glint in her eyes. Raw anticipation. He turned away and clenched the wheel, trying not to pass out.

"Sure, yeah, you can meet her."

* * *

She stood on the cliff where they'd had their first date, where they'd celebrated their first anniversary. Staring out over the black waters, the moon casting halos about her hair and her arms folded around her torso. She said nothing as Alfred dragged himself up the path. Fire gnawed at his bones from within, and his hair was sparse and wispy from the chemo.

"You're trying to kill me," he gasped. "It's not like I have long left anyway, why are you trying to kill me?"

She turned and smiled from within the dark circle of her face, her hair tracing jet streams in the wind. "You're not going to die," she said. "I think we did it."

"Did what?"

"What do you think, dummy?"

"You...?"

"It might not strictly be a cure. I don't think so. But it doesn't matter anymore."

He stood before her, and the wind whipped her dress about them, wrapped them together like a tandem mummy. She threw her arms around him as he struggled to lift his own and settled for resting them against her hips. Her face still lost in the darkness except for her grin.

"It doesn't matter?"

"I think we just made the disease irrelevant. Maybe all disease. I'll know when we get you back to the lab."

"Wait, like now? Tonight?"

"It's up to you," she said, and her mouth widened. The smile of an elder god who has just made the world. "When would you like to stop dying?"

* * *

Inside Alfred's apartment, motes of dust rode the air like locusts, and light poured feebly from an antique green lamp Sophie had bought him for a birthday, or maybe for Christmas. The girl sank into a black leather chair and looked idly for a remote control while Alfred rummaged through a kitchen drawer.

"Nice digs. I see the housekeeper is on leave."

"I don't spend much time here. You're welcome to leave if it offends you that much."

"No, sorry. Just commenting." A drawer slammed and another slid open and Alfred muttered something profane. After a minute he grunted and there was another slam and he walked into the living room and sat on the sofa across from her.

The girl eyed the syringe in his hand. "You sure that's clean?"

"Yeah. Doesn't much matter anyway. Ready?"

She started to say something, but he'd already unbuttoned his shirt cuff and rolled it up past his elbow. The needle sank into flesh, and the syringe filled with crimson fluid. He pulled it out, held it up and tapped it for reasons he had never quite understood.

The girl had already removed her jacket and was leaning over with one elbow resting on her knee, her fist clenching and unclenching.

Alfred took her wrist in one hand, the pulse beneath his fingers fast and fevered. He brought his face in close and stared at the crook of her arm, then lanced the fat, blue vein with a clumsy jab.

"Ow, damn," she said. He thumbed down the plunger until the syringe was empty, then removed the needle and set it on a dusty glass end table and leaned back. "You could learn to be a little gentle."

"Now we wait," he said.

"How long?"

"Ten minutes." He shrugged. "Fifteen. It'll be pretty obvious."

"Can we watch the TV or something?"

"Nothing on. I don't have cable."

"A movie then...?"

"Don't have a DVD player."

"Oh. Wow. You're loads of fun."

The girl leaned back and held her arm with one hand. A bead of blood grew to the size of a pinhead and then to the size of a ladybug before stopping.

"So this is what cured you, then? That's what I heard, that this was some cure for something?"

"Acute myeloid leukemia," said Alfred. "Pretty rare. Has a five-month survival rate around forty percent. I got diagnosed after Sophie and I had been together a couple years. Her team had already been researching blood disorders. It was sort of her thing."

"I guess it was like fate."

"Whatever. Anyway, the treatments they'd been working on had looked promising. It was nowhere near ready for human trials, but..." Alfred closed his eyes and sank back into the couch. "I just trusted her. She was pretty smart."

"I guess so," said the girl. "Curing disease. Inventing the high to beat all highs. Sophie was one helluva overachiever."

Alfred shook his head. He could feel the blood squelching inside him like napalm. "She didn't really cure disease. She just made it so it didn't matter anymore. She figured out how to slow down the metabolism, basically stop it. She thought if she could slow things down, maybe the leukemia wouldn't move so fast, maybe she could buy me a few more months, or years."

"So how's it work?"

"How would I know? I was a paralegal. Something goes in the blood, makes everything slow down. The rest is all jargon to me."

"I, umm." Her voice worked for a second, and her eyes rolled upwards like she was searching for the right word. Then they kept going until there was nothing visible but white.

Her mouth opened into a silent scream, and her fists pounded against the couch. Her legs kicked, and she fell from the chair onto the floor with a muted thump. Fists pounding the rug, the table. Legs kicking over a magazine rack filled with year-old issues of *Time*, *Newsweek* and *Popular Mechanics*. Her chest heaved in and out like something was trying to tear loose from her lungs, gasps of air whistling between her lips. Then her chest stopped and her legs stopped and her fists went slack and she stared upward with unseeing eyes like some game animal, dead and discarded.

"Like I said, pretty obvious."

He pushed aside the magazine rack and knelt beside her and

drew a syringe-full of blood from her other arm, then tapped the syringe and rolled up his other sleeve.

* * *

"Babe? You awake? Alfie?"

Things went from black to gray to a muted fuzz of insinuated shapes and finally to a blurred approximation of Sophie's face. His tongue felt like a wadded sock, and every limb was dull and throbbing. He closed one hand into a fist and then opened it again.

"Can't move well. Thick... Like... Moving through... Syrup... Sophie?"

The blur resolved into a grin, and her hand was on his face, soft and cool, rubbing what little hair he had away from his forehead and behind his ears. She stared down at him, triumphant. Blue eyes like the crystal sheen of ponds in winter.

"It'll take some getting used to, probably." White, antiseptic light shone from behind her head. "The process makes your blood more viscous. It'll make moving around a bit stiffer at first, but I think you'll build up the muscle mass to overcome it. The real trick was getting oxygen to your cells without the blood actually flowing. Keeping electrical impulses moving. But I think I got it now. I think this'll work. Here's some water."

She held out a paper cup.

Alfred pushed himself upward on his elbows and grimaced at the pain in his joints and the weight of his paper gown. He sat up and took the cup. It weighed a thousand pounds, and as he moved it the six miles to his mouth she went on.

"You won't really need food anymore, but it won't hurt to eat. You won't metabolize anything, because you don't need to. Water is still important. I don't think dehydration will kill you, but it can make you feel like hell. I'm guessing at a lot of this." She peered down at him. Her smile didn't falter. "We'll just have to wait and see."

"I thought this was all still really early? You didn't tell me you guys were this close."

"I didn't want to get your hopes up. Anyone's, really. The stuff I was trying wasn't exactly in accordance with established practice, so..." She shrugged. "The first batch of rats saw an increase in expected survival time of seventy percent. I ramped that up a little."

"A little? How much is a little?"

"Umm...as of today...twenty-eight hundred percent. And going. The little buggers won't die." She laughed and her eyes shimmered. "God, I'm giddy. If this takes, Alfie, it's just—"

"I'm not going to die, then? The leukemia, it's...?"

"Still there," she said. "But like I told you, it's irrelevant. No metabolism to spread the disease around. No way to wear out your organs, no way to keep poisoning you."

Sophie stood and walked to a steel table littered with gleaming tools of unstated purpose. She picked up a needle and walked back to where Alfred was stretching his legs and his arms, spreading his fingers outward and wiggling his toes and smiling.

"The ache is going away already."

"Yep. Pretty soon you should feel more or less like a pro athlete. And it'll stay like that."

"So how long?"

"A really long time. You won't get sick. You won't die. Don't know if I can do anything about the hair, but I think you'll look cute clean-shaven. Give me your arm."

He held it out and felt as if he could hold it there forever. "What are you doing?"

She stabbed his arm with the needle and he winced.

"It's my turn."

"What?"

"If I'm right, then I just turned you into the fountain of youth, baby. And now I want a drink."

* * *

The girl lay on Alfred's sofa with her arms placed neatly at her sides and a mostly-flat pillow beneath her head. He thought back to Tobias, lying on his bed in just the same way. The flesh slashed across his wrists and up his arms in a long T-shape, weeping striations of skin and fat and muscle and frayed ligament. A great slit opened up across his throat like a parallel smile, glinting with exposed tissues in the dirty yellow light of Tobias's bedroom.

The girl's eyes flickered open, and Alfred blotted her forehead with an old washcloth that had been a vibrant blue fifty wash cycles ago. He smiled at her and helped her sit and offered her a paper cup of water.

"Drink this. It'll make your tongue feel less horrible. Water's important."

Her lips smacked a few times and turned down at the taste and the feel. She tried to lift her hand to the cup and failed. Alfred held it up to her lips and tilted it back as she took greedy swigs. Water ran down her chin and neck and dripped into her shirt.

"Wha. Fuh."

"I told you it hurt."

"Wha-fuck? Was. That? God."

"The pain'll subside. It's probably mostly gone already. You'll feel tired for a few minutes, and then you'll feel fine. And then you'll feel incredible. More water?"

"Yeah." She sat and wiped her forehead with her hands, wiped the sweaty mop of hair back from her face, swung her legs down to the floor and twisted her neck left and right.

"Like I said, water's important." From the kitchen came a liquid roar and then the plip-plop of ice cubes. Alfred walked over and sat in the leather chair and handed her the water. She emptied the glass in two gulps, and this time most of it went down her throat.

"Hey," she said, "can I, you know, stay here a few minutes? Or do you have someplace to be, or...?"

"You can stay here for awhile, yeah. I have nowhere to be."

"God, that was...that was intense. Glad it's over." She laughed, and the pink hair-tongue flopped over her face. She seemed not to notice. "I so hate needles. I'm almost surprised I went through with it."

Alfred watched her, and she looked around self-consciously, somehow smaller now. Her eyes crystal blue. She still smacked her lips and licked at them.

"You know this isn't the last time, right? You know you have to keep doing this, right?"

* * *

Sophie was quiet and clinical the first few weeks as they went about their days in hopeful uncertainty. She ran tests and poked him and prodded him and ran more tests and nodded thoughtfully and explained things in impenetrable science-speak. After that she grew confident, then proud, and after four weeks, as she and Alfred and Xander and Tobias sat in her uptown apartment playing cards and emptying their third bottle of Grey Goose, she let slip.

"So hey, Alfie's cured now. I thought I should mention it." She smiled at her hand. "And Tobias, I can see your damned cards. This is why you're still just a lab assistant."

"Wait. Cured? What? Huh?" asked Xander. He sat askew on the couch in a black shirt and black pants, black hair swept back with sweat and product, tongue thick with vodka.

Tobias rubbed the perpetual stubble on his chin and tried to will his eyeballs into focus.

"The treatments." said Sophie. "I tweaked them a little."

"Tweaked? How'd you get from where we were to curing Alfie's leukemia? Where were the human trials?" Xander questioned.

"I skipped them."

"You fucking what?" Xander's jaw dropped in apoplexy while Tobias grinned and poured himself another drink.

"It was Alfie. It was getting bad. Tell them, Alfie."

"It was getting bad," Alfie agreed.

"And now?" Sophie offered.

"Now...not so bad."

"Jesus Christ, Sophie, Jesus. Fucking. Christ. I mean, okay, glad you're not dead or whatever Alfie—"

"Thanks."

"But...Sophie, what you did. I mean, how do you know what you did is even sustainable?"

"I know. We're not dead, right?"

"Wait, we?"

"I did us both."

"What? Why? You don't have cancer, Soph. Why the hell would you treat yourself for a condition you don't even have? Are you god-damn crazy?"

She explained the process and her methods. She spoke of cures and of immortality in the cold, white diction of experimental medicine. Tobias nodded occasionally as if he understood more than every fourth word. Alfred stared at Sophie with a big, toothy grin. Alcohol still affected him in those days, but his drunkenness that night had little to do with vodka.

Sophie stopped speaking. Everything was quiet.

"Good Christ. That's, that's crazy. And it worked? It's stable?"

"It's stable."

"And you two..."

"We're gods now, Xander."

Xander poured himself a shot and downed it, poured another and downed it, and then the bottle was empty.

"Gods. Shit. I'm your partner, Soph, and you never told me all this? You just go and make yourself fucking immortal and this is how I find out? How long we been together, Soph? Since grad school, that's how long. And you don't even tell me. Fucking hell."

"I'm going to the board with it next week," she said.

"You can't. Not with what you did, Soph. They'll fire you. If you're lucky. We need to take this through proper testing first. We need to get this to human trials. Make it legit."

"Okay, fine, we'll make it legit. Getting approval for human trials is going to be months, though. Years. You know how they are." She downed a shot.

"All this time," said Xander, while Tobias lay on the couch with his eyes closed and his jaw working silently. "And this thing works."

"Of course it works. You know me. You know I'm sure."

"Been on it a month?"

"Yep."

"How are the rats?"

"Little fluffy super-rodents."

"Fuck it, then. You owe me. Let's go."

They called a cab and stumbled out into the gray haze of an urban midnight, and by the time the early morning sun was jabbing through the blinds and across their flesh, they were a pantheon.

Two months later, Alfred and Sophie were laying in bed recovering from a weekend of clubbing while some movie played on the television. The sound of Xander pounding against the front door echoed down the hallway. Alfred pulled on sweatpants and slogged down the hall and opened the door. Xander stomped in with a black towel wrapped around one hand like a swollen boxing glove and sat on the couch and opened the towel. Something small and pink rolled out and tumbled to the floor as Sophie walked in wearing a robe.

"What the hell, Xander? It's...I dunno, some time or other..."

"What the hell? Look at this!" He reached to the floor, then held up the tiny nub that used to be the top inch of his thumb. "I was working on some goddamn shelving for my room and the saw slipped and now this. What do I do with this, Soph, huh?"

Alfred stared in horror.

Sophie dropped onto the couch next to Xander and looked at the shredded gore of his hand and the orphaned digit between his fingers and laughed.

"What? This isn't goddamn funny, Soph. No metabolism means no healing, right? There's no way to fix this. I get to start the rest of eternity with nine goddamn fingers and you sit there laughing your head off."

"No," she said, wiping at eyes that no longer knew how to shed tears. "It isn't funny. Wait, wait, yeah, it really is. It's completely hilarious." More laughter. "But no, I have an idea. I thought something like this might happen. We need a cosmetic surgeon. I know a guy, back from in school. He's really good."

"Wait," said Alfred. "What are we going to tell him? We can't just have him fix us up. He's gonna wonder why the thumbless guy isn't actually bleeding. Why there's no healing or clotting or anything going on."

"No," said Xander, "this is good. This'll work. I think we can make a pretty compelling argument for him to help us." He mimed pushing a needle into his arm. "You know, with the right incentive."

The surgeon's name was Tony, and he was a little Italian guy with a nose like an old yam and big eyes that always looked on the verge of tears. He was as good as Sophie promised, and he snatched the opportunity for immortality with a zeal that Alfred found just a little scary. Xander was patched up good as new, and the seam on his thumb where the laser melted his flesh back together was only visible with a careful eye.

The pantheon metastasized after that. Xander opened up to a lab assistant who wore her skirts too short, her top too small and giggled like a beach girl from some fifties surfer flick. He converted her and then he fucked her and two weeks later he left her with nothing but a blur of memories and the gift of life everlasting. Tobias offered up godhood in exchange for some dental work he couldn't afford, to his buddy from back home when he came to visit one weekend and to the cute girl at the bar down the street from his grungy apartment.

Meanwhile, the research continued at a snail's pace as Sophie and Xander tried to grant legitimacy to her brainchild. It was conducted in the spare hours between clubbing and parties and long weekends that stretched ever longer. The study of life-everlasting gradually edged out by time spent living.

It was six months before Alfred felt the first twinge of pain in his bones and in his veins, like the sting of antiseptic on an open wound. At first Sophie thought the process had failed, then she ran a battery of blood tests.

"It's temporary," she told him one night as he sat huddled in her bed, an empty bottle of ibuprofen dimpling the comforter at his feet. Pain killers didn't work on them anymore. Anesthetics didn't work. "The process, it...apparently it doesn't last forever."

"So, what, I'm going to die anyway?"

"No. You won't die. That part's permanent. But the pain will grow. It's a little bit like withdrawal."

"What about the rats?"

"The rats are still fine. This is...I don't know. Humans are...different. If you don't get another hit, the pain will keep ramping up. But you'll never die. I'm so sorry, Alfie, God. I'm...I had no idea."

He put his hand on his face, pressed it hard against his forehead and down to his nose, down to his chin, trying to blot out the pain with pressure and failing. His eyes closed, everything black and empty, and when he opened them again Sophie was there, mouth turned down and eyes wide.

"Why aren't you going through this?" he asked.

"I will. Xander and Tobias would too, except they keep doing conversions. The fresh blood, it kind of reboots the process. If you want to kill the pain, we need to find you someone."

"Find someone to do...this to, you mean. Find someone to subject to all of this."

"Find someone to grant eternal life," she said and stretched her mouth into a false smile.

"Eternal life." Alfred closed his eyes. In the deep black behind his lids all he could see was the pain.

* * *

"So how often?" asked the girl. She sat on the couch hunched over, rubbing her palms between her knees as if there was a chill in the room.

Alfred lay draped over his own chair, feeling hot but not sweating, his face not flushing. He stood and walked towards the kitchen.

"The pain sets in after a few months. Maybe six at the outside. You can do it as often as you need to, just has to be someone new. However the process works, it needs fresh blood."

"Can I just, you know, stockpile? Get a big vat or whatever, just draw from that?"

"No. It doesn't work that way."

"Well, why the fuck not?"

"I told you, I don't know." He pulled down a tall, cleanish glass from the cupboard and filled it with bottled water from the refrigerator. "I don't know how this stuff works, or why. But it has to be from a new source still pumping fresh blood. You inject them with your blood, the stuff takes effect, and then you take some of theirs and shoot it back into yourself, and it resets the clock. That's what I know."

The girl looked at Alfred and then at her own feet clad in sneakers that were once white. Black socks in rumples around her ankles.

"You asshole."

He took a swig and wiped his mouth on his sleeve.

"Yes."

* * *

He hadn't seen Sophie for two weeks when he went to Tobias's place and knocked on the door. The fluorescent light down the breezeway flickered, the left half burnt out, an eye in mid-wink. Across the way a moldering gray mattress was propped against the wall next to someone's door. The handrails leading downstairs painted in pigeon shit.

He did a mental twenty-count and rang the bell, then counted again and pounded against the door hard and yelled for Tobias to open up. Finally he tried the door himself, and it was unlocked. He went inside.

The smell of rotting food struck him. He turned on the lights and things skittered for cover of darkness. Dishes piled in the sink, plates crusted with food that looked untouched by anything with fewer than four legs.

"Tobias?"

He walked into the back of the apartment, to the bedroom, and pushed open the door. Tobias lay on a naked bed, sheets and blankets crumpled at the foot, his arms sliced open to the elbows and his throat slit. The knife on the floor beside the bed brown with old blood.

"I can't die," said Tobias. He had nicked his windpipe and the air whistled through the hole as he spoke. "I tried but I can't. It hurts so bad."

"Jesus, Tobias. How long have you been here?"

"A few days. I don't know. I've been trying to just will myself to death, and it's not working. I can't do this to people, Alfie."

"You talked to Sophie."

Alfred moved to the bed and sat down. He took Tobias's hand in his own and held it. The flesh around the wounds rippled and pulsed from the pressure. "How long ago did you talk to her? I can't find her."

"She was here a while ago. Maybe a day? Or a few hours? We talked, and then she said she had to go. She didn't say where."

"You need to get yourself fixed up. You can't just stay like this. Go find Tony, get him to take care of you."

"I don't know where he is. I think he's with Xander somewhere, but I don't want to talk to Xander."

Xander had been busy, sweeping through clubs, planting gossip and rumor, building a mythology. He spread the process through the young and beautiful, through models and aspiring actresses, investment bankers and agents. It seeped through the city's veins and the word spread and the pantheon grew. Last Alfred heard, Xander was building followings in Italy and France. Setting down roots. Creeping into the cultural marrow.

"I'll find him. Just...just don't go out like this, okay? I'll get Tony to help you out."

"Alfie, don't leave me here. It hurts, please, just…it hurts. I don't want to be alone."

"I'll be back, I promise." He squeezed Tobias's hand and could hear the squish of flesh and layers of fat, feel tendons scraping together.

"Don't, Alfie." But by then he was already up and out the door and into the night.

He found Xander in some club, sitting at a booth between a pair of pretty girls with white corsages on their wrists, talking and laughing with an arm around each one, hands floating above barely-concealed breasts. Alfred sat at the table across from him, and Xander flagged over a woman in a short skirt and asked her for a gin, neat.

"I don't want a drink, Xander. I want to talk to you."

"I'll take the gin, then, and give my girls more of whatever they're drinking. Don't skimp on the umbrellas."

"Stop this, Xander. We can't do this."

Xander's smile remained fixed. The girls were probably flying blind by now, but Xander was dead sober behind the pyramid of shot glasses piled on the table.

"No, we have to do this. The more people we get, the better the chance to find a cure. Make it permanent. Right, girls?" Their heads lolled and their faces brightened with precarious smiles.

"Bullshit. You're not looking for a cure; you're looking for a goddamn army. You're building a staff of groupies. When was the last time you were even in the lab? Making it legit, remember? Hell, do you still even have a job?"

"Screw legitimacy. I'm building our pantheon, Alfie. I'm building a paradise."

"You're hurting people."

"The best things in life are borne of suffering."

"What the hell is that? Did you make that up?"

Xander shrugged and detached an arm from one girl long enough to throw back his gin.

"Do you tell them?" Alfred asked. "Before you convert them? I know Sophie talked to you about it, I know you understand. Do you tell them?"

Xander leaned forward and set his elbows on the table, his fingers pressed together in a teepee. "I am making gods, Alfie. Do you get that?"

"We're not gods. There's a word for what we are, and it's not gods."

The smile again.

"Whatever. Did you have anything else to say, or did you just come here to shit on my good time? I think my girls are getting bored."

"I think they're past the point of feeling much of anything. Where's Sophie? Have you seen her?"

"Not for maybe a week now."

"Damn it!"

"You two have a spat or something?"

"Never mind. If you see her, tell her I'm looking for her. Meantime, call Tony and tell him to get over to Tobias's place. Guy messed himself up bad."

Alfred got into his car and drove to Sophie's house for the umpteenth time and revisited her favorite places and found no leads. Nothing but loud people living loud lives, and everywhere he went there were one or two people with white flowers on their wrists, some waiting patiently or maybe looking at their watches, some chatting with beautiful strangers with wide smiles and expensive clothes.

He was returning to Tobias's place when the phone buzzed in his pocket, and he pulled it out. It was Sophie.

"I'm so sorry," she said, and the words were almost lost against a symphony of roars. "I can't do it, and it hurts. I'm just so sorry, I didn't mean for any of this."

"Sophie, where are you, let me come get you. Sophie—"

"I'm sorry. I love you, and I wish I could—"

There was more, but it was swallowed in the din, and then the line clicked off. Silence.

* * *

Alfred drained his glass. "You said you wanted to meet Sophie. That still the case?"

"Whatever. Yeah, introduce me to her. May as well get the five-star experience while I'm here, right?"

"C'mon. She's in the bedroom."

Alfred stood and walked towards the back of his apartment, and after a moment the girl stood and followed him. He opened a door into a square of blackness, reached inside and flicked a switch. Light washed over a carpet specked with detritus, a few items of dusty furniture, an empty bed.

"Hey Soph, we have company."

"What's this?" asked the girl. "Where the fuck is she?"

* * *

Alfred pulled over and closed his eyes. In his mind he heard the roar from the phone—the rhythmic crashing, the howl of wind.

He was at the point in twenty minutes. He leapt out of the car with the lights still on, the door still open and the engine popping in the cold. He ran up the path to the cliff. He could see the end, and nobody was there, but he ran anyway, trying to will her into existence, standing at the apex of the cliff like a figurehead, good old Sophie, strong and reliant and eternal.

The moon was out and nearly full. It shone down like a beacon, illuminating the rocks below. Alfred could see her with digital clarity.

Minutes passed like hours as he crawled over the staccato terrain at the cliff's base, drenched and freezing from the mist, deaf from the crash of waves and the claxon of the wind.

He saw the mess of her smeared across the rocks, jagged things bared at the night sky in an idiot's grin. One hundred feet above, the point loomed over him like an accusation.

He scrambled over pebbles and over bits of Sophie that hung in tatters, licked by waves. Counted her limbs and they were less than four. Her stomach ripped through by one great spire and her head bent at a crazy angle. Crystal eyes stared at him, and speckles of seawater on her face might have been tears.

Her mouth moved.

"Alfie."

She smiled.

"God, Soph, my god, what...we could have fixed this, baby."

"No fix. Hurts." No sound came from her lips, but it didn't matter against the pound of the surf. "Kill me."

"I can't! I, I don't even know how!"

"Kill me, please."

"How?"

Her lips moved again, but Alfred couldn't make out the words. Then her mouth fell still, and it was just her eyes, staring at him. Blinking and pleading.

He stood and held the spike of stone piercing her gut, slippery with water and other fluids, and kicked at its base. Bits of shale flaked off, and he kicked again and again until his foot was numb. The feeling came back and it was a fire in his heel and in his ankle and up to his knee. He kicked until the rock splintered and gave. He knelt beside her head and smiled and told her he loved her.

Then he stabbed at her neck with the makeshift dagger until the flesh gave, until the tendons ripped loose and the bone shattered and her head came free. Her mouth still worked and her eyes still stared and he cradled her head in his lap and wept phantom tears and screamed and wept some more.

Hours later her mouth grew still, and the last light winked from her eyes. He pitched her head into waters that grew gray with the coming dawn, then drove to an all-night club and found a young girl with pale blue eyes and a flower on her wrist, took her home and made her a goddess.

* * *

"What's the game here, guy?"

Alfred walked to a dresser on the far wall and picked up a little wooden box from atop it. He brought it to the girl and opened it. Inside was a lump of cloth the size of a fist. He set the box on the bed and pulled it out.

"She was the last one to try it," he said. "No more suicide attempts after her. Not even Tobias. Because even now, they're not sure she's dead."

He held the lump in one hand and started to unwrap it, pulling the cloth off one layer at a time.

"Last I heard, Xander's numbers were about six hundred strong. This was months ago. By now it's probably in the thousands. Eventually he'll get around to converting some doctors. Maybe then someone will get around to finding a cure."

"Oh fuck, what the fuck?"

The little red heart sat in Alfie's hand, pristine, like something from a jar of formaldehyde. "It's all I could save of her," he said. "I keep it to remind me."

"Jeez. Jesus." She was backing away now, looking towards the door.

"First, go slow. Do it when you need to. Don't do it for kicks, like Xander and his goddamn legion. It'll buy us more time if you go slow. And second, don't try to end it all."

Her eyes trained on the heart and then on the door and back again.

"You ever stared at the hour hand on a clock until you can just start to see it move? It looks stationary, but it's not. I've stared at her heart before like that, for hours. Until I swore I could see it move. Remember that."

The girl nodded and then ran as Alfred carefully wrapped Sophie's heart again, set it in his box and placed the box back on the dresser.

Grabbing a bottle of water from the refrigerator, he walked down to his car and drove to the cliff where so many memories dwelled. He sat and watched as the sun birthed itself from the sea, and he bore the weight of paradise.

SARAH L. JOHNSON

Sarah L. Johnson lives in Calgary, Alberta, Canada where she reads, runs, blogs about Vladimir Nabokov and writes everything from literary fiction, to horror, to erotic stories she can never show her mother.

Johnson's work has appeared in several magazines and anthologies, including her story "Santa's Claw" in the Rainstorm Press anthology *The Undead That Saved Christmas: Vol. 3 Monster Bash*, "You're Bleeding," featured in Recliner Books' *Freshwater Pearls* and "Why (Y)" in the anthology *Curcurbital 3* from Paper Golem Publishing.

Her interests include eating cookies, mowing the lawn and wondering how her earphones got so tangled up.

THREE MINUTES

BY SARAH L. JOHNSON

Wake up, wake up, wake up…

John's breath scraped his throat, and his hands ached from the sheets twisted tight around his fingers. His silent chant looped through the dark.

The Dream Eater was close. It bashed the gates of the real world and clawed at him through the bars. In a fading whisper, it told secrets he didn't want to know, in words he couldn't understand.

Every night, for as long as he could remember, the Dream Eater chased him through the black nothing of sleep. He'd done the math and had since then kept track. At twelve years, seven months and three days old that was 4,599 nights of jolting awake with his heart trying to crack through his chest like an alien baby.

Tonight made it an even 4,600.

Sweat pooled in his ears as he stared at the ceiling and listened to the roar of the fan, churning thick summer air. By the time his heart relaxed, he wasn't sure what made it spaz out in the first place. The memory was gone. It dissolved that way every night, leaving him with a skull crammed full of bad feelings he couldn't explain.

It was after midnight, but the room still baked with the heat of the day. The four boys he bunked with were motionless lumps in their beds. John was wide awake. He sucked at sleeping. It was called insomnia. He had a book about it hidden under his mattress. The book said chronic insomnia was rare in children. The book also said kids who couldn't sleep were usually messed up. John figured foster care was enough to warp anyone's brainpan. But it was all he'd ever known.

A shaft of light from a streetlamp fell across the crucifix on the wall beside his bed. John didn't believe in God, but felt sorta bad for plastic Jesus, melting on His cross.

Hot as Hell, John thought. Then he turned his face into the pillow and laughed. It *was* hot as Hell. He'd long since kicked away the covers, and his pajama pants clung to his skinny legs like wet towels. Even in the dark he could see the dinosaur pattern.

Too freaking babyish to believe.

It sucked to be a shrimp when you were stuck having to wear what fit from the hand-me-down heap. He flipped his pillow and sighed as the cool surface cradled his head.

The fan growled.

Sleep? Yeah, right. Waste of time, anyway. While the world snored, he could do whatever he wanted. And there were better things to do than lay in the dark and sweat. He rolled out of bed, ditched the dino-pants and pulled on a t-shirt, cut-off jeans and his sneakers. Then he bundled an extra blanket under the covers. Good enough to pass an open-door bed check.

From the wall, plastic Jesus saw everything and said nothing. When John was halfway out the window, however, he heard the squeak of mattress springs.

Wendell's paper-plate face hovered in the darkness. "Where you goin'?"

"Go back to sleep."

"I'm gonna tell Monique."

John gritted his teeth.

Monique, the housemother, was a holy tank of a woman who could roll over a land mine and not feel it. Monique treated John more or less like a catastrophe in human form, like he'd personally nailed plastic Jesus to his plastic cross. Sneaking out was high on her list of Very Bad Things, and Wendell was a well-known snitch. If he tattled, it would be the kiss of death for John's nocturnal walkabouts.

Wendell was a problem.

"Tell anyone," John said, "and I'll cut your goddamn tongue out."

Wendell's paper head vanished under his blanket.

John rolled his eyes and dropped onto the lower pitch of the roof. The lattice creaked as he climbed down to the flower bed. He was careful not to squash the plants. When you were up to Very Bad Things, it was smart not to leave evidence behind.

He brushed soil over his footprints. Then he ran. Frame houses gave way to dented trailers and empty lots full of ragweed. He held his breath as he sprinted past the latter, a runty orphan with allergies. At least he'd been spared freckles and red hair.

At the edge of town, he flew onto a path curling through a grove of aspens. His sneakers thumped on the dirt in a steady rhythm. He slowed to a panting trot when the path ended and the trees opened onto the shoreline of a man-made lake. The "beach" was nothing more than rocks and sour mud squishy enough to slurp the shoes off your feet. He hopped stone to stone until he reached the dock. There, he took a minute to catch his breath and scrub the sweat from his eyes with his shirt. Starlight glinted off still, black water.

He'd tried so many times, come so close. Three minutes.

He stripped to his underwear, raced down the warped planks and dove headfirst into warm water that tasted like bagged grass clippings after a week in the sun. When he surfaced, he took a dozen rapid breaths. It was a pearl diver trick he'd read about. Carbon dioxide was the automatic breath trigger, not oxygen. If you scrubbed most of the carbon dioxide out of your blood, you could hold your breath a lot longer.

He filled his lungs one last time. He pulled and gulped and packed the air in until it pushed his stomach out and stretched his ribs apart. Then he went under. Starlight disappeared as he flipped himself head down and kicked.

Since he didn't have a waterproof watch, he had to count in his head. One hundred eighty was the magic number. The closest he'd ever come was one hundred sixty-four. On the bottom of the lake, he pulled himself along by grabbing handfuls of slimy grass. Pulling and counting, pulling and counting. He hit eighty-three seconds when he located the cluster of man-sized rocks.

Glacial erratics — that's what they were called. Chunks of mountains chipped off and carried away by traveling glaciers during the ice age. When the ice melted, it dropped them wherever. All alone in a place they didn't belong. Odd rocks. Misfits. John knew what that was like.

One hundred twenty. Two minutes.

The need to exhale pounded at the base of his throat. Bubbles flew from his mouth as his lungs partially deflated. Like a freshwater starfish, he latched onto one of the rocks. Sharp edges, slick with algae, bit into his arms and legs. Mud squelched between his toes as they wedged in at the base.

One hundred sixty.

Almost there. His heart banged against his ribs, and the numbers slopped around in his head.

One hundred seventy.

He pressed his forehead hard into the rock.

One hundred seventy-five.

Dirty air raced up his throat.

One hundred seventy-eight...nine...one hundred eighty.

Three minutes.

He braced his feet and pushed off. Only instead of launching upward, his foot sunk deep into the mud. The rock shifted onto his ankle. Not enough to crush, but enough to pin. He tugged at his leg and shoved at the rock. Panic swept his oxygen-starved brain. One thought. Three words.

Up. Air. Breathe.

Nothing worked anymore. His legs went limp, and his head fell back to face the surface. Too dark. Too far. His arms flopped like they had minds of their own. Maybe the arms thought they could swim away and save themselves. But it was too late for them. Too late for everything.

His throat gasped open. For a speck of time there was relief—until water boiled into his lungs. The reflexive cough pulled in another scalding wave. Then, like a drawstring pulled tight, his windpipe closed. His body strangled itself even as he continued to suck water into his stomach.

Air hunger, serious air hunger, was the weirdest thing. It transformed time into a melted marshmallow that stretched out forever on a single sticky thread. It also hurt more than he thought anything could. Still, he managed a few clear thoughts.

He'd read about drowning. Now he wished he hadn't. He'd rather not know about the freshwater rushing into his veins, fattening his red blood cells until they exploded, and that with each second of increasing hypoxia, his brain cells were croaking by the zillions. His throat remained sealed. It was called laryngospasm, and it wouldn't release until he passed out or went into cardiac arrest. But he didn't black out.

Instead, he felt the last link between his mind and its meat suit snap. Then he felt nothing at all.

Interesting.

Death was a dark, floaty place, like the bottom of the lake, except he didn't have to hold his breath, because he had no body that needed to breathe. If there was a white light, he had no eyes to see it, and no legs to walk toward or away from it. As he floundered, it occurred to him that his last words were, *"I'll cut your goddamn tongue out."* It was only meant to terrorize that snitch, Wendell, but what if there was a God? *He* probably wouldn't like that.

Monique made Hell sound like an overgrown, spider-infested garden, with each descending circle weedier than the last. Then again, what if Heaven was a giant church, with a giant bloody Jesus hanging from the wall? What if you had to sit between God and Monique on those hard benches and read the Bible forever and pretend you liked it? He'd rather spend an eternity sneezing in the weeds.

And what about reincarnation?

If that was the deal, his Karma was a problem. The foster home looked civilized on the outside, but within those walls, the law of the jungle reigned. To survive, you kept your claws sharp and used them. John was a survivor, or he had been, before he died.

No one would care much. He'd be remembered as a bad seed. People would think of all the Very Bad Things he'd done and say it was for the best. No one would consider that he'd done most of those bad things for good reasons.

In terms of reincarnation, he figured the best he could hope for would be an intelligent animal. Something that couldn't drown would be cool. His argument for manta ray was coming together when a voice punctured the silence. A voice he knew.

The Dream Eater.

It called his name, his real name. The one he had before some dud of a social worker labeled an abandoned baby 'John.' But every time the Dream Eater said the name, it would slip away before he could slot it into his memory.

"Why can't I keep it?" John asked.

"Names change, they are not important."

"Then why keep it a secret."

"You place value on that which has none," the Dream Eater said.

"I don't believe you."

"So you have indicated, rather stridently, every night of your life. We haven't much time. Abide with me now, and I will reveal all that I am able."

"I'm not going anywhere with you."

"Even if the alternative is death?"

"Who are you?"

"I am that I am."

John had more questions, angry sorts of questions, but the Dream Eater was taking him somewhere. It pulled him. Not up or down, forward or back. It pulled him through and out. Beyond. The soft marshmallow of time stretched and twisted and folded back on itself. Seconds, years, hours, days, it was impossible to know.

The mineral smell of water tickled John's nose. He was surprised to find he had a nose again, and arms and legs, and eyes, which were closed. The moment he opened them, he was horribly dizzy.

Eyes shut. Breathe deep. Try again. Eyes open. The light was wrong. An orange sun blazed in a hazy, red sky. He was dressed, and dry, and standing, not by the lake, but on the bank of a river. The green water rushed fast and wide through a valley of dead trees and yellow earth.

John was alone on his side, but across the water there were people. They were filthy, with blood on their hands and faces. A woman stumbled out of the crowd. She stood at the edge of the river, clutching a dirty towel to her chest.

Not a towel, a baby.

Her eyes met John's. She jumped into the river. He held a breath for them, but they never surfaced.

The others screamed.

They called his name. They cursed him and begged for help in a language he didn't know but somehow understood because the words were a noose around his neck. It tugged him forward, until his toes hung off the edge of the steep bank. Gravity teased him closer and closer to a tumble into the rapids. Then a hand closed on his shoulder.

"Your part in saving them is long done," said a soft voice, and the hand pulled him back from the edge. In his ungentle life, it was the kindest touch John had ever felt. The hand belonged to a man or someone man-shaped, but not a man at all. He had gold skin and eyes with no whites. They glowed, like the sun glinting off shards of blue glass.

"Am I dead?"

The man-that-was-not-a-man sighed and shook his head. "You weary me, stubborn thing."

"Sorry," John said, and meant it, though the very word felt strange in his mouth, and he couldn't ever remember saying it sincerely.

The man shrugged. "Faith is a fool's virtue."

John didn't know what that meant.

"You think me disingenuous."

He didn't know what that meant either.

"But I kept only what you were not prepared to see. Look around."

John scanned the valley. No birds, no bugs, only a bone yard of barren trees and baked dirt. He listened to the heavy rush of the river and the cries of the people on the other side.

"These are my dreams?"

"You are strong enough now to be shown what is true." The man gestured to the wailing mob. "Wretches. Like human names, human life is worthless. Their souls, on the other hand, are pearls of great price."

"What does this have to do with me?"

"To be saved, they must suffer." The man's blue gaze swung away from the mob. "But nature seeks a balance, and its laws are not easily subverted. I designed it to be so. As such my power here is limited. On the mortal plane, I must work through men."

John's heart fought for space between lungs that felt bloated and stiff. For forty-six hundred nights, he thought he'd been running from a monster, or a demon. He crumpled to his knees on the cracked earth.

Balance? What the hell?

He had to drown for this? A bitter taste crawled into his mouth. He spit in the dirt.

"Why don't you leave us alone?" John said. "Go burn some ants with a magnifying glass or something."

"What I speak of is no triviality. The balance must be maintained."

Balance this, was on the tip of John's tongue. "What are you talking about?"

"I made this world," He said. "It must now be unmade. Dust to dust, as they say."

John's gut tumbled like a clothes dryer full of loose change.

He dropped to one knee in front of John. "In your first incarnation, you spread my word, that as I had loved them, so should they love one another. In your short life, you suffered and sacrificed yourself to save their souls. Now I call upon you again, to reap them."

John was a glacial erratic. No one knew where he'd come from. He realized this might be the only chance he'd ever get to learn more. "Who am I?"

His eyes dimmed and sadness poured off Him like frozen rain. "Names change. But always, you are my chosen."

John shivered and rubbed his eyes. The river, the mob and the dead valley—they weren't just dreams. Very Bad Things would happen. It would start here.

John wondered if being chosen meant he had no choice.

"You desire the truth, and the truth is this." He bowed his head. "They will not understand this second coming any more than the first. There will be atrocities. They will spit on your new name as they do the old. I ask too much of you, and I weep at the thought of your burden." He took John's shoulders in a gentle grasp that saved him from the river. "I chose you with great care. But your will is your own."

John didn't know whether to laugh or faint. A powerless god was kneeling in front of him, asking him to choose his side of the river.

* * *

Water spewed from his mouth and nose. He coughed until he thought his chest might break apart. When it passed, he was shocked to find himself in the dark, sprawled near the tree line by the lake, twenty yards from where water licked the shore.

He whipped his head back and forth.

Trees. Mud. Water. Mud. Trees.

Nothing. No one.

Somehow he'd pulled his foot free and, with a chest full of water, climbed the dock, stepped across the stones to the grass, and passed out.

Runny foam bubbled into his mouth. Words and images skipped across the surface of his mind like flat rocks. He couldn't remember. On wobbling knees he tried to stand. That wasn't happening. Instead it seemed like an awesome idea to slump to the ground, roll to his side and puke.

* * *

A few blocks from the house, John sagged against a chain link fence, panting. He felt heavy, like he'd swallowed an anvil. His raw, leaky lungs worked for every breath. Nothing about it felt right. Then he realized his face was six inches from a tangle of weeds and enough pollen to make his head explode.

Oh hell, he thought. But his nose didn't so much as itch.

By the time he dragged his carcass over the windowsill, he felt almost good again. The fan still growled in the shadows of the now almost chilly bedroom. Everyone remained asleep, and no sign of Monique. Situation normal. There was just one thing he needed to set right before he crashed.

From under his quilt, he pulled out the extra blanket he'd used as a decoy. He tucked it under his arm and crossed the room to stand over a huddled form. Wendell's blonde hair trailed over his forehead and his breath whistled around the thumb between his lips. He looked like a baby, innocent like that.

John wished he'd been nicer to him. Wendell was just a little kid who hadn't learned the ropes yet. Beneath their lids, his eyes flicked back and forth. It was called Rapid Eye Movement. It meant he was dreaming. What might a snitch like Wendell dream about?

On impulse, John bent and kissed Wendell's hot cheek.

Then he shook out the blanket, refolded it into a thick square and truly hoped Wendell was having the best dream of his life.

The alarm clock said 4:09. Earlier, John held his breath for over three minutes. Permanent brain damage started after five. Wendell fought some, but John was older and stronger. He didn't know the exact reason he had to do it, only that if he didn't, Wendell would go on to be a problem for him, a big one. The hot stink of piss burned John's nose. He held the blanket down until 4:20.

Wendell was a problem now solved.

John thought he'd feel different, maybe guilty or scared. Why though? Nothing that easily squished could be worth much. He unfolded the blanket, spread it over the body, and yawned as he plodded to his own bed.

The only witness hung from a cross on the wall, silent as always. John reached out and traced the crown of thorns. Suffering and sacrifice. *He* wasn't the only one.

John's throat felt tight. His stomach lurched like it was full of tumbling rocks—or loose silver. This wasn't the first time he'd done a Very Bad Thing, a dirty job.

Plastic Jesus wouldn't betray him though. He understood. Someone had to do it.

"I'm sorry," John whispered, and meant it.

RAY GARTON

Ray Garton has been nominated for the Bram Stoker Award and is the author of more than sixty novels, novellas, short story collections, movie novelizations and TV tie-ins. His exceptional portfolio of work spans the genres of horror, crime and suspense.

Garton's 1987 erotic vampire novel *Live Girls* was called "artful" by the *New York Times* and was nominated for the Bram Stoker Award. In 2006, he received the Grand Master of Horror Award at the World Horror Convention in San Francisco. His 2001 comedy thriller *Sex and Violence in Hollywood* is being developed for the screen.

His most recent novels, *Trailer Park Noir* and *Meds* (a thriller with deadly side effects), are available in paperback and as ebooks from E-Reads. And his seventh collection, *Wailing and Gnashing of Teeth*, was recently published by Cemetery Dance Publications.

Garton lives in northern California with his wife Dawn.

Second Opinion

BY RAY GARTON

Do you know what it's like to cut up your best friend with a hacksaw? Probably not. Most people don't. The narrow metal blade, with its fine, sharp teeth, makes a very distinctive sound while it's cutting through human bones. I know that sound very well, and I'm not bragging. Not at all.

The food is very bad today, worse than usual. Instead of eating, I've been going over and over things in my head. One of the orderlies gave me this crayon and some paper, so I decided to start writing it all down. After all, that's what I do best, isn't it?

I called him Hank, but everybody else called him Henry Carr. His work had won a lot of awards, including the Pulitzer, which he called, with a characteristic blend of sarcasm and self-deprecation, the "Putzpuller." He was a truly great writer, one of the best ever in my opinion, and I don't give a damn what any of those bonehead critics wrote or said about his work. The man was an artist with words, a genius.

Aside from being a great writer, he was a great man. Just a great person, plain and simple. He was my best friend and my mentor. He took me under his wing after reading one of my stories—the third that was actually published—and tried his best to prepare me for the rejection that every writer has to tolerate with ease if he or she is to succeed. Hank recognized my talent and tried to make sure that I remained true to it. I very likely would have been a much different person if I had not known him, and a much different writer, as well—certainly not as good, if I'm any good at all. In fact, I might not have been a writer, period.

Yes, Henry Carr was a great writer, a great man, and my best friend and mentor. And I cut his arms and legs off, then cut those into small pieces, and wrapped his severed head in aluminum foil and plastic. I hate myself for it, but I've never forgotten the reason I did it.

* * *

When I heard Michael's knock at the front door, I hurried from the kitchen to answer it, still wearing my apron, which bore splotches of tomato sauce like battle wounds.

"Come in, come in," I said jovially as I opened the door, working hard to cover my anxiety, my discomfort.

Mikey shuffled into the house nervously, still behaving as if this was our first meeting and he was still nothing more than a young beginner. That wasn't the case at all.

I'd known Mikey for seven years, and he *always* behaved that way, showing me deference that I didn't deserve. It bugged me a little, because he was every bit my equal. The fact that he didn't realize that yet was a bit annoying.

Michael Anderson's latest novel was number one on the *New York Times* bestseller list, and it wasn't his first trip to the top of that mountain, no, it was his third. He'd consulted me several times on the first two novels, but not at all on his third, and I saw that as a good sign. He'd found his voice, his rhythm. It told me he'd developed confidence in his work. He'd set sail on his own, and that was good.

When I first met him, he'd written a couple of critically acclaimed novels that sold about a dozen copies. I encouraged him to keep writing in spite of that, because his talent was obvious. I knew he just needed some seasoning and a little guidance—not unlike the guidance I had gotten from Hank.

"Jeez, Greg," he said, "I haven't seen you in so long."

"Yeah, I know. Been busy."

"Well, that's good, but...*nobody's* seen or heard from you in a long time. We've all been kind of worried about you, Greg. I was really surprised when you called me out of the blue. Pleasantly surprised, I mean. Are you sure everything's okay?"

"Fine, just fine, everything's fine."

It was raining hard outside, and Mikey's black overcoat was soaked. After closing the door against the storm, I peeled the coat off of him, put it on a hanger and hung it in the open doorway of the hall closet to dry.

"You don't look so good, Greg," Mikey said, frowning as he looked me over. "Are you sick?"

He was right. I was pale and had lost weight, and I'd been pretty thin in the first place.

"Oh, no, not sick," I said. "Just tired. I've been working too hard, haven't slept well lately." That was putting it mildly. I hadn't slept at *all* in the last week, and every time I ate, I threw up the food a few minutes later. I'd been a wreck for a little more than a year, to be honest, but especially in the past couple of weeks. Mikey was right; I hadn't called or seen anyone in about a year and I hardly even listened to messages anymore. I never answered the door when the doorbell rang. I hoped he couldn't see my hands shaking.

"You cooked Italian?" Mikey asked, sniffing the aromas coming from the kitchen.

"Spaghetti. With my own special sauce. Which, by the way, if I may say so myself, is the best you'll have in this lifetime."

I set the table and served up the salad, spaghetti and garlic bread. Before we began to eat, I put Vivaldi's *The Four Seasons* on the stereo.

"This is *great*," Mikey said as he ate. "I mean, this is delicious, really, Greg." He took a few more bites. "You said you wanted me to come here because something, um...well, you said something important had happened."

I shook my head as I chewed my food. "No, no, that's not exactly what I said. I said I wanted you to come here so we could discuss something important."

He began nodding rapidly, apologetically, and said, "Okay, yeah, that's what you said. I'm sorry, really, I'm—"

"Dammit, Mikey, would you stop apologizing. You didn't do anything wrong. Quit treating me like I'm, I don't know, a member of the royal family, or something. All right? I mean, my god, you've never figured that out have you? I'm just another writer, just like you."

He nodded slowly, surprised by my harsh tone.

I sighed and shook my head. "I'm sorry, I didn't mean to snap at you like that, I've just been...well, kind of tense, on edge. But Mikey, you and I have known each other for a while and, hell, you've got more pull now than I ever had. You're hot shit, Mr. Bestseller. So no more of that."

He chuckled appreciatively, and we continued to eat.

"I do want to discuss something important," I said.

He gave me a questioning look as he sucked a string of pasta into his mouth.

"I wanted to talk to you about a story," I said. "A story I've been working on for a long time. But I...well, I can't seem to end the damned thing. It's been hounding me. Haunting me. I know it's a good story. A *great* story. The kind of thing that could really revive my career. Bring me back. But this ending...well, it just keeps slipping away from me. It's been eating at me so much, I can't sleep well, and I can't work on anything else. But I just can't crack it. So I wanted to ask for your thoughts. If, of course, that's all right with you. I mean, if you don't mind."

He stopped chewing and stared across the table at me for a moment. "You mean, uh...you want my opinion of this story of yours?"

"That's right. And don't act like it's a big deal, because it's not."

His smile grew slowly and he said, "Sure, Greg, sure. You want me to read it?"

"Not yet. I want to tell it to you. Would you mind?"

"Sure."

"Okay, then. Eat your food and listen up."

I told him the story.

* * *

Hacking through bone is not like cutting wood. For one thing, when you're cutting wood—if you know what you're doing—it's usually dry. For another, wood isn't wrapped in skin and muscle tissue. It's a messy business, wet and tedious and sickening. It's especially sickening when you're cutting up the bones of someone you care about.

I don't think I can emphasize too much just how deeply I cared about Hank. And I still do, even though he's gone. But what I did had nothing to do with my feelings for him. My decision and subsequent actions were entirely divorced from our personal relationship, sort of like competing for a promotion with a coworker who also happens to be your friend.

Even though I'm a writer and words are my business, I can't seem to find the right ones to explain why I did what I did. I've never had this problem before. I did it for selfish reasons, of course, to breathe life back into my career, which had been wheezing along for years, barely alive. The success I'd once known, thanks in part to my mentor's tutelage, was gone, and I was a has-been. My last three novels had barely broke even, and advances had withered in comparison to those I'd gotten during the height of my career.

That was it, simple as that. The height of my career was well behind me, and I wanted to bring it back. I wanted it desperately. I wanted to reach another peak, and I wanted the notoriety and fat advances that I knew would come with it. This sounds odd, but I knew in my heart that Hank would have wanted that for me, too. That's why I killed him, because I knew that he would want me to have the success that his story would bring me. I know how that sounds, and I know it says nothing good about me, but...there it is.

I knew right away that Hank would have to be dead. I certainly don't want to lead anyone to believe that I heard voices—for months now, I've been trying to convince my doctor of that, but I'm not sure he believes that it was anything but my own internal voice, the one that has spoken to me every day of my life, the same internal voice possessed by everyone, yourself included. That voice told me that Hank would have to be gone. It told me there was no other way.

If Hank had moved to an island in the Caribbean and become a recluse, his life, his very existence, no matter how far away, would have been a constant obstacle. The possibility that he might discover my theft and publicly accuse me of plagiarism would forever hang over my head. The only way it would work would be if I killed him and hid his body someplace where it would never, ever be found.

I didn't own a gun—I've never possessed one—so I used a length of rope. I brought him over to my house one evening in my car, ostensibly for dinner. Early in the evening, while he was looking at a gift I'd received from a friend—a first edition signed copy of *Naked Lunch*—I wrapped the rope around his neck from behind and strangled him.

It certainly didn't go the way it does in the movies. He did not make a simple gagging sound, struggle for a moment, stiffen, and then fall limp and dead to the floor. He fought like the devil. He kicked and tried to scream and threw his fists backward over his shoulders to hit me. He knocked over a bookshelf, a table lamp, poked me in the eye with his thumb, scratched my face twice with his fingernails and kicked my shin hard with his heel.

When he finally died, he emptied his bowels into his pants with a wet farting sound and smelled up the entire room.

Dinner was still cooking, so I hurried to the kitchen and turned off the stove. But when I returned, I had the hacksaw and was prepared to do what I had to do.

I dragged him to the bathroom and stripped off his clothes, then hefted the corpse into the tub. I cut him up in there, running the faucet to wash the blood down the drain. I wrapped each piece in foil and plastic.

I did not stop until I could fit his entire body into a suitcase.

Late that night, after I'd cleaned up the mess and had dinner, I drove with the suitcase to a dense patch of woods about thirty miles away from the city or any residential neighborhoods. I hiked deep into those woods, dragging the suitcase and a shovel, and buried his remains at least five feet underground between two monstrous redwoods. I covered the grave well and made sure there was no sign of freshly dug earth. Then I went home.

I'm not a violent person. I've never raised a hand to anyone, and I've never been in a fight, not once in my life. But killing and dismembering my friend was pretty simple, I'm afraid. Not once, not for one moment during the entire process, did I ever doubt that I was doing the right thing. And not once after that, either. In fact, even now, I have no regrets. Something deep inside me says that I probably should, but I don't.

I can honestly say that I would do it again. I so passionately wanted, once again, the success I'd known before. It didn't work out that way, of course, but I would still do it all over again.

* * *

"Would you like more spaghetti?" I asked. Mikey's plate was empty, and he was slumped in his chair staring off into space.

For the last twenty minutes, I'd been pacing as I told the story, acting out the roles, changing my voice from one character to the next. He'd eaten slowly the whole time, watching me, listening intently. Now his plate was empty, and he looked exhausted, his face kind of...empty.

"More spaghetti, Mikey?" I asked again.

He blinked a few times and lifted his face to look at me. "Oh, yeah. Please. That was delicious. Yeah, I'd like some more."

"Okay," I said, taking his plate. I was on my way out of the dining room and into the kitchen when he stopped me with a question.

"Why did you tell me that, Greg?"

I stopped and turned to him. "What do you mean?"

"That story. Why did you tell me that story?"

I saw something in his face at that moment that made the skin at the back of my neck shrivel up. His eyes were different, no longer as open and eager as usual. Now they were dark, shaded, as if some protective membrane had closed over them.

"I just wanted to hear your take on it," I said with a shrug. "Like I said, the ending has been driving me nuts, and I wanted an outside opinion."

"But why me? I mean, you've been at this a lot longer than I have and you—"

"There you go again," I said testily, taking my seat at the table again. "Every writer, at one time or another, asks another writer for his opinion. I've done it before, I'll do it again. Haven't you done that? Hell, even Hank came to me for advice a couple of times, god rest his soul."

I regretted saying it even before the words had come all the way out of my mouth. I didn't want the conversation to go down that road, but it was too late.

"What?" Mikey asked, frowning.

"I said, even Hank used to—"

"No, not that. You said 'god rest his soul.'"

Every muscle in my body tensed, and I stood from my chair and began pacing again. "Well, yeah."

"But I thought he hadn't been found."

The words poured from me in a rush. "He hasn't Mikey, but my god, he's been gone for nearly two years, and I know Hank well enough to know that he wouldn't just disappear like that without contacting someone if he could, especially me, because we were really close. I knew him better than anyone, and I haven't heard from him, so I'm just assuming the poor guy's dead, that's all. That's why I said that, okay?"

After a moment, he asked, "How long have you been working on this story?"

"Oh, I don't know. A year and a half, maybe."

"So you didn't show it to Hank?"

"No, of course not. I would if I could, just like he used to come to me with stories. Just like Leonard used to ask Hank for advice on his work. We all do that, Mikey, so what's the problem? Why are you so surprised by this?"

"You mean Leonard Avery?"

"Yeah. Leonard took Hank under his wing, just like Hank took me under his, and like I've tried to help you out. But age and experience don't mean that much when it comes to writing. Sooner or later, we all need some advice, or an opinion. Now I'm coming to you."

He frowned thoughtfully. "They never figured out who killed Leonard Avery, did they?" he said, his voice quiet and distant, as if he were suddenly preoccupied with something.

I stopped pacing and stared at him, confused. "What the hell has that got to do with anything?"

He shook his head as if to jar his thoughts back into order, then looked at me and smiled. "I'm flattered that you've asked me to help you, Greg. I guess I'm just a little surprised. I figured you'd go to someone with more experience, but if you think I can help, then I want to." He stared at me silently for a moment, still smiling, then asked, "You haven't shown it to anyone else?"

Once again, I saw something in his eyes that chilled my blood, something much stronger than before, something deadly.

"No," I said, my voice a mere whisper now. "I haven't shown it to anyone."

He nodded silently, smile never faltering. "Can I read it, Greg?"

I was filled with a dread that clogged my throat for a moment, but I finally said, "Sure, if you'd like. I'll get it."

The manuscript was on my desk and I went to get it, all the while suspecting that I was making a horrible mistake, doing something so wrong that it would alter the course of my life, even more so than my experience with Hank.

I returned to the dining room and handed him the manuscript as I asked, "Do you still want some more spaghetti?"

"Yes, please. It was delicious."

I took his plate to the kitchen to dish up more for him.

I'd scarcely touched my own meal, and I knew I wouldn't eat any more, not tonight. After seeing what I'd seen in Mikey's eyes, I was sick with fear, and I began thinking thoughts that made me suspect the lack of sleep had finally gotten the best of me, that I'd gone around the bend, over the edge. They were the thoughts of a madman, but they were insistent, and they grew rapidly, filling my mind with a scenario that suddenly seemed so obvious, I could not understand why I hadn't thought of it before.

For the first time, I vaguely began to consider myself a victim. As much a victim as Hank had been. And who else?

Just as Hank had mentored me, he had been mentored by Leonard Avery. I'm sure you've heard of him. His work was quite popular during the 1950s, and three of his novels had been made into successful movies, one of which was directed by John Huston and starred Humphrey Bogart and was nominated for a slew of Academy Awards. When I met him, he was old and in ill health, and he would have died soon even if he had not been brutally murdered.

Leonard was seventy-eight when he was killed in what the police concluded was an interrupted burglary. He was shot four times, but the fatal wound came from a large knife in the chest. It was amazing to everyone who knew him that he didn't die instantly, because he was suffering from pancreatic cancer at the time. But according to the medical examiner, he'd struggled and fought with his attacker, and it had taken that knife in the heart to do him in, even after two bullets in the chest and two more in the gut.

I remember talking to Hank the day after Leonard's murder. He wasn't as emotional as I'd expected him to be; rather, he was quiet

and reflective, and he kept looking at me with a sad smile and saying, "He fought, Greg, can you believe that? He already had a foot in
the grave, but he fought like a man half his age, maybe younger. He
struggled and kicked and fought like the great man he was."

I didn't think much of it at the time. To me, it was just Hank talking with admiration about the tenacity of his dearest friend, nothing
more.

In fact, I thought of Leonard as I was tightening that rope around
Hank's neck. I remembered what Hank had said about Leonard
fighting so hard at the very end, and it occurred to me that Hank was
proving himself to be every bit the man Leonard had been, because
just like Leonard, Hank had gone out with a hell of a fight. I remember thinking that if Hank were still alive to talk about his own death,
he would have spoken of it just as admiringly as he had of Leonard's.
He would have been proud of himself.

Leonard had been killed two years before I killed Hank. During those two years, Leonard's death was nearly all Hank could talk
about. That, and the story.

In the last year of Hank's life, he'd been consumed by that story.
He mentioned it to me in conversation, just in passing, but never
gave any details. All he ever said was that it was something big, a
story that might very well bring him back from the dead.

In spite of his many awards and years of critical praise and com-
mercial success, Hank's career had been swamped for a long time.
The editors of magazines that once fought over his short fiction
wouldn't even return his calls. Hank could not, as they say, get arrested. But he kept working, picking up what work he could while
his savings from the glory days were whittled down to nothing.

By the time he finally shared the story with me and asked for my
input, he was a mess. He hadn't been out of his house in months, all
of his groceries were delivered, and he never answered the phone. In
fact, there were times when I'd dropped by his place and knocked on
the door but got no answer, although I knew he was inside because
I could hear him moving around, and sometimes the television or

radio was playing loudly. But finally, he opened up and admitted to me that he had a great story that could put him back on top...if only he could come up with an ending. It had been killing him, he said, trying to find a way to tie up this absolutely perfect story, the best thing he'd ever done in his life. He'd lost sleep and couldn't eat, he said, and all he needed was a little advice, a pair of objective eyes to look over the pages he'd written so far, the opinion of someone he really trusted. So he showed me the story. And I killed him for it.

All of that ran through my mind as I was in the kitchen, dishing up Mikey's spaghetti. He was out in the dining room reading the story and waiting for his second helping, and I was standing there over the stove, suddenly not sure I wanted to go back out there.

I didn't think he suspected anything, that wasn't it. No, I was suddenly worried about how much he would like that story. That damned story.

The thoughts shooting through my mind were insane, the stuff of nightmares and campfire stories. And those ugly thoughts made me quite afraid of the young man sitting at my dining room table. Just as Hank might have been afraid of *me* if he'd had the same thoughts.

But I don't think he did. I suspect he had no idea what was coming, which would account for his incredible struggle. It was a surprise. In fact, I don't even think he knew who was killing him. I was behind him the whole time. He didn't know who was killing him...but did he know why? In those last moments, did the reason for his death come to him in a flash?

Once I'd filled Mikey's plate, I set it on the counter and crept back through the kitchen and across the hall to look through the doorway into the dining room. He didn't hear me. He was hunched over that manuscript with all the intensity of a doctor performing brain surgery. I backed away and returned to the plate on the kitchen counter, picked it up, and walked into the dining room with a smile on my face, hoping it didn't look forced.

"Here it is," I said.

He didn't move, didn't look up, didn't even seem to know I was there.

I stood beside him, holding the plate in one hand, waiting for him to move the manuscript so I could set it down.

"Mikey? Here's your spaghetti."

He flinched and lifted his head, looked up at me and stammered, "Oh, oh, yeah, uh, yeah, sure, um, thanks, Greg, thanks." He pulled the manuscript away and set the plate down.

When he turned and swung his fist up holding the fork, aiming straight at my throat, I surprised myself by moving quickly, almost as if I'd expected it. I grabbed his wrist and stopped the fork with it, the tines only a couple of inches or so from my throat. Then I made the mistake of looking at Mikey's face.

It was a fright mask, tense and wide-eyed and determined to kill me. I knew there was only one way I would survive this: I would have to kill Mikey.

My left hand was clutching his right wrist. With the thumb of my right hand, I pulled his little finger back, away from the fork, just kept pulling until the finger straightened out, and I kept pulling after that. The wild expression on his face began to pinch until it was screwed up with pain. I pulled the finger back until it broke with a thick pop.

Mikey screamed like a child, dropping the fork as he fell off the chair. The manuscript fell from his other hand and the pages scattered across the floor.

I pressed a knee to his chest, holding him down, and shouted, "Why did you do that?"

He struggled, crying out in pain, but did not answer.

"I said, *why* did you *do* that, Mikey?"

He looked at me, his eyes showing nothing but agony, and whimpered, "Jesus, Greg, help me, please...my finger...it hurts."

I nearly whispered the question again. "Why did you do it?"

"*The story!*" he screamed. "The...story. Dammit, I can...I can handle that story...the end...I can do it."

"And you were gonna kill me for it?"

"No, Greg, jeez, you...you just misunderstood, that's all. I was just...I guess I moved too fast, and...that's all...I moved too fast and you thought I wanted to hurt you, but...I didn't...not at all, Greg, I...I wouldn't do that."

As he spoke, I guess I relaxed my hold on his wrist and gradually leaned back just enough so that my weight was no longer fully on his chest. My fault entirely. Hey, I'm just a writer, not a fighter.

Mikey swept his left hand up and grabbed my crotch in his fist, squeezing my testicles hard as if they were nothing more than bread dough. I cried out and fell backward to escape his grip. Before I knew it, my back had hit the floor and Mikey was on me. We'd traded places. But now he had the fork in his left hand.

I watched as Mikey lifted his left hand high, then brought it down with an ugly sound from deep in his chest, and I fought back my own pain to lift my hand and stop him. I grabbed his arm and pushed it back, but he was younger and stronger and I knew I didn't stand a chance.

I grabbed his right hand and pushed his broken little finger with my thumb.

Mikey screamed.

I wrapped my fist around the finger and pulled, as if I were trying to remove it from his hand.

He screamed even louder and fell backward in a faint. He wasn't out for long, but long enough for me to get to my feet and grab the fork.

I have no idea how many times I stabbed him. I've been told it was forty-three times, but I find that hard to believe. I just wanted to stop him. Sure, I wanted to kill him, because I knew that I needed to. I knew exactly what was happening, and if I did not kill him, he would kill me, because he had to, just as I had to kill Hank, and just as Hank had to kill Leonard. But forty-three times? No, I can't believe that. I can't imagine I would do *that*.

All I know for sure is that I killed Michael Anderson with that fork. Beyond that, I remember little. I have a vague memory of leaving my house, covered with his blood and screaming for help. My neighbors came out of their houses one at a time, stepping cautiously onto their porches, their porch lights coming on one after another as I cried for help, begged for help. And someone called the police.

But that wasn't what I wanted. I wasn't screaming for the police to help. I was screaming for the kind of help that I knew I could never get. I wanted help because I knew I was a victim of something no one would understand. In fact, I remember what I was screaming:

"Help! Please help us! It's killing us! It's killing us all! My god, it's killing us all!"

That's what I screamed to my neighbors. They had no idea that I was talking about a story. A simple, exquisite, absolutely perfect, but unfinished—and maybe unfinishable—story.

* * *

As I sit here in my room with its mattressed walls and locked door, I can't remember everything that happened that night. But I remember why it happened. It was the story. That was the only reason.

All of my crazy, insane thoughts were not so crazy and insane after all. I know now why all those lives were lost. Leonard Avery, Henry Carr, and eventually Michael Anderson. They all died because of that story. The perfect story with no ending.

I wonder how many others had died before Leonard, and I wonder how far back it all goes. After all, the story, set in a village in no particular country, no particular time period, is absolutely timeless.

And absolutely perfect, as well. I must admit that I've still been trying to crack that unreachable ending, even here, in my room, in this place.

I have no idea what's happened to my copy of it, but it will most likely fall into the hands of another writer. In any case, I can do nothing from this room. And I know the more I talk about it, the longer

I will be in this room, in this hospital. I have to behave the way they want me to so they won't keep thinking that I'm crazy.

But that won't change anything. It's still out there, waiting to be read.

* * *

My doctor just visited me. Dr. Culley is tall and rather round, soft-spoken and apparently kind. At least, he's been kind to me, and I still consider him kind in spite of what I know is happening.

This was our third conversation, and he still seemed intensely concerned about my well-being. He asked how I was being treated, what I thought of the food, things like that. Then he started asking the questions that make me see my future.

"I've gone through your personal effects," Dr. Culley said, "and I found a story. It's very interesting."

As I watched him and listened to him, I realized that he was trying hard to make me think that the story enabled him to understand me better, but posed some sort of mysterious question that he hoped I would answer. All of that was so obvious that it was difficult not to smirk. But I did not.

"I am intrigued by this story," he went on. "It is untitled and unfinished. Do you know which story I'm talking about?"

I couldn't hold back a smile. "Yes, I know."

"Did you have an ending in mind? I'm very curious, because I think this story might provide some important information about your problems. So...did you? Have an ending in mind?"

Sitting on the edge of my bed, I looked up at him with a big grin and said, "No, I didn't. Do *you*...have...an ending? In mind?"

He flinched and took a step backward away from me, then smiled and chuckled and said, "No, no, of course not." He chuckled again. "Look, Greg, just wait right here. I'll be back in a minute."

I shrugged and said, "I'm not going anywhere."

* * *

Dr. Culley has just returned. He's smiling and saying something, but his words make no difference. I see the syringe in his hand.

So that's how he's going to end it.

JASON S. RIDLER

A seasoned author and veteran historian, Jason S. Ridler is known to pen some pretty damned provocative horror fiction.

A former punk-rock musician and cemetery groundskeeper, Ridler holds a Ph.D. in War Studies from the Royal Military College of Canada.

Ridler is the author of *Blood and Sawdust*, the Spar Battersea thrillers—*Death Match*, *Con Job* and *Dice Roll*—and the short story collection *Knockouts*. In addition, Ridler has published over fifty stories in magazines and anthologies that include *Beneath Ceaseless Skies*, *Brain Harvest*, *Not One of Us*, *Chilling Tales*, *Tesseracts Thirteen* and more.

His popular non-fiction work has appeared in *Clarkesworld*, *Dark Scribe* and the *Internet Review of Science Fiction*.

THE LAST ICE CREAM KISS

BY JASON S. RIDLER

Dedicated to Melanie Tem

Roaches run from the last bowl you set. One scoop for him, two for her. You lick your fingers, lay down the spoon, and head to the basement with the tub.

The scattered remains of battle prickle your feet before you secure your safe spot to sit. Before the sun rises, you take a deep, sweet bite. The ice cream bites back and…

* * *

It's Saturday morning!

The bursting sun warms the bed like a Christmas oven. Outside the winter moon melts slowly but steadily before it becomes toast. Throw off the sheets and jump into the day of rays! The smell of flapjacks flipping and bacon sizzling is almost visible, riding the radio waves of Looney Tunes cartoons that bounce through the room. No time to wait.

The hallway's moving sidewalk zips you past the other room—

the locked one on the left. You can hear their sweet seductive whispers.

"*Tommy...we're waiting...*"

It's not time for the icing on the cake, no need to dally. Sweat drips as soon as you leap into the kitchen.

Mom is sky high with the frying pan in hand. Mountains of pancakes crowd the mighty kitchen table. Rivers of syrup splash over the rim and onto the floor. A stolen bead tastes like bliss.

"Eat it while it's hot, my love," Mom says, and you climb the wooden chair with the grace of a veteran monkey.

"It's good to have you back, Tom," Dad says from behind the morning paper. The headlines are nice and blurry. "You've been gone a long, long while."

"Not anymore," you say.

Above him, a dozen TVs tuned to a dozen different channels blast the best cartoons the world has ever seen, shimmering into one amazing show. The sticky fork spears a chunk of pancake as Mom puts the bacon at the side, mixing it in with the buttery syrup.

She is beautiful. Ruby lips with a pale, pale face, her brown hair curly and free. "How about some milk for my growing boy?" she asks, her smile widening.

"Ab-so-lutely!"

She pours a giant glass full of pink milk. Dad better not see. Strawberry milk is for babies and girls.

"Drink it all up, my love." She winks and you wink back and the newspaper never drops.

There's an extra chair at the table, making four. "What's that doing here?" You ask.

"What's the trouble?" Dad's newspaper head responds.

"Oh, Tommy just thought he saw a bug. You know how he hates them," Mom says, taking the extra chair away with a knowing smile.

Dad mumbles something about fear and courage.

When Mom comes back it is just you three.

Three.

That number tugs. You grab the milk and gulp and...brr! The milk bites with frigid teeth, and frosty soreness flashes as the avalanche burrows down your throat. The hammer of an ice cream headache pounds as she returns. She always used strawberry ice cream.

The world waves in and out of focus. When the pain leaves, her eyes sparkle and shine like fresh cut diamonds.

"Tommy? Is something wrong? Did I do something wrong?" She covers her mouth in worry.

"Not you. Never you." The strawberry-ice-cream headache burns as the glass is drained, and the world stays as sparkle-sharp as before.

"Better get outside and do what needs done, Tom," Dad says, turning a page. "You left the war on yesterday, and everyone is waiting."

Mom kisses your forehead, and the warmth spreads fast and even. "Run along, my love. We'll see you tomorrow morning."

The morning world glows in summer reds, blues and greens. Freshly cut grass crunches under foot like packing snow as you run through the old neighborhood to the war grounds at the diamond. The happy nobodies wave. Sweet wind blows. No bugs ruin nature's sweetness.

The armies are wandering about, the ref in the middle enjoying a Twinkie. In the distance you see the Clown Army dressed in important suits, phony smiles grease-paint thick, tickle hands on standby.

Sir Growls-A-Lot, CO of the Teddy Bear Brigade, waves. "Commander Tom! Commander Tom returns!"

A roar from the toys crams you full of pride. Sir Growls-A-Lot rests a soft but matted claw on your shoulder. "Where have you been? The war is almost over and we're scared you might miss it!"

"Never, old friend," you say. "When I reach the command bike, stand ready. Today, we charge."

The bear salutes. "Sir, yes sir!"

Everyone salutes until your arm is sore: there are the Joes, armed for Armageddon and ready to go; the heroes, costumes bright and about to take flight; the Lego Legion Engineers, ready to be blown up and smashed together again.

And a strawberry dragon alone on first base.

"Number one!"

"Here, sir!" Ferret Jones pops up and salutes.

"Who is that?"

The beady eyes squint. "Not sure, sir. If I may be so bold, it looks like a dragon."

"I know it's a dragon, Jones! Whose is it?"

"Um, yours?"

"I think I'd know if I had a dragon, you stuffing head!"

"Well then, I don't know whose it could be."

"Bring it to me."

Jones dashes out and snaps back like an elastic-band slingshot. "Here's the culprit. Might he be a spy, sir?"

You snatch the dragon from Jones's hand. It isn't alive. The chest is covered in filthy pink fur and it smells like dirt and tears and… strawberries.

"Spy. Maybe." The head comes off without a whimper. "Bury the dragon behind the dugout."

Jones takes the dead toy and scurries off. The field is full of wonders. *But could there be any more spies?* At the command BMX bike, it matters little. Today is the day. You climb on up and scream. "Sir Growls-A-Lot! Commence the war!"

The crowd roars like a thousand lions as you hit the kickstand, raise the wooden sword, and charge toward the enemy. The ref blows the whistle and runs like hell.

Hours of clown massacres fly by before the white flag of cowardice is raised high on Fool Hill. Victory is yours.

The sun is fat and coming down. The toys cheer the parade through Tommy Town square. Sir Growls-A-Lot, now armless, stands close as the Triumph nears the end of Spectator Street, lined with the girls who once snickered at you, eyes now full of wonder. "You done good, sir. I think those clowns will stay put for a while."

"Until tomorrow," you say. "But we'll be ready. Right, old friend?"

"Indeed, sir. Just like always."

The radio-watch blurts out that it is almost two o'clock in the afternoon. "Afraid I have to leave," you say. "Got an important date."

"Of course, sir. I'll have the gang in shape for your return. See you tomorrow." The parade marches on as the afternoon heat thickens.

* * *

A giant oak at the far end of the battlefield bathes in the rich afternoon sunlight, strong and smelling of granola bars and burning leaves. Carol sits in its shade, reading *To Kill a Mockingbird*. She's wearing jean shorts and her brother's work shirt and if it were two years before this moment she'd be mistaken for a boy. But her china-doll face, small, budding breasts, and dark red hair led to a different conclusion today.

She lifts her face. "Hey, Thomas."

"Hi, Carol. How's the book?"

"Awesome. Jem and Scout are about to see Boo Radley. Do you want me to read it to you?"

Head in her lap, you say, "Ab-so-lutely!"

"Then will you tell me one of your stories? The one about the pirate girls and their awesome Captain Carol?"

"If you're good to me."

"I'm always good to you, Thomas."

You smile.

As Carol speaks, the scenery drifts from the tree to the clouds. They are cars. They are jet planes. They are pin-up gals dancing in the sky for free. Carol runs her cool fingers through your shoulder-length hair, soothing the warm scalp. Body aches and quivers emerge. Just when Boo Radley is discovered, you kiss her hand. The book goes down. Honeydew fills your mouth as you kiss her for the first time. She tastes like electric sugar with a pinch of salt.

She whispers in your ear. "First love is true love, Thomas. Right?"

"Ab-so-lutely!"

Tongue wrestling commences until the current snaps. Terror contorts Carol's face. "What's that?" she asks.

From behind lurches a shambling form in red and black flannel, dark jeans filling the air with the friction of fat legs burning against each other with every step. Its presence turns the grass to ash and the blue sky to sauerkraut grey as it lumbers toward you.

"Thomas," Carol whispers, "I'm frightened."

It's cold in the Summerlands of Tommy Town.

"Commander Tom's Toy Corps," you scream. "Assemble!"

No army arrives. No cavalry stampedes. The shambling form approaches.

Grabbing Carol's hand, you dash into the ravine, jumping the root beer creek and the bushels of candy grapes.

"He's still following us!" Carol screams.

You dash across the rickety bridge of the Rocky Road River. The bridge falls with one blow of your wooden sword and disappears in the chocolate current, just as the lumberjack arrives.

"Ha! Too slow, you sneaky, fat bastard!"

The lumberjack stands there. Face full of zits like a hornet's nest, dandruff-sprinkled hair pushed over his big ears. He's sweating grease in the late afternoon sun.

"What kind of monster is he?" Carol asks, holding you tight. "A zombie? A gargoyle?"

"The kind that can't reach me."

"Let's leave. He looks awful, probably smells worse."

"No. I'm done running. This is my place.

"You're so brave, Thomas."

"Hey! You! Get out of my neighborhood!"

The lumberjack looks around. His face is pinched and sour. "You make it yourself?"

"Yeah, and I didn't invite you."

"Nice digs. Sure beats my house on Shady Pine," says the lumberjack. "Ever been there?"

"What's he talking about?" Carol asks. "There's no Shady Pine here. No pines at all. Go away!"

"That must be Mrs. Tanner," says the lumberjack. "Found the old photo in your toy trunk, in the den, under the *Playboys*. Along with her letters. I thought you said she'd moved to Kansas, but they say she's still in town."

Carol shivers and hugs tighter. "He's awful. Make him stop. Please? He doesn't know about first love."

"You better shut your mouth," you say.

The lumberjack crosses his arms. "Or else what?"

You hold your breath and wish him away. Wish for the army to smash him. For the sun to melt him. For the earth to open and drag him to Hell. The lumberjack spreads his stance like a gunfighter and spits in the river. The chocolate hisses.

"I learned about this daydream junk years ago. Guess I got that from you," he snorts. "Not that you'd noticed."

"Daydream?" Carol says. "Thomas, please, make him go away. Why can't you make it like it was?"

There is no good answer.

Carol and her copy of *To Kill a Mockingbird* vanish. The river gurgles between you and the lumberjack.

"You've been playing with my head all day," you say. "The chair. The dragon. That's you."

The lumberjack snorts. "Just clues. To help you remember who you are."

"I know who I am!"

"Right. Commander Tom. My hero." He walks across the chocolate river in his filthy white sneakers and the water blackens. You stumble back and hit another oak tree. Then he's staring down at you.

The lumberjack crosses his arms. "It's time to come home, Dad."

You give chase. You hide. You call for every clown monster hiding in the caves of the storm giants. The robot monsters of Sky City. But nothing works, as if the world has an ice-cream headache.

There's only one place to run. You slam the door to the house, and the echo dies in the emptiness.

* * *

The lumberjack's in the kitchen, eating bacon, licking his fingers. "Nice place. Kinda messy, though. Guess that's your style."

"Just go away."

"I'm not leaving until you get out of here."

"No. Never. I live here."

He stands with shaking fists. "Then I'll make you."

"No way you can do that!"

"Goddamn it! I can't take care of the house and look after Rebecca on my own and go to school. We have mail stacked to the roof. We...got a letter from Mom."

You hug yourself and roll on the sticky floor.

"Shut up, shut up, shut up!"

The lumberjack's boots are like anvils smacking your backside.

"Pay attention! I read it, when I couldn't find you."

Hope rises, and the world dulls to a black-and-white picture.

"Is she...is she coming home?" Your face relaxes. "She is, isn't she? We could do like we did. I'll take care of you like when you were small. I'll be good, won't wander, just like..."

"No." The lumberjack is back in awful Halloween black and Christmas red. "Said she was tired of raising three kids by herself. Now I know what she meant."

You run to the moving sidewalk, hoping to reach the bed. He's too big to follow you under there. You'll try to reach your secret lair, miles beneath the city. You'll call Doc Savage, Batman, everyone will come to help. "Leave me here! Go away!"

He yanks you in the air by the overalls, his breath like chimney smoke.

"You pathetic shit. We need you. I can't do this on my own. We're out of food. Even the cereal's gone." He shakes you hard. "Grow up, Dad!"

Ice-cream tears snap from your lids. "I don't wanna!"

"You want Rebecca to starve?"

"Don't say that name!"

"Do you know what you look like? Hiding in the damn closet?" He shakes the tears out of you. "Look!"

A black hole emerges on the once serene blue wall. A skeleton sits in a closet, hugging an ice cream tub. "Stop it!" Pain flashes but the hole won't close. "That's not me! That's not me!"

"You selfish fuck. I'll drag you back if I have to."

Head smacks floor. Down the hall, the locked door clicks. A slender hand emerges from the dark crack. A red, sharp fingernail beckons you closer then vanishes inside.

"Fine." You stand up and take stock. "How old are you?"

"Jesus." The lumberjack grabs his head. "Fifteen, Dad. I'm fifteen."

The door closes, but does not lock. "I missed your birthday. Didn't I?"

The lumberjack holds himself.

"I'm sorry. I'm real sorry. Not really a good father, am I?" You shoegaze. He coughs. "I'll make it up to you. I have a present in my room."

"I don't want a present, Dad. Just walk through the hole. Don't make me—"

"Please," you beg, "I've been so rotten, it just isn't fair. Let me make it up to you. Let me try and fix this." You hold your hand up. "Please? Then we can go. I'm not going anywhere. Please, son?"

The lumberjack's crossed arms slowly unfurl. "No funny stuff?"

"Nothing funny about this at all," you say, inhaling the perfume drifting from the door. "Let me do good. Please? Michael?"

His giant right hand holds yours as the sidewalk moves you along. The door begins to creak open. "Know what your grandfather gave me when I was fifteen?" you ask. "My first *Playboy*." Michael laughs nervously, and his giant hands are soon wet. The room on the left gets closer. He doesn't notice what's up! Ha! Too young! "Yup. Lot of good times with that magazine over the years. You say you found my collection?"

Mike's face reddens. "Well, I was looking for, uh, you, and..."

You laugh. The door opens a tad more. "It's ok. It's normal. It's what you're supposed to do. It's a great time, that first year. When all the women are gods." The door opens wide. "And no matter how ugly you are, they all worship you."

Beauty crams the door: angelic faces with devil eyes, giant breasts with eager nipples, blood red lips curved in knowing smiles, legs wrapped in stockings and balanced on dagger heels. Michael's face hangs off his skull like melting cheese. You slip out of his wet grip as they pull him into the dark room, giggling. Their lips descend, their limbs tangle. His mouth is permanently kissed, and his face turns blueberry.

"Happy Birthday, Mikey!" you say, the door closing.

Delicious submission flushes Michael's face, but he resists enough to turn around and see you before the door closes. His eyes redden as a word slips out.

"Rebecca!"

Darkness floods.

It is very cold.

Weak arms and sticky hands cling to the giant tub. Coats rub your head as you sway back and forth on the closet floor.

Michael's body twitches beside the old toy trunk, four feet away, surrounded by fast food garbage, toys and *Playboy* magazines. The stink is unholy. Roaches dart toward him from you, disappearing beneath his shaggy hair.

A thumping comes from outside. Feet descending stairs. Getting closer. The melting tub is iron on your lap, your fist rammed inside.

Only a few scoops left. Steps get louder. Your hand is pushed deeper, until there's nothing but the frigid handful at the bottom of the tub. A figure walks in, a strawberry dragon in her mitts. "Michael?"

You shove some in. It melts easy and loose. Too warm. Too old. Too little. Too late.

She drags her dragon behind her until she sees you. "Daddy?"

Tears swell as you bury your face in the tub, ramming it hard until you breathe ice cream.

Her voice muffles. "You hurt Michael?"

You bite the frigid bottom until the shimmering pierces your mind, until it's Saturday morning!

You jump from bed, onto the floor, and run face first into a strawberry dragon. It looks down at you from heaven.

"You said you wouldn't. If I played with you."

Chills kill the sun. The dragon's once fuzzy teeth are now butcher sharp and the size of tusks.

"You play hide and seek too much." Two massive scoops of ice cream drip from the creature's mouth like rabid lava, its voice like a sing-song children's song. "But I found you, Daddy. Yes I did. You hurt Michael and I found you."

Dragons teeth clench, and the pain burns cold as the Summerlands melt in your eyes.

DAVID A. RILEY

David A. Riley lives in England and is both an acclaimed editor and author of horror fiction.

Riley's first short story, "The Lurkers in the Abyss," was published in 1970 in the *Eleventh Pan Book of Horror Stories*. The story was later selected by editor John Pelan for inclusion in *The Century's Best Horror Fiction*, published by Cemetery Dance in 2012. Riley has also had a number of articles published in David Sutton's prestigious fanzine, *Shadow*, including pieces on Franz Kafka and William Morris.

His first collection of short stories, *His Own Mad Demons: Dark Tales from David A. Riley*, was published in 2012. Riley's Lovecraftian novel *The Return* and a second collection, *The Lurkers in the Abyss & Other Tales of Terror*, will be released in 2013.

Over the years, Riley has had numerous stories published in Britain and the United States, with many of those having been translated into other languages. His work has appeared in magazines that include *World of Horror*, *Fear*, *Whispers*, *Fantasy Tales*, *Aboriginal Science Fiction*, *Dark Discoveries* and *Lovecraft eZine*. With his wife Linden, he edited and published the science fiction/fantasy magazine *Beyond*.

He and his wife now run a bookshop in Oswaldtwistle, Lancashire.

SCRAP

BY DAVID A. RILEY

It was a month since Gary and his older brother moved into their new house in Edgebottom, and he hated it. Although the council estate was similar to the one they'd been brought up on in Blackburn, that was where all their friends lived and they couldn't get on with the lads here, who seemed to be a close knit bunch of inbred country bumpkins. Edgebottom was miles from anywhere, stuck out in a valley in the middle of the moors like a big grey canker. Gary liked the word canker. Then again, he had a fondness for words that puzzled others, especially Eddie.

While a year older, Eddie was so slow he'd been kept back a year in school and was now in the same class as Gary. That always struck Gary as hilarious. Some people thought they had to be twins because they were in the same year, till he explained that, no, he wasn't the runt of the litter—Eddie was two inches taller than him—it was because Eddie was thick. Not that he ever let Eddie hear him say that. Thick or not, Gary loved him in a way only brothers brought up by arsehole parents could, even though one of those arseholes was dead.

A mean little man, their father had always either been drunk or on drugs, and never worked. It was a bright day for the boys when he'd overdosed, which was how they came to leave their council house in Blackburn and ended up in Edgebottom, where their mum grew up.

Their old home might not have been heaven on earth, but this place was shit as far as Gary and Eddie were concerned, especially when their mum shacked up with another loser. Ten years younger than their mother, Pete didn't look it, with bad skin and bags beneath his eyes. So far he hadn't hit the boys, but they had had more than a few warnings, and Gary was wary. It wouldn't be long before something happened, though time was on their side. Eddie would be fifteen at the end of the month, and they were getting big enough to stand up for themselves, especially if they looked out for each other.

Gary gazed across their garden with its tufts of dead dandelions, nettles and scraps of garbage—most of it rusting—that Pete had dumped in it, like the engine of a crashed motorbike that was seeping oil or the fridge whose insides stank and were full of mould. It was impossible for Gary to imagine anyone ever putting food in there.

In the distance he could see the grey rooftops of Grudge End, a derelict area of terraced streets that rose up the same steep slope as the estate. Some of Grudge End's streets had been demolished, which was where the estate had been built. The rest loomed like a drab ghost town, about which he had heard enough tales from the boys at school to give him the creeps. It had a bad reputation, even though no one lived there anymore. From what he'd heard at school no one had lived there since long before any of his classmates were born. It was supposed to have been demolished by the council years ago, but for some reason no one seemed able to explain why they hadn't. One word was that the council couldn't find anyone who was interested in developing it, so the houses stayed, decaying in their own good time, but that seemed unlikely to Gary.

His jeans tight about his knees, Eddie hunkered down next to him. He was struggling to roll a cigarette using tobacco he'd collected from dog ends discarded outside pubs. Eddie had only just taken up smoking and was rubbish at rolling them. His thick fingers were too clumsy, and more strings of tobacco fell out than stayed in as he tried to do it. Gary laughed at him.

"You're shit."

Eddie glared at him, then grinned. He passed him what he'd managed so far. "You do it for me."

"Only if I get a couple of puffs when it's done," Gary said, accepting the remnants. Though far from proficient, his fingers looked nimble compared to his brother's as he remade it.

"Wish I had enough money to buy new ones." Eddie sounded wistful.

"Not much chance of that."

Their mum never had any money to spare, and what she got from the social and from child benefit went on her own habits first— the usual Trinity of fags, drugs and booze. As for her boyfriend Pete, neither brother had the guts to ask him for anything. He even begrudged the badly cooked food their mum gave them.

"There's a scrap yard in town that'll pay good money for any odds and ends of metal," Eddie said. "Some of the lads at school were telling me about it. They make a few quid every week, easy peasy."

Gary looked up, his interest piqued. "Where do they find it?"

"Here an' there," Eddie said. He knitted his brows as if trying to remember what he'd been told. "They go down back alleys where someone might've been mending a car or thrown stuff out."

Gary considered it for a few moments. "Might be worth a try," he said. "We could go and see what we can find now." Their mum and Pete were at the pub and wouldn't be back till late. He handed Eddie the reconstructed cigarette. His brother put it in his pocket for later. They stood up and dashed down the path, batting the gate open.

"Where do you think we should look first?"

Gary shrugged, unsure. "Anywhere, I s'ppose."

They wandered down the avenue, scanning its gardens, not sure for what they were looking. Eddie spotted an old-fashioned pram someone had left by a gate. It was rusty and one of its wheels was buckled. The kids inside the house sometimes used it as a go-cart. Gary grabbed hold of it, tilting it on its undamaged rear wheels. "We could put what we find in this," he said.

"We'd look like a pair of sissies."

"Do you know how heavy scrap metal is? If you want to lug it in your arms…"

Eddie grunted.

"Hey, you! That's my sister's pram." A plump little redhead, Angelica Louise, stood at the front door of the nearest house, fists on her hips.

Eddie stared back at her and grinned.

Gary's words might not have convinced him to take the pram; Angelica Louise's had. Waving two fingers at her, Eddie set off at a run, the pram wheels squealing. They tore down the avenue towards the road at the bottom where the estate ended. Eddie took the corner at full pelt, missing an elderly couple by barely an inch. Gary followed behind, laughing as the old man shouted, shaking his fist.

"Go fuck yourself!" Eddie shouted back as they wove around shoppers on the pavement. Two blocks later they stopped, panting.

Gary grinned at his brother. "Let's start."

Eddie's forehead creased in puzzled ridges. "Where?"

Gary nodded across the road to where rows of terraced streets surrounded a church steeple. "It's no good this side. There's only Grudge End and I'm not looking there."

"Why not? There could be loads of scrap there and no one to stop us." Eddie looked too cocksure for the blankness in his eyes. "You're not scared, are you?"

Gary was—he'd heard too many tales at school—but he wasn't eager to admit this to Eddie. "It's been empty too long. Everything'll have been scavenged years ago."

"You think?"

SCRAP 119

Gary nodded. "'Course it will."

When there was a break in the traffic they wheeled the pram to the opposite pavement. The houses on that side only went back for several blocks before they ended at farmland—or what passed for farmland hereabouts: steep-sloping fields from which rocks jutted through the thin soil. Most of the houses were empty, FOR SALE notices shaking in the wind. Eddie wondered if being close to Grudge End put people off buying them. It was dispiriting here, especially when there was almost nothing worth putting inside the pram. After more than an hour they had only a few scraps of iron: a useless padlock welded with rust, some back door hinges and part of a car exhaust so full of holes Gary was sure it would be laughed at by the scrap metal dealer if they took it to him.

"We're wasting our time," Eddie said, stopping the pram and leaning on it. He looked irritable and tired. Eddie always got bored easily. If they found any metal worth anything at all he would soon cheer up, but there didn't seem much likelihood of that, not here.

"We'd be better off across the road," Eddie said.

"How d'you know? Grudge End's been empty for years."

"It's big. No one could've scrounged everything. Besides," his brother added with a knowing wink, "if no one lives there, there's no one to stop us going inside some of the houses. There'll be water pipes and stuff like that we could nick. We only need some lead pipes to make us loads. How long would that take?"

Gary stared across the road to where Grudge End rose in row after row of terraced roofs, gloomy, cramped, inhospitable, its streets disjointed in haphazard lines as if planned by a madman determined to make sure that anyone who didn't know them well would soon get lost. Gary did not want to go there. Even if what he had heard whispered about the place at school wasn't enough, there was something about it that gave him the creeps.

"Pete would kill us if we got caught breaking in," he said.

Eddie shook his head. "Who'd catch us? No one lives there. There won't be any police or anyone else to get us. It'll be easy."

Easy peasy, Gary thought, unconvinced.

Eddie shook the pram, rattling the scraps of metal they had gathered so far. "D'you think this is enough for all the time we've wasted? We could fill it from just one house. Betcha."

Gary stared at the odds and ends inside the pram. He knew his brother was right. It was just that he knew he felt frightened. Not that he would admit this to Eddie. He'd never hear the end of it.

"C'mon," Eddie said. "If we don't find something in the first two houses, we'll call it a day. Okay?" Eddie punched him conspiratorially on the shoulder.

"Just two? No more? Whatever we find?"

Eddie grinned at him. "You're scared of the fucking place, aren't you?"

Gary shook his head. "Like fuck I am. If we get nicked, Pete would kill us. That's all."

"Yeah…" Eddie turned the pram and ran across the road through a gap in the traffic. Gary followed, outpacing a Ford Mondeo that barely slowed. He ignored its horn.

Eddie laughed as he led them along the street.

"You've heard all about the murders in Grudge End, haven't you?" Gary asked, still hoping to dissuade his brother from taking them there.

"Yeah, yeah. I've heard about them. Who hasn't?"

"Whole families were murdered, Eddie—always killed by one of their own, before he topped himself."

"Ancient history."

"Not that ancient, you pilluck. The kids would have still been around if they hadn't been killed. The place was full of shit like that."

"Which is why it's deserted," Eddie said. "Lucky for us, eh?"

They turned a corner. Ahead of them loomed Grudge End. Entering its deserted streets felt like stepping back in time. Gary realised that little had probably changed here since long before he was born. Unlike the streets in Edgebottom there were no cars by the kerbs, and most house windows had been boarded up, row after row of them as far as he could see. Those that weren't had slovenly curtains hung behind them, grey with mould, like limp eyelids.

Gary wondered which of the houses might have had murders inside them. He knew there had to be scores of them from what he'd been told. The area had been a hotbed for rival cults, brimming with violence for as far back as anyone could remember, with witchcraft scares in earlier centuries to the dark religious fanaticism of later years. At first, Gary thought his leg was being pulled when he heard about the place at school, before he realised his new-found friends were serious. None of them would come here, he knew. Not like him and Eddie. Which made him worried that he was letting his brother get him into something he'd have been better off staying well away from. They needed money, but he was sure they could scrape together enough scrap metal without coming here.

Eddie looked behind them.

"Told you there'd be no one here," he said.

Gary followed his gaze. Now that the main road was hidden behind a bend in the street, they were alone. Even the sound of traffic had muted to a drone. Gary shivered. It felt colder here, but he was not sure if this was what affected him.

"Let's make it quick," he said.

Eddie snickered. "Slick and quick."

He pointed at the nearest house, but Gary shook his head.

"Not a boarded up one," he said. "It'll be black inside. There won't be any lights working."

Eddie nodded. It was obvious he hadn't thought of that.

The nearest houses that hadn't been boarded up weren't far away. Gary glanced up at a name plate bolted to the top corner of the terrace. Hope Street. Not much of that here, he thought, wondering whether to mention it to his brother, though he didn't suppose Eddie would see the joke.

Eddie tried the door of the first house. It was locked, though its panelled door, stripped bare by the weather, looked weak and rotten. He stood back and gave it a savage kick with the sole of his shoe. It burst inwards, ripped off its hinges.

"Easy peasy," Eddie shouted. His cry echoed from the brick walls of the surrounding blocks, though for a moment Gary had the odd impression that at least one of the echoes came from a different voice, as if someone else had joined in, mocking him.

"Let's be quick," Gary said as Eddie dragged the pram inside the house.

The vestibule reeked of damp and decay. The front room smelt even worse, and Gary felt like gagging. A square of carpet covered the floorboards. It squelched beneath their feet. Above it, a hole gaped in the ceiling, fringed with rotting paper, laths and plaster. Water was dripping from it, black in the half light. It splashed into a stagnant puddle that had spread across the carpet.

Eddie wrinkled his nose.

"The kitchen'll be where there're any pipes worth nicking." He bustled through.

Floor tiles curled up at their corners from the asphalt floor, tripping them as they dragged the pram through. A row of kitchen units sagged beneath their heavy work top. A shattered tea mug littered part of the floor like broken teeth.

Eddie squealed with delight. He pointed at the copper water pipes fixed to the walls.

"Help me rip these out. They're worth loads."

Together, they yanked them away from the wall, working them back and forth till they snapped free. No water leaked from them. That must have been cut off long ago, probably when the house was abandoned, Gary thought. They worked on bending the pipes into manageable lengths they could load into the pram. Eddie found some lead ones under the work units, which he kicked apart, then added to their cache. They cleared the kitchen of everything of any value they could work loose. Already the pram was almost full.

Eddie looked at it with pride.

"All it took was one house," he said.

"Let's call it a day." Gary felt uncomfortable here, not just because it smelt bad, but because somehow he didn't feel they were alone. He gave the pram a hefty push. "Let's get out of here."

Even though the buckled wheel made it difficult to steer the pram along the pavement, they were soon back on the road into town. Even Eddie wasted no time in pushing the pram away from the house, cursing every time it cockled to one side. He was red-faced and panting by the time they reached the edge of the town centre, where they headed towards the scrap yard.

*　*　*

"The fucking bastard cheated us, you know," Eddie grumbled an hour later as they sat on one of the benches in Crows Nest Park, which overlooked the town. His fingers trembled as he puffed at one of the cigarettes they'd bought from the ten pound note they'd got from the scrap yard.

Gary shrugged. He had no idea how much the metal they'd collected was worth, though it was just like Eddie to be convinced they should have got more. If the guy at the yard had given them more Eddie would still have been sure they'd been swindled.

"At least it got us a pack of fags — and some change."

"Only just, the tight bastard," Eddie said.

Eddie stared at the ground. The pram stood only a couple of feet from them.

"We could go back for more, now we know how easy it is," he said. "Like taking sweets from a baby, only easier," he added with a grin. "Old houses don't burst into tears."

Gary shook his head.

"I'm not going back, not today. I've had enough of that place for a while. It gave me to creeps."

"You're chicken."

Gary shrugged. "You can call me what you like, I'm not going back. Perhaps in a few days," he said, in the hope he could put Eddie off for a while.

Eddie puffed hard on his cigarette, agitated. "Who needs you anyway? I did most of the work while we were there." He flexed his fingers. "I could do without you whining about getting away. If I'd been by myself I'd have stripped another house and got even more from that tight bastard."

"How'd you know he'd have paid any more? If he's as tight as you say, he might've given us a tenner no matter what we'd piled in that pram."

Eddie snorted. "You're scared," he sneered. "Like a soft little girl."

Gary felt like hitting him, though he knew he'd get the worst of it. He always did; with his brother's height and weight advantage it was no contest. Even so…

Eddie gazed across the valley to where Grudge End spread in a dark grey blotch across the hillside. Gary followed his eyes and shuddered.

"You could act as lookout if you don't want to go inside," Eddie said.

Gary wondered how much of what his brother had been saying was hot air. He felt like asking if he was too scared to go by himself except he was unsure if that would have been a good idea. Eddie could be a vicious bastard when he wanted to be, just like their dad.

Their dead dad.

Gary shrugged. "If you wanna."

"You're not too scared?"

Gary felt like telling his brother to fuck off, but shook his head instead. He was already regretting he had let Eddie manipulate him. The last thing he wanted was to go back to Grudge End.

"We'll have to hurry. The scrap yard shuts at six; it's half four now."

Eddie drew in the last inch of his cigarette, expelling the smoke with gusto, then stood up, grabbed the cheap plastic handle of the pram and set off downhill at a pace that forced Gary to run to catch up.

For all his moans, Eddie had never had as much as ten pounds in his hands before, even if half of it belonged to Gary. Though they had spent most of it on cigarettes and a plastic lighter, they still had enough left over to share out nearly three pounds between them, which was more than enough for him.

Why was Eddie so keen on going there again? Gary knew it wasn't just the money. Or was it?

* * *

A light rain was falling by the time they reached Grudge End. The end of a perfect day, Gary thought, feeling wet already. Eddie didn't seem to mind. He was already thinking about the next ten pounds he felt sure they would get when they returned to the scrap yard.

Eddie headed straight to the house next door to the one they pillaged before. Its door was no sturdier, and it was only a few seconds before they were dragging the pram inside. Even more damp-stained than the other, there were great streaks of fungus hanging on wallpaper that had begun to fall free, and on the exposed plaster beneath. There was a smell of dead rodent and the skeletal remains of what looked like a cat by the hearth. A metal pin, like a rusty knitting needle, but longer and heavier, had been hammered through its blackened ribs.

"Jesus! Who did that?" Gary whispered.

Eddie laughed. "Some sick bastard."

He laughed again when he spotted a copper pipe down one wall. He grabbed it, wrenched it back and forth till it broke free. Using leverage he folded it in two. He looked back at Gary. "This should get us a fiver at least."

Not waiting for a reply, Eddie pushed the pram towards the

kitchen, kicking the door open. It swung with a thud against the wall, loosening plaster.

The smell grew worse.

"Something's dead in there," Gary said. "Something big."

Which was when, over Eddie's shoulder, he caught sight of the body curled beneath the kitchen sink. It was bloated, its utilitarian feminine clothes straining against swollen, elephantine limbs. Something wet had spread across the linoleum from under the body like rancid syrup that had dried into dark brown, yellowish crusts at the edges.

Gary turned away from it, felt his stomach begin to cramp, before he threw up against the wall. Whatever he had eaten all day was heaved onto it, splashing his jeans. Abandoning the pram, Eddie blundered into him. His face looked bleached and scared. He could barely speak, gesturing at Gary to get out of the house while making inarticulate sounds at the back of his throat like a strangled hen. At any other time Gary would have laughed at him, but now he turned and scrambled onto the street. Rain showered his face as he stared up at it, gasping for breath. Drops of it washed away some of the vomit from his lips, but not enough. He could still taste its acidic bite.

He saw Eddie staring at him, his eyes grown huge and frightened.

"It had no head." His brother's voice barely more than a whisper, Gary was unsure if he heard him correctly.

"No head?" Even as he said it Gary felt his gorge rise again, even though he was sure he couldn't have anything left in his stomach. He grimaced as his muscles cramped.

Eddie stared into the house. "Do you think we should tell the police?"

"And tell them we broke in?" He took a deep breath; the nausea finally started to seep away. "You sure there was no head?"

Eddie nodded. "There was just a stump." He grimaced at the memory, and Gary could tell he was only just stopping himself from being sick as well.

"We should get away from here as quick as we can and forget about it. We don't want the police to know we've been here. You know what Pete would do if they came to our house. He'd go mental."

"Big time."

"We need to get the pram," Gary said. "If they find that here it might link us to this place."

"How? It's only a battered old pram."

"And how many people saw us today? No one's likely to forget it, especially Angelica Louise. Anyway, our fingerprints are on it."

Eddie swore beneath his breath.

"I'll get it," Gary said. He was starting to feel better. Perhaps an empty stomach helped. He wiped the rain across his face, took a deep breath before going inside again, then strode to the kitchen. All he had to do was grab the pram and drag it back after him. He didn't need to look at what was on the floor. He could keep his eyes fixed on the pram. That was all.

But he couldn't help it. Even though he did not want to see them again, remembrance of the swollen limbs drew his eyes to the floor as his hands took hold of the pram. But the floor was empty. Too startled to react straight away, Gary's fingers tightened around the pram's handle, ready to jerk it towards him, except that he couldn't move. He stiffened as he stared at the stained linoleum. He could see where the body had been. He could even see it in his imagination, curled like a grotesque, oversized foetus, gross with decay, but there were only the huge stains on the floor like spilled gravy, mouldy with age.

"Eddie!" His voice cracked, brittle with hysteria. "Eddie!" He was relieved to hear his brother lumber through the house behind him. "It's gone," he shouted, pointing to the spot where the body had been.

More scared than before, Gary pulled the pram's handle but the thing wouldn't move. Panicking, he wrenched at it, but it was as if someone was tugging it from him, and for the briefest of moments he could have sworn he saw someone on the other side of the pram, staring at him—an old-fashioned Teddy Boy, with slicked back hair, shiny with Brylcreem.

"The pram's stuck," he shouted to Eddie. His brother took hold of one end of the handle, adding his weight. Even then it was a struggle.

"Come on, you bastard," Eddie snarled; his teeth ground together with the effort, before the pram suddenly came free, almost bowling them over. Panic-stricken, Gary backed as quickly as he could out of the house, dragging the pram behind him.

"Whoever killed her must have taken her body," Eddie said when they were outside.

Startled at the thought, Gary's head swivelled to the door behind them, suddenly scared that her killer might come for them too. That must have been who grabbed hold of the pram, Gary thought, though the image of the youth he thought he'd seen was fading from his mind's eye, as if he had never been there. And Eddie never even seemed to notice him.

"Do you think he heard us?"

Eddie shook his head. He pushed the pram down the street so fast he was almost running. "Fuck knows," he said between breaths. "Let's get out of here, Gary."

* * *

Back on their own estate, they rammed the pram against the gate of Angelica Louise's house, abandoning it before hurrying home in time to catch the tail end of a raging row between Pete and their mum. Both sounded drunk. The boys ran upstairs, knowing there would be little chance of anything to eat tonight, though they had enough money left for a bag of chips and some sausages from the chippie later, which was probably better than what they could expect from their mum, even if she did manage to put something together. They had had burnt offerings too often in the past when she got like this to have any illusions. Empty stomachs they could live with. It was what Pete might do that worried them. He was an unknown quantity, and they meant to keep away from him for the rest of the day if they could.

Picking through dog-eared comics in their bedroom they talked over what had happened. It seemed like a dream to them now, already beginning to doubt that they had really seen a body.

"It was dark," Eddie said, scratching his forehead where an archipelago of pimples marred his skin. "We might've imagined it. Yeah?"

Even though he could still vividly see the rot-thickened legs, bursting through their laddered tights, Gary had doubts as well. It was more like something he'd seen in a film, too gross to be real.

"Besides," Eddie said, "how could a body disappear without us hearing?"

Gary frowned, wondering about the certainty he'd had that someone had been tugging the pram back into the kitchen. "They could have used the back door," he suggested, weakly.

Eddie shook his head, scowling.

Could they have imagined it? Gary wished he could believe it, but he knew, deep down, that they hadn't. There'd been a body or something that looked like one, though how it disappeared during the few minutes it was out of their sight he had no idea.

In an effort to think about something else, Gary flicked through a copy of *The Spider-Man*, but his eyes glided over its graphics. Clearer was the body. He could smell it. Its powerful odour seemed stuck inside his nostrils.

* * *

"What's this about you selling scrap metal?" Pete stood in the doorway to their bedroom, their mother behind him, a can of lager in one hand.

The brothers made exclamations of denial but Pete shut them up.

"You were seen, you stupid arseholes." Pete smirked. "Where'd you get it? And don't try telling me it was lying in the street. Not these days. It's worth too fucking much."

"Have you been nicking?" Their mother's lined face, looking years older than she was, was dominated by her eyes that flashed anger at her sons. "You'd better not, you little bastards. I'm not having the police coming here after you."

"Any filth come here," Pete added, his eyes darting from one boy to the other, "I'll leather you." His fists looked hard and knobbly. He clenched them as if barely restraining himself from using them now. "So where the fuck did you get it?"

"We weren't nicking." Eddie told them what they did, stammering badly, though he did not mention the body.

"Can you fucking believe them?" Pete's laugh was a humourless bark. "They've been breaking into houses in *Grudge End*!" He shook his head at them. "You must be fucking mental. How long have you lived here? Has no one warned you about that fucking place?" He whipped the back of his hand across Eddie's face, making him yelp. "Fucking morons!"

Still swearing, he trundled downstairs. Their mother cast the boys a mixture of pity and scorn, then followed, calling Pete's name. Seconds later the front door slammed shut as they went down the path, arguing.

Eddie stared at his brother. "What've we done?"

Gary shrugged, uncertain. Though baffled by Pete's reaction, he was more concerned by their mother's. It wasn't just that they had broken into empty houses that seemed to bother her but that they'd done it in Grudge End.

"Why are they frightened of that place?" Gary asked.

"Everyone is in this soddin' town." Eddie grimaced. "Kids'll laugh about it at school but you can tell they're scared."

"And you still insisted we went there?"

Eddie shrugged. "You've heard the tales too."

"I don't believe them."

"Me neither." Eddie grinned. "They're all retarded in this place. So what's it matter?"

Gary thought about what happened at the house. "That body had been dead for ages, hadn't it? It was rotting. Stuff had leaked from it." He felt nauseated telling his brother this. It brought the images back too vividly.

"So?"

"So why'd someone shift it while we were there? Why wasn't it moved earlier?"

"What're you talking about?"

Gary wasn't sure. "Could it have been a ghost?" he suggested.

Eddie laughed. "The ghost of a dead body, you loon?"

Gary shrugged. "Maybe."

"You're bonkers."

"You have any better ideas?" he asked.

Eddie turned away, angry. Gary wondered if something about what he had said scared him. Eddie always got bad tempered when he was frightened.

"I heard that loads of weird things went on when people lived there."

"That's shit."

"Is it?" Gary wasn't so sure. "Everyone says it. One of the lads at school was rabbiting on about Hope Street."

"Where's Hope Street?" Eddie stared at him with puzzled annoyance.

"Those houses we broke into, they're there. I saw the sign. I wish I'd remembered what he told us about it before we broke in. He said there were murders there years ago. This lad went crazy, killed his family. Butchered them. Hacked off their heads."

"That's bullshit."

"There were others. Grudge End was full of shit like that."

"*Bull*shit, you mean. I wouldn't listen to what any of those mongs at school told me. The town's full of retards. We shouldn't have come here. We were okay where we were."

Gary agreed with this. He missed their estate. It wasn't as if mum was any happier here. If anything, since she hooked up with Pete, she drank even more. She'd be drinking now, and it would be well past midnight before she got home with Pete, pissed out of their minds, scrapping and screaming. It made him sick. One day they'd go too far and one of them would get killed.

Outside Gary heard something bang against the gate, forcing it open.

He jumped to the window, though he couldn't see anyone, just a shadow by the gate, which looked half open.

"Someone's dumped something outside," he said.

Eddie pushed against him, his breath steaming the window pane.

Together they bounded downstairs, unlocked the front door and ran outside. The pram they had used was jammed inside the gate.

"That bloody little sod Angelica Louise," Eddie muttered, without conviction. Gary didn't even bother to ask him why she should have done this. They both knew she hadn't.

Eddie went to the pram and kicked it out onto the pavement, then again till it rolled into the road.

"Fucking thing stinks like shit," Eddie said in disgust, wiping his mouth with the back of his hand, but Gary knew it wasn't shit they could smell. He felt a squirm of fear in his stomach. He recognised the smell as he stood by the gate. It was the spoiled meat stench that had filled the house in Grudge End.

"I'm going in," he said. He heard Eddie behind him as he hurried inside. They locked the door behind them, breathing hard. When they exchanged glances Gary could see that his brother was as scared as him.

"We shouldn't have gone there," Eddie said.

"Too fucking late for that, isn't it?" Though neither of them had been superstitious, Gary knew they shared the same fear for what they had seen in Grudge End.

Outside, they heard the garden gate creak open. There was a squeal of metal as the pram's buckled wheel was forced to turn on its ruined axle. It was being pushed towards the door.

But by whom? Gary wondered. And why?

Pulling it open with his fingers he peered through the letter box, but could see nothing. Then he heard a bump as something small hit the bottom of the door. Even without opening it he could smell the stink of spoiled offal outside.

"What have we done?" Eddie's face was slack, as if all its muscles had begun to dissolve.

Gary did not know what to say. One hand clutched the door handle as if he was about to fling it open or jam it shut. He wasn't sure which impulse to follow; they both tugged at him. He wanted to see what was there, whether it was only an empty pram, but he also wanted to keep whatever might have bumped against the door out of sight, as if that was all that kept them safe.

In the end he let go of the handle. He felt an overwhelming need to use the bathroom. He clambered upstairs. Afterwards, feeling sick, he saw some of Pete's underwear piled inside the door to the main bedroom. On an impulse, Gary snatched some of it and ran downstairs.

Ignoring Eddie's stare of disgust, Gary prised open the letter box and forced the underwear out through the hole. He heard it land inside the pram.

"Pete'll kill you when he sees that," Eddie said. Then his jaw dropped open as the pram began to squeal again. They rushed to the front window. The pram was stood on the pavement again as if it had never moved. Lit only by street lights as the night darkened, Gary felt sure he could see someone stood by the pram.

Gary squinted through the gloom.

"It's gone," he said.

"What do you mean, gone?" Eddie had slumped onto the sofa. He returned to the window, peering through it.

"Can you see it?"

Shadows from a windblown tree jerked back and forth across the gate, making it difficult for them to make out details.

"It must've blown away. Or that bitch came back and took it."

Either reason made sense, though Gary felt unsure, just as he was unsure why he had dumped a pair of Pete's underpants inside the pram. Where the hell had that idea sprung from? If Pete found out he'd never hear the end of it.

Not wanting to be up when their mother got home, it wasn't long before the brothers went upstairs, which was where they were hours later when Gary heard voices outside. He shook his brother awake in the adjoining bed.

Downstairs they heard their mother crying. She sounded hysterical. There were other voices. Some were men's. There was also a woman's.

The boys crept to the landing, where they glanced down to see a uniformed policeman in the hallway. Hearing them, he looked up. Although his face looked tense he managed a brief, perfunctory smile before calling into the front room. Seconds later a uniformed policewoman ran upstairs to the boys and told them what had happened.

Pete was dead.

* * *

No one seemed sure what had happened except that Pete left the pub he had been drinking in with their mother, angry that the taxi he had ordered was late. When she went out a few minutes later he was lying on the ground. Not only had he been killed, but someone had severed his head, which was still missing. Even the glee Gary felt at Pete's death was soured by this detail. He hated the man, yes, but this was something that scared him.

"Don't be stupid," Eddie said when they talked about it later.

Their mother was in bed, drugged on pills prescribed by her doctor. Her sister, Eileen, had come from the other end of the estate to see they were all right. A chip off the same block that had made their mother, her idea of seeing that "they were all right" was to send the boys out for a bottle of gin and some fags while she fried some bacon and made sandwiches dripping with fat. She had commandeered the front room, television and sofa and was watching *Jeremy Kyle* with a glass of gin in one hand and a cigarette in the other while the boys washed up in the kitchen.

"You don't think dropping a pair of Pete's old underkecks into the pram had anything to do with what happened?"

Eddie grunted. "You're soft in the head."

But he wasn't sure, Gary could tell. "It's here again, you know, back at the gate."

"That'll be Angelica Louise, the little bitch."

"You think?" Gary asked, knowing that he didn't. "It stinks," he added, quietly, though there was little enough chance of Aunt Eileen hearing them. Jeremy Kyle was telling someone to *"grow a pair"* at the top of his voice. They could hear Eileen's raucous laughter.

"You've been to look at it?"

Gary nodded. "To make sure I was right."

He was surprised at the look of admiration on his brother's face.

"I'd have been scared shitless," Eddie said.

Gary didn't say how scared he was. It was only because he'd been too curious he'd had the nerve to do it.

"Why's it there?" Eddie asked. "It's already had Pete."

Neither of the boys laughed at the daftness of what he said, as if they knew there was nothing daft about it. Gary smirked at the thought of Pete's underpants acting as a lure.

"We can't send it after someone else," Gary said. "If we ignore it, it'll go away."

"Do you think?"

"Course it will."

* * *

Aunt Eileen was keen on them going back to school, even though they felt they should have stayed off for a few days after the "trauma" of what happened to Pete. There was no pulling the wool over Aunt Eileen's eyes, though. She saw through them straight away. Besides, they could tell she wanted them out of the way. Their mother was beginning to pull herself together, and they suspected Aunt Eileen would probably suggest they should go for some drinks as part of her recuperation. Whatever happened after that, she wouldn't want the boys around the house. They had seen how Eileen liked to enjoy herself when they visited hers.

Whether it was Aunt Eileen's cooking or what had happened to Pete—or maybe both—the brothers suffered bad dreams that night, lying awake for hours before they got up the next morning to go to school. They ran past the pram at the gate post. Even though Gary tried to hold his breath, its smell trailed him. He glanced back as they raced for their bus, grimacing. If anything the smell was even worse.

"There'll be another useless bastard living with us by the time we get back," Eddie said as their bus trundled through Edgebottom.

"What d'you mean?"

Eddie smirked. "Pete *mark two*."

Gary punched him in the ribs. "You're kidding, aren't you?" Gary thought about it for a few minutes. "If there is we could find out if dropping underkecks into the pram really works. That'd sort him out."

The brothers laughed.

Gary wondered if there was something odd about their laughter. Eddie did not seem to be troubled by it, though Gary noticed that others on the school bus with them cast wary glances.

When they got home that night, after rampaging through a couple of town centre shops, where they managed to lift some bars of chocolate and a handful of comics, they saw the windows were wide open. Rock music—the stuff their mother loved—thumped through them, audible as soon as they could see their house.

"Fucking hell," Eddie whispered. His shoulders slumped.

Gary's reaction was to feel his stomach contract with apprehension, knowing the chaos they would find.

"At least they might have got some take-outs," Eddie said.

"And scoffed the lot."

A thin man dressed in baggy jeans that hung off his scrawny buttocks, a t-shirt and boots, opened the door before they got there, staggered out into the garden and was violently sick, though he still managed to hold a spliff in one hand. He turned as the boys approached the gate. For a few seconds he gazed at them with incomprehension as he balanced himself against the house with one hand, before understanding sank into his eyes. He had a deeply wrinkled, pale yellow face, a crooked nose and stubble across his bony head. He looked even meaner than Pete, and Gary hoped this wasn't *mark two*.

"You must be the boys," the man slurred. He winked at them. "Your mother's a wonderful woman, a wonderful, wonderful woman. You don't know how lucky you are."

He waved them to the door, which he'd left wide open. Resentful at being invited into their own home, the brothers barged past. There was a strong smell of marijuana inside. Gary hadn't smelt it since his father's death. It brought back bad memories, memories he thought he had forgotten till now. People—strangers most of them—pottered about the house; some lounging against the walls as they laughed and smoked and drank from cans, others sat on what few chairs there were or on the floor and at least one was asleep.

The music from the front room was deafeningly loud, and Gary could not understand how any of them could talk or sleep with a heavy metal anthem pounding through their ears. He nodded to Eddie, indicating that they should go upstairs, but their mother forestalled him. Mascara daubed in smears around her eyes as if she was auditioning for a horror flick, she tripped in front of them, precariously holding herself against the doorframe. Ash sparkled from her cigarette as it hit the wallpaper; gin sloshed onto the carpet from her glass as she looked at her sons, shaking her head as if chastising her clumsiness.

"Help yourselves to some food in the kitchen. Karl got fish and chips."

"Okay, mum," Eddie said.

The boys left her and went into the kitchen, which was slightly quieter. There were only four people there, in deep conversation while they helped themselves to cans of lager from the fridge. A pile of greaseproof paper bags had been left on the side of the sink. Inside, they managed to find one bag of chips. All the rest had been emptied and screwed into balls.

"Let's eat outside," Gary said. His head was already starting to ache from the noise and the overwhelming smell of drugs, cigarettes and alcohol inside the house. If he had tried to eat any of the chips there he knew he'd be sick.

"She's got over Pete," Eddie said matter-of-factly as they squatted on the edge of the pavement, feet in the road, the chip bag opened between them.

Gary said nothing as he chewed. He had known it wouldn't take her long. It hadn't after the death of their father. Only a few days after his funeral Pete had moved in. "A home needs a man inside it," their mother had told them; it was all the explanation she had ever given.

"A home needs a man inside it," Gary repeated. He saw Eddie stiffen.

"You don't think that scumbag's the one?"

"If he's here when the rest have gone, what do you think?"

Eddie gazed down the street, deep in thought. He flicked a chip into the road, watching as a pigeon fluttered down to attack it.

* * *

It wasn't till the following night when they returned home from school that they saw the newcomer slumped on the sofa, drinking with their mother as they watched TV. Little of the debris from the party had been cleared away, and the house stank of lager, stale smoke and sweat.

"You boys get yourself something to eat from the cupboard," their mother called without stirring. When they lingered at the doorway, she turned to the man—the thin-faced skinhead who had greeted them the previous day. "This is Karl."

Karl grinned gap-toothed at them and waved a can of lager in salute.

"Hi, lads," he drawled.

In the kitchen, Eddie opened a can of baked beans and Gary prepared some toast. Gary whispered: "A home needs a man inside it."

"Pity mum can't find one," Eddie whispered back.

Suppressing their giggles, the brothers hurried outside while their beans heated in a saucepan.

Later, when they'd eaten their singed beans and dry toast, they wandered into the front room to watch TV, but after an hour Karl made it obvious they weren't welcome; in any case, it was embarrassing to see him with one arm around their mother, fondling her— and to hear her giggle. Both of them were spaced out on drugs and drink, though Gary suspected Karl was less affected by them than her. After a few minutes, Eddie nudged his brother in the ribs and they went outside again.

"I can't stand the prick," Eddie said as soon as they were out of earshot.

"Won't be long before we'll be dodging backhanders again."

Eddie grimaced. "If I were a year older I'd give him one back." He told Gary that Karl had already threatened him. When he was checking the beans, Karl was going for a can of beer from the fridge. He grabbed Eddie by the scruff of the neck and told him to watch himself.

Even Pete hadn't been as blatant as this.

It was a sign of what they would have to expect.

Desultory, they trudged down the path. Gary kicked the pram to one side. It had again been jammed into their gate, blocking it.

"Who keeps putting this fucking thing here?" Gary grumbled.

Eddie grabbed his arm. "Don't!"

Gary stared at him till comprehension began to dawn, then he shook his head, laughing. "You're not serious, are you, you soft lug?"

Eddie shrugged. "What's to lose?"

Gary laughed again, louder. "Only a pair of Karl's old underpants."

* * *

They were easier to get than they expected. Within a couple of days items of Karl's clothes were spread over the floor of their mother's bedroom, discarded wherever he saw fit. Disregarding the funk that had begun to fill the room, Gary crept in when everyone else was downstairs. Wearing a glove, he scooped up a pair of boxers lined with skid marks. That night he threw them inside the pram. The next morning both were gone.

"Unless we've rats that'll eat anything..." Gary said as they clambered onto their school bus.

Eddie guffawed, which was the first time he'd laughed since Karl's arrival.

* * *

"If nothing happens," Eddie whispered as they lay in bed that night, trying to sleep, "I'm going to do him myself."

Gary was worried that his brother was serious. He knew Eddie would be no match for someone like Karl. If he tried anything, the man would kill him. He shut his eyes, thinking *Please, please, please, just work once more.* He pictured the pram with its buckled wheel. Whoever or whatever was linked to it from Grudge End, he hoped was still there. *Don't let Eddie have to do it.*

Outside, he heard something squeak.

* * *

It was barely dawn when the boys were wrenched awake by hysterical screams from their mother's bedroom.

His heart thumping, Gary threw aside his duvet and leapt out of bed, bare feet skidding on the thin carpet. The door into their mother's room was already open. In it, lit by a single bedside lamp, he could see his mother. She was sat up in bed, hands clamped to the sides of her head as she screamed and screamed. Other than this she seemed unable to move. Her eyes were transfixed on the other side of the bed.

Bumping into each other in confusion, the brothers jammed the doorway. Karl's side of the bed was dark and wet. There was a narrow lump where he lay beneath the duvet. Gary took a step nearer. There was no mistaking that the wetness was blood. It was so bright and shiny it must have only just drenched the cover.

Eddie took hold of his mother's arms, weaning her out of the bed and towards the landing. Gary took a quick look at where Karl was laid, then ran downstairs. Stammering, he phoned for an ambulance. As soon as the ambulancemen looked inside the bedroom, they called the police. By this time, having drunk what was left of a bottle of gin, the boys' mother was a wretched, squawking, pitiful wreck, sat cross-legged on the living room floor among last night's beer cans, pizza boxes and overfilled, spilt ashtrays.

After their mother had been taken to hospital, and the medical examiner was upstairs doing whatever he had to do with the body, the boys were handed over to social services, following their mother to the hospital to be checked over. When Eddie objected, one of the doctors asked, "Did you get any blood on you?"

Eddie looked at his arms. There were splashes of what could have been blood on them.

The doctor nodded. "We need to see if anything could have been passed on through contact with bodily fluids."

Eddie paled even more than he already had. "D'you mean AIDS?"

The doctor shrugged, point made.

After that, neither of the brothers objected. Stunned by everything that had happened, and feeling certain that they had been the cause of it, they said little.

Too ill to be released that day, their mother was given a bed at the hospital. It was obvious that the police suspected her of having something to do with Karl's death as she was given a private ward with a policewoman at the door. After being interrogated, the boys were sent to Aunt Eileen's house as theirs was a crime scene, filled with forensic investigators trying to sort out what had happened. A neighbour had donated a bunk bed so they could share a room with their cousin, Jake. This, though, was the least of their worries. Both of them knew they had been responsible for Karl's death, even if they did not understand how.

Unlike before, Aunt Eileen was more subdued this time. She'd known Karl longer and, though she seemed to have had no particular fondness for him, a second violent death was too much even for her to get over with a few cans of lager and a funny fag.

More importantly, though, Gary sensed that she suspected he and Eddie knew more about what had happened than they let on. She didn't say anything, but he caught her taking some strange, speculative glances at them now and then.

Back at her house, Gary couldn't wait to get outside, just him and Eddie. He felt overwhelmed by all the questions they'd been hectored with and needed space in which to think.

Despite the cold, they wandered through the estate till they could see their own house. Lengths of police tape flapped in the wind around it like the leftovers from a shabby carnival. Two police vans still stood outside, and there was a policeman at the gate, so the boys stopped some distance away and sat on the pavement.

"Do you think we made it happen?" Eddie asked, chewing his fingernails. He had been doing that a lot recently; they'd been bitten to the quick and some were bleeding.

Gary shrugged. "How should I know?"

Eddie cocked his head at him. "You think it, don't you?"

Gary thought for a few moments. He couldn't lie to his brother, not about something like this. "Maybe."

Eddie released a pent up sigh. He gazed at their house, looking bleak. "Do you think it'll stop?"

Gary shook his head, looking even bleaker.

"Why should it?"

There were tears in Eddie's eyes. "It's my fault. I shouldn't have made us go. I was stupid. Greedy. For a few fucking quid." He wiped his eyes with the back of his hand, sniffled, then squinted again at the vans. "We need some petrol."

Gary didn't ask why. He nodded his head instead, his mouth set in a determined scowl. Neither of them liked what they were talking about doing, but they had no choice. As if in affirmation, the pram they had borrowed from Angelica Louise was stood by the gate of their aunt's house when they returned as if it was waiting for them. Gary felt his bowels loosen and had to dash inside for the bathroom, only just reaching it in time. Eddie was still stood outside when he returned downstairs.

"Ready?"

Gary shook his head, resigned.

They walked round to the side of the house where their aunt's husband, Uncle Rhys, kept their car, a dated Ford Escort he usually left parked on the concrete drive as the garage was too full of junk for anything bigger than a bicycle to be wheeled inside. Eddie rummaged about till he found a length of rubber pipe hidden among their uncle's tools. He told Gary he got the idea from hearing their cousins talk about how their dad used it to siphon petrol from people's cars. Next to the pipe was a green plastic can.

"Do you know how to do it?" Gary asked.

Eddie shrugged. "Sort of." He grinned, then, making sure that no one was looking, unfastened the petrol cap on their uncle's car. He slid the pipe inside till it reached the petrol, took a deep breath, exhaled just as deeply, then started to suck on the pipe. A few seconds later his face reddened and he spat out, looking disgusted.

Gary laughed as he smelt the petrol Eddie had almost choked himself on, before hurriedly holding the plastic can under the pipe as petrol poured from it.

Afterwards, with their aunt yelling at them to come in for dinner, they put everything back, except the can, which they hid under a piece of old carpet.

"When we've finished eating we'll go," Eddie muttered as they went inside. "We'll do it tonight."

* * *

It was gloomy outside when they were able to leave the house again. Gary managed to hide one of Aunt Eileen's boxes of matches inside his pocket. A chain-smoker, she left them all over the house, so one of them going missing would never be noticed, he was sure.

They retrieved the petrol can, dumped it inside the pram and set off downhill at a brisk pace. Grudge End was a good fifteen-minute walk, and already they could feel the first spittles of rain that the heavy clouds warned could turn into a downpour soon. Though neither boy relished the idea of getting drenched, at least the rain might reduce the number of people out on the streets.

They didn't speak as they hurried towards Grudge End. Somehow, through some empathy between them, they knew what they needed to do, even if they dreaded doing it.

When they reached the house its door was still open. Inside it looked darker than before, though Gary suspected that this was because of how gloomy it was outside. It was bound to be, wasn't it? he thought, trying not to be put off. Eddie seemed to have more resolve, pushing the pram over the front doorstep without hesitation. Inside, he shoved the pram to one side and reached for the petrol.

"You got the matches?" His voice sounded as if he'd got no saliva inside his mouth.

Gary brought the box out of his pocket.

There was a sound upstairs as if something shifted its weight on one of the floorboards.

"Kids?" Gary asked in a whisper.

"Here?" Eddie shook his head, but he looked uncertain.

"We have to be sure," Gary said.

Eddie cautiously stepped to the foot of the stairs and looked up to the narrow landing. He cleared his throat and shouted, "Who's there?"

His words sounded flat, as if absorbed by the damp wallpaper that clung to the walls on either side of the stairs, mottled with mildew. Spider webs hung in dirty drapes.

"Hoy!" he called out again. He glanced at Gary, when there was another creak.

"They could be scared of us," Gary said. "Perhaps they're hiding."

Even though Eddie shook his head, Gary was insistent. They couldn't set fire to the place if some local kids might be trapped upstairs. It was bad enough Pete and Karl getting killed, about which he felt sicker than he had expected.

Still holding the petrol can, Eddie started to climb upstairs using the loosened banister rail for support on the steep wooden steps. Lengths of paper had peeled from the walls in mouldy strips like rotten skin. Gary shuddered when he brushed against them or one of them touched his face.

At the landing, Eddie turned towards the front bedroom. Gary heard him gasp.

A youth sat in the far corner on the bare floorboards. His clothes reminded Gary of a style he'd seen in old documentaries on TV about Teddy Boys battling the police in street riots. He wore tight-looking trousers and pointed shoes—Winklepickers, he remembered they were called, a name that had amused him when he first heard it. His leather jacket looked old. It was creased and dirty, and there were gaps where it seemed to have dried and split. The youth's face was pallid, with dirty, unwashed, pimply skin. In front of him, making Gary's stomach clench with the urge to throw up, was a row of heads. Three had decayed so much they were featureless, a gelatinous gunk that might have been flesh sticking to them. The other two were recognisable, even if Pete's eyes looked as if someone had tried to crush them flat. Karl's head looked almost like it had in life. Trickles of blood had clotted at the corners of his mouth, and there was a look of protest on his scraggly face. His skin looked waxen.

Grunting, Eddie opened the can and began to fling petrol onto the floor as near as he could manage to the corner. An imbecilic grin spread across the Teddy Boy's face as some of it splashed his clothes.

"Give me the matches," Eddie said.

Gary passed them over; his hands shook so much he almost dropped them. More calmly, Eddie struck a match. "Get out of here," he whispered as he turned and flung it through the air.

There was a high-pitched whoosh as petrol fumes exploded, hitting both boys in a blinding gust of searingly hot air. Gary's eyebrows shrivelled, and he could smell burnt hair as he was hurled onto the landing. He made a desperate grab for the banister rail for support, missed it and found himself tumbling downstairs, his spine jarring against the edge of each step till he finally managed to stop himself near the bottom, winded and shocked.

His face hurt where it had been scorched, and for a moment he thought that his eyes had been damaged till he managed to force them open. He looked up the stairs. "Eddie!" His voice was little more than a croak. There was a strong smell of petrol as flames lit the top of the stairs, growing brighter. "Eddie!"

Gary struggled to climb back to the landing, shouting for his brother. But the heat from the front bedroom scorched him like an opened furnace. He tried to move against it, but it was too intense. He couldn't breath and his skin hurt. He could feel it burn. And, however much he wanted to help Eddie, he had to retreat as the fire suddenly lunged through the bedroom door and across the landing.

Sobbing, Gary fled the house. Smoke had made the air inside unbreathable and his eyes were stinging so much he could barely see. Outside, he shouted for Eddie, even though he knew he was wasting his time. He couldn't seem able to make himself stop, as if by shouting his name again and again he could alter things.

Smoke billowed out of the house and across the street. The bedroom window burst apart, showering glass all around him. One shard struck his face and gashed his cheek, making him flee to the safety of the opposite pavement as the smoke grew denser.

With a cry of despair, Gary ran up the street. The rain was falling even heavier now, sluicing down the gutters in black torrents. More poured from broken drainpipes out across the pavement, making him dodge into the road to avoid getting hit. He felt tears on his cheeks, mingling with the rain as he remembered.

"Get out of here," Eddie had whispered to him before he hurled the match at the petrol. It was the last he saw of him before he was flung onto the landing.

Why hadn't Eddie been flung there as well, where he would have tumbled down the staircase to safety like him? But his brother had been stood away from the door. When the fumes exploded, Eddie would have been pummelled into the wall, not out through the doorway. Gary tried not to think what happened next, how Eddie would have been scorched by the searing flames that filled the room.

Gary sobbed. His legs were beginning to feel weak, and he stumbled to a halt. He looked back down the street. Most of it was hidden behind clouds of smoke. They billowed above the rooftops, so frighteningly huge he was sure the whole town would see them now. The scale of what he and Eddie had done overwhelmed him with fear, and he was unsure whether he was more scared by this than what had happened to his brother. Eddie should have known better than to do what he'd done. He was his big brother. It was up to him to look out for both of them, even if Gary knew that Eddie was thick.

Still sobbing, Gary started to run once more, though he knew he was heading further into Grudge End. Eventually, he would veer sideways to return downhill once he had put enough distance between him and the fire. Already there were sirens, faint in the distance, growing louder. He looked at his hands; they were covered in soot. There were probably more splotches on his face. Anyone seeing him would know where he'd been, he was sure. He tried to wipe it from him, but the rain only seemed to smudge it, dirtying his clothes.

Feeling exhausted, he stopped once again. The street was getting steeper. He looked up it to where the block finally ended. *Were there people up there?* He wasn't sure. Even here wafts of smoke were blowing through the rain. The smoke, the rain and the growing gloom as night drew in made it difficult to see, but he seemed to be able to make out people stood in ones and twos higher up the street, thin, perhaps stick-like. He thought Grudge End had been deserted, that no one came here anymore, but it seemed he was wrong. Perhaps they had been drawn by the smoke.

Gary made himself start to run again. It wasn't far to the end of the block. Too tired to lift his feet high enough, the uneven paving stones stubbed his toes. He felt as if he had been climbing forever. And the further he went the steeper it became. He wondered how cars ever managed to drive up here—if any had.

Somewhere nearby something squealed, metal against metal. And for a moment he was sure it was the pram again. But he'd left that at the house. It would have been destroyed by now.

Something poked him in the back.

Like a finger.

Gary screamed, running faster. Reaching the corner, he turned right, his feet skidding on rain-wet cobbles where the road suddenly went downhill at a sharp angle before rising again. A muddy torrent, created by the rain, thrashed along the bottom of the slope. Little more than two feet across, he leapt over it and scrambled at the cobbles on the opposite slope as he slipped to his knees, grazing them.

He heard the squealing again, a pram's wheel spinning on a twisted axle only yards behind him. But that was rubbish. The pram had been burned or crushed in the house by now. It must have been. Gary looked behind him, saw nothing. Only trails of smoke, fainter now. Diffused.

More scared than before, he ran even faster. He wanted to get back into town and away from Grudge End, but the street ahead of him turned back towards the fire. He took a gap to his right, but this led him into a winding ginnel that made him even more confused than before. Backyard walls teetered above him. Decades of nettles, growing between the cobbles, pricked his legs, tripping him. Here and there old dustbins, riddled with rust, had been abandoned on their sides like barricades. He grazed his knee on one of them.

Limping now, Gary finally exited the ginnel. It opened out into a small square where a number of streets met at odd angles. In the middle, raised on stone steps, was an old-fashioned lamppost which was dimly starting to flicker into life. At the end of one street stood an abandoned chapel, with a domed roof and thin, pretentious stone pillars either side of its boarded-up door. Gary felt repelled by it as he hobbled towards the furthest street away from it. He remembered what he'd heard about cults in this area and wondered whether the chapel might have been used by them.

More worryingly, he had the impression of being watched. When he stopped at the edge of the square he heard a metallic squeal again, close behind him. Startled, he looked round and for the first time saw it. In the street beside the chapel a crouched figure, pushing the pram in front of it, emerged from the gloom. Gary felt like screaming when he saw the buckled wheel. The pram looked black as if it was covered in soot or had been scorched till whatever paint still stuck to it had been reduced to cinders. A second figure emerged behind the first. They were too far away for him to make them out properly in the dusk as he watched the pram move towards him. Suddenly he was running downhill, heedless of slipping on paving stones or the wet cobbles that rose towards the middle of the street. The pram was moving so slowly he knew he could easily outpace it—and the figures behind it.

The street rose again as it twisted rightwards, veering away from the way into town and deeper into Grudge End. He turned at the first corner, hoping to go downhill, but the street meandered between unbroken rows of terraced houses that hemmed him in on either side without even so much as the gap of an alley for as far as he could see. None of the street lamps along it was lit, even though the smudge of sky he could see was darkening quickly. The rain was falling heavier now. Yet, in the distance, he could still see the occasional figure stood on the pavement. He was sure they were peering at him.

Spotting a gap between the houses to his left, Gary dashed straight for it. He reached out for a lamppost to propel himself around the corner, but he used it instead to bring his feet skidding to a halt.

The pram had stopped there. The pale-faced Teddy Boy leaned on its handle. Behind him a figure lurched unsteadily. Its face was no more than a charred ruin. What features it had, including its eyes, had been burned. All that Gary could recognise were the remnants of clothes that clung to its flesh. Tears filled his eyes as he stared at the blackened, twig-like fingers that curled into the mockery of a fist and at the rain trickling through the fragile crusts of its hair.

"Let him go, you bastard!" Gary faced the Teddy Boy. Unlike Eddie, the flames had done nothing to the pallid youth, whose face was the same unhealthy grey as before. If he had been holding something, Gary would have hurled it at him, but his hands were empty. "Let him go, you bastard!"

The pram moved nearer, and Gary saw a broad bladed carving knife lying inside it. The Teddy Boy reached for the knife. He swept its blade across Eddie's throat. His brother's flesh could have been no more than cinders, because the blade snapped through it with a loud crack. The boy's head toppled from his shoulders, hitting the ground with a heavy crunch.

Gary ran. But the pram shot forwards, hit his heels, and he fell with a scream. He tried to get up, but the paving stones were wet with rain and his hands slipped. Panicking, he barely managed to roll out of the way of the pram before the Teddy Boy kicked it to one side and loomed above him.

* * *

It was not till the next morning that a police patrol found Gary's body, or what remained of it, nailed to the door of a disused chapel. Spokes from the wheels of an abandoned pram had been driven though his arms and legs, pinioning him to the thick panels.

His head had been severed.

It was never found.

MILO JAMES FOWLER

Milo James Fowler is a teacher by day and a writer by night.

A native of San Diego, California, Fowler currently resides on the Pacific coast with his beloved wife. When he's not grading papers, he's imagining what the world might be like in a few dozen alternate realities.

Fowler's disturbing, speculative work has appeared in more than sixty publications, including *AE Science Fiction, Cosmos, Shimmer* and *Nature*. Milo's story "The Coyote's Word" can be found in *The Big Bad: An Anthology of Evil* from Dark Oak Press. A novella, *Immaterial Evidence*, was recently published by Musa Publishing.

WHAT DO YOU NEED?

BY MILO JAMES FOWLER

John's eyelids flutter, then jerk wide open in the jittery light of the television. The plaid bedspread beneath his face is wet with drool. How long was he asleep?

He sits up with a start.

This room... Where the hell am I?

Groggy, he slides off the bed and staggers toward the console television on the floor, its screen a flurry of static.

"Hello?" The echo of his voice is muted by thick drapes over the two windows and the popcorn ceiling and the shag carpet—a motel room from the '70s. "Is anybody there?"

Silence.

He storms toward the door and tries the knob, but it doesn't turn, not even a jiggle. He pounds with his fists, but there's no hollow thud. He's hitting concrete.

"What the hell?" He takes a step back.

The windows. *What's outside?*

He throws the drapes aside, but there is no window. Only a dingy wall.

Am I still sleeping? He glances at the bed, then back at the TV.

He moves to the other window, but the drapes there are a ruse as well. The wall mocks his growing panic.

What is this place?

His knees swim in their sockets. His throat tightens. His chest—he can't breathe. He stumbles over to the telephone, an old green rotary device like his grandmother had when he was a kid. He grabs the handset and stares at it for a long moment, trying to remember how the ancient thing worked. He digs his finger into the dial to call 9-1-1.

Placing the receiver against his ear, he finds only silence. No dial tone.

As if trying to force it into life, he shakes the handset. Nothing. He curses and pounds it against the nightstand. Still nothing.

Then, a voice on the other end.

"What do you need?" The voice cracks across the wire. It could be that of a small child—or a very old woman. Or both.

John blinks and clears his throat as the hairs rise on the back of his neck. "Hello?"

"What do you need?"

"Where am I?" he asks. "How did I get here?"

Dead air.

"Hello? Are you still there? I'm in a motel room, there's no way out—"

"What do you need?"

"I need help! Call the police! Call somebody! Tell them where I am!" John screams, short of breath. "Who are you? Do you work here?" He gestures toward the drapes. "There aren't any windows, and the door, it…" He pivots on his heel, glances at the static coming from the television. "Hello?"

"What do you need?" The tone of the ninety-year-old girl's voice doesn't change. It could be a recording for all he knows.

John curses again. "I need some answers, that's what I need! Can you help me or not?"

No response.

He slams the receiver down and runs his hands through his hair, raking his fingers down his unshaven jaw line. He traces his stubble and, with a sudden epiphany, staggers into the bathroom. The wall switch snaps upward under his palm, and a fluorescent tube jitters to life. The light flares from the ceiling, exposing mold and hard water stains on the walls. He leans over the sink to inspect the sides of his face in the cracked mirror. As a sundial tracks the course of the sun, so does John's facial hair show the passage of time. With less than a centimeter of growth, he knows the longest he could have been here is a week.

A week? And I slept the whole time? It's not possible...

He stares hard at his reflection and turns his head side to side, pulling down the skin beneath his bloodshot eyes, checking them one at a time. He grips both sides of the sink and drops his head, releases a sigh.

His stomach gurgles, and for the first time John realizes how hungry he is. He returns to the bedroom and tugs open the drawer on the nightstand. Empty. He checks the doors on the TV console, but they don't open. They're as much a façade as the drapes on the wall.

What do I need? A fat, grilled burrito would be real nice right about now.

"Hello?" He shouts at the ceiling and pounds on the door again. "Is anybody out there? Can you hear me?"

His gaze returns to the flickering TV.

Nana had one just like it — an old Zenith. The morning game shows, those soap operas she called her 'stories,' the afternoon talk shows. I must have been seven at the time.

He crouches down in front of the screen; its glow washes across his haggard features. There is no remote control. The knob clicks clockwise, counter-clockwise, turning through static, every channel broadcasting the same snowstorm. He flips the power switch. No change. On, off, on, off. The blizzard remains on the screen.

He rises with another curse, glancing back at the phone. He picks up the receiver.

"Hello? Are you still there?"

No dial tone.

"What do you need?" the voice asks.

"Listen, I don't know what's going on here, but I need your help. I need you to get me out."

Silence.

His fingers drum along the nightstand. He stares at the carpet.

This room is a real throwback to 1976—the year I was born...

"Hello?"

"What do you need?"

He slams the receiver into its cradle. The coiled cord dances. He throws himself around the room, screaming, pounding, trying to get the attention of someone, anyone.

"You can't keep me here! I don't know what kind of game you think you're playing, but it's over! You hear me? OVER!"

Will my starved remains lie on the floor three or four weeks from now? How long can a man go without food and water?

There's a sink in the bathroom, but even if there's running water, should I drink from that faucet?

He beats against the walls until his fists become sore. Tired of storming around the room and shouting impotent ultimatums at the ceiling, he collapses onto the bed and lapses into unconsciousness— a pathetic child who's cried himself to sleep.

Hours pass in silence, broken only by his intermittent snores. Static flickers on the TV, alive and alone.

* * *

The phone rings three times before John stirs, wiping saliva from his chin. For a moment he looks around, bewildered, as if he's forgotten where he is, but then he shakes his head. The nightmare hasn't ended. Groggy fingers grapple to bring the receiver up to his ear.

"What do you need?" the familiar voice asks.

John's stomach churns. "Grilled California burrito. And a Coke." He licks his lips and grimaces. "Think you can handle that?" He doesn't wait for the silent treatment, dropping the receiver into its cradle, almost laughing at himself. Even if the voice on the phone belongs to an actual person, how would she make his special delivery? There's no way in or out of this room that he can see.

How the hell did I get in here?

He has to use the bathroom, but something stops him halfway there—a sound from inside the closet, a quiet click. He pushes the sliding door aside, and it jiggles along its track. The smell of something both impossible and wonderful wafts upward. There, sitting atop the small closet safe, is the meal he'd requested.

He stands rooted to the carpet, eyes unblinking. He leans forward to smell the food, reaching a tentative hand toward the white wrapper stained with splotches of grease. He doesn't spend more than a moment weighing the pros and cons of the situation. He dives in, greedily consuming the burrito, pausing only occasionally to drink from the can of soda. On his knees, he devours the meal as an act of devotion to the closet—a source of sustenance. When all that remains is the soggy wrapper, he closes his eyes and smiles. He reaches forward, presses the paneling at the back of the closet.

Is there some type of hidden compartment?

It feels like solid steel.

"Thanks," he says to the silence as he finishes the Coke.

* * *

Time passes. Without a clock, John doesn't know how long. He paces the length of the room, returns to the bathroom at untimed intervals, sits in the armchair next to the TV, often turning his gaze to the phone. Eventually, he picks it up.

"What do you need?" the voice on the other end asks.

This time, he places a much taller order: grilled halibut over

baked potatoes with a zesty lemon cream sauce and crispy aspara-
gus. He plants himself in front of the closet to watch and wait.

In the hours that follow, he begins to weave, to lurch. He starts
to nod off and fights it. Eventually he loses the battle and falls asleep,
snoring into the shag carpet. He doesn't notice the steel panel at the
rear of the closet slide open. He doesn't see the pale, emaciated arms
set the meal he requested atop the closet safe. And he doesn't notice
the hands withdraw through the opening or the hidden panel slide
closed.

John finds the meal still warm when he awakes.

* * *

Hours, days, maybe weeks pass as John moves around the
room—from the bed to the bathroom to the chair to the now well-
worn carpet in front of the closet—in a ceaseless attempt to endure
the endless tedium as best he can.

Will I spend the rest of my life here?

Using the telephone, he orders his meals three times a day. They
never arrive while he's watching, but they're the only thing he can
use to gauge the passage of time. When he falls asleep and wakes up
hungry, that's got to be morning.

He paces, stares at the TV, the room's only source of light.

*It's always the same time of day here—well after midnight, when all the
stations have signed off. That's what they used to do, back in the 70s; late
night infomercials and sex hotlines had yet to hit the airwaves.*

His eyes grow hollow and dark. His skin pale, sagging from his
bones. The reflection in the bathroom mirror and in the TV screen
doesn't look familiar anymore. Despite the requested meals—no
matter how extravagant—John appears malnourished. While the
food is delicious, his intestines cramp up at times, sending him re-
peatedly to the bathroom. He mumbles to himself about the potential of slow-acting poisons. Trembling, he reaches for the phone.

"What do you need?"

John clears his throat. "I know you can't help me—or won't. I mean, thanks for the food. Sometimes it doesn't agree with me, but that's probably just nerves. I don't feel much like myself. I don't...I wish I knew what is going on...why I'm here." He exhales. "I guess I need somebody to talk to, you know? I can't tell for sure how long I've been in this room. The days all run together. I...I think I might be losing my mind."

There is no response.

He drops his head against his open palm. "I guess it's good just to have somebody listen. Whoever you are."

More dead air.

"Yeah," he says, nodding.

What did I expect?

From the closet, he hears the sliding panel click shut. Of course, he's missed it again.

Then his eyes widen. He fumbles with the phone, returning it to its cradle as a woman steps out of the closet, ducking her head.

John steps toward her, stammering, "H-hey there..."

The woman's gaze is focused on the carpeting at her bare feet. Her pale, emaciated arms cradle her middle. Her long, angular face is expressionless. Her hair appears dark in the flickering glare of the TV.

"How did you get in here?" John asks. "Through the wall?" She says nothing, appearing not to understand the question.

"Do you speak English?"

No answer.

"My name is John." He pats his chest, taking another step forward. "I've been here for...for too long." He swallows. "Were you in the room next door? Do you know what this place is? There aren't any doors or windows—no way out. I've checked." He stares at her. "How did you get out of your room?"

The woman frowns, her long, crooked fingers squeezing her sides.

"I'm sorry," he says. "I'm rambling. I just wish you'd say something."

She blinks, gestures back toward the closet as if to explain everything.

"Right." He watches her, but she avoids eye contact. "Don't be afraid. I'm not going to hurt you." He takes another step closer. "Can you tell me your name, at least?"

Her eyes linger on the TV. Her lips part, then close.

"Do you know why you're here? How you got here?"

Again she gestures toward the closet.

"Yeah, the closet. I know. But before you came here, to this place, do you remember anything?"

She casts another sidelong glance at the television.

"Me either." He sighs, running a nervous hand through his hair. "Nothing about this is right, that's for sure."

He notices the gooseflesh prickling up her bare legs. "Are you cold?"

She shakes her head.

"Can't you speak?"

Her eyes dart back and forth between the television and the closet.

"Are you hungry? I can get you something. Anything, really. The room service here is pretty good."

She thrusts both arms forward, palms out, and stares into his eyes.

"I don't understand." He looks at her arms. They are smooth, white marble. "What are you trying to tell me? I don't know what this means." He mimics the position of her arms, and they stand together in the silence.

She drops her hands to her sides and returns her gaze to the floor.

"We're getting nowhere fast, aren't we? You can't tell me where you're from?"

She points at the closet, emphatically now.

"Right. But you can't speak, or you won't. Which is it?"

She meets his gaze without blinking and walks toward him toe to heel like a dancer. She seems to float, glowing in the TV's glare. John resists the sudden urge to back away.

"What is it?"

She opens her mouth wide. Her lips parting wider than possible, her jaws almost unhinging like those of a python. Jerking her head back, she reveals her teeth. So many teeth, glistening and even. He sees the back of her throat and the torn fleshy root where her tongue should have been. He staggers backward, reflexively. She closes her mouth and hugs herself tighter.

"Who did this to you?"

Her only response is to stare at the floor.

"Did they do this to you?" He points at the phone. She doesn't react. "They did this to you! Why?"

John runs to the phone and snatches it up.

The voice on the other end barely has time to ask the question he has heard so many times, "What do you—?"

"What the hell kind of game are you people playing here? What kind of monsters are you? Answer me!"

Silence.

The woman shivers, standing at the foot of the bed.

"Why don't you come in here and face me? You think you can hurt this girl and nothing will happen to you? Well, think again!"

He slams down the phone. The woman jumps, startled.

"We've got to find a way out of here." He gestures toward the closet. "Can we go back the way you came?"

She shakes her head.

"No? Why not?" No good. She can't answer. "You're saying it only goes one way?"

She nods.

"This doesn't make any sense." Squeezing his temples fails to alleviate his throbbing headache. "Okay. I'll stick to yes or no questions. You have no idea how you got here, this place, whatever it is. Right?"

Yes.

"But you do remember your name, right?"

Yes.

He starts guessing, running through the alphabet a letter at a time. Once he arrives at M and she nods, he goes through every name he can think of, finally arriving at the winner:

"Michelle?"

She almost smiles when he says her name.

"Michelle." He nearly smiles himself. "That's who you are. It's a beautiful name." He gestures toward the armchair. "Would you like to sit down, Michelle?" She appears agitated at the offer and refuses to sit.

"Okay, you'd rather stand. Fine, we'll stand." He pauses. "You came in from next door. Did they send you through?" He points at the phone.

No.

"So you came on your own. It was your idea?"

Yes—she darts another glance at the TV.

"And where you came from, it's a room like this?"

No.

"Did you know this room would be here? That I would be here?"

She nods several times, again checking the snow on the TV.

"Did they tell you I'd be in here?"

Yes.

"Who are they?"

She looks to the TV.

"What?" He crouches down to look into the jittery light. "Somebody's watching us from in there?"

He looks over his shoulder and sees her rub her protruding ribs, squeezing pale flesh. There isn't much to spare.

"Hey!" His knuckles rap against the convex TV screen. "Are you watching us?" He jumps to his feet. "Yeah? Well, watch this."

John grabs the armchair and slams it into the television. The screen cracks, but doesn't shatter. The static continues. Michelle releases an urgent grunt. Her mouth forms the shape of a letter 'O'. She shakes her head, attempting a warning.

"You don't think they'll like that?" He chuckles. "Yeah, probably not."

John slams the chair into the screen again. The fractures expand, yet the snowstorm of static rages on. Nervous and more frightened than ever, Michelle shuffles back to the closet.

Caught up in his fury, John doesn't notice her retreat as he kicks at the television screen over and over again, but it refuses to shatter.

Muscular arms clothed in black emerge from the opening in the wall. Gloved hands seize Michelle's wrists and pull her through. The panel slides shuts with a resounding click behind her.

"Michelle?" John gasps.

Silence.

John stumbles to the closet. "Michelle!" His fists thunder across the steel wall. "Bring her back, you bastards!"

He dashes to the bed, the nightstand, and snatches up the phone.

"What do you need?" the voice asks.

"What have you done with Michelle? Bring her back, damn it!" He pulls the cord taught and kneels before the TV, the phone still at his ear. "Do you see me? Are you watching this? What do you want? Tell me what you want!"

"What do you need?" The crone-child's voice is as emotionless as ever.

"You've taken everything from me!" *My life...my friends...the world.* He curses, tears sliding down his face and through the thick beard on his cheek. "Just tell me what you want from me. Please. That's all I need."

No response.

"Bring her back," he said, begging. "Don't hurt her anymore. She didn't do anything wrong. It was me." He traces one of the cracks on the screen with a fingertip.

Even with her limited capacity for communication, Michelle had provided a glimpse of the human companionship that John craved.

She gave him a few of the answers he wanted so desperately. But she also frightened him.

Was she a preview of my own future?

How long has she wasted away in this place?

John hangs up the phone and drops onto the bed. There he remains, catatonic for days, curled into a fetal position, his head buried under the pillow to block out the flickering light of the all-seeing television.

* * *

How many days has it been…since Michelle?

John's lost all track of time, lying in the bed, refusing to order meals. His beard has grown thicker than ever before in his life.

I can't keep this up.

Ultimately, if he is to survive—and survive he must; he won't let the voice on the phone or her minions beat him—he must resume his routine, such that it is: moving from the bed to the armchair to the bathroom to the floor in front of the closet.

Regaining his appetite, he orders his meals just as any guest at any hotel would. Each time, his meal is delivered through the secret door. And every time, he is just a fraction of a second too late to reach the closet and grab hold of Michelle's alabaster arms.

He's provided with everything he could possibly think to ask for. He is delivered books, music, and devices to play the music, a Betamax VCR and videotapes of the old films he remembers watching as a child. The TV screen remains fractured, but the static snow-storm no longer rages. There's always a movie playing now through the cracks. Even on mute, it provides the companionship he lacked for so long. The characters go about their business, reciting lines he knows by heart and often recites in his best impersonations. He asks for light bulbs for the table lamps. There is now a comfortable warmth in this room that was once cold and alien. The motel prison cell is no more.

Feels almost like...home.

* * *

John sits in the armchair wearing a comfortable robe and slippers, his feet propped on a plush corduroy ottoman. The lamp beside him casts an amber glow across his lap, reflecting in his reading glasses. His sight is no longer what it once was. Neither is his beard. It's now a full three or four inches long, thick and well-groomed. As is his hair, fastidiously maintained and combed back from his forehead. No longer thin or pale, he sits under the reading lamp equipped with an ultraviolet bulb as he thumbs through an Arthur C. Clarke novel: *A Fall of Moondust.*

The rear panel of the closet slides open, but he makes no move toward it. Two emaciated arms reach in, holding a tray of steaming chow mein, chicken breast marinated in a lemon sauce and a cup of herbal tea. The arms pause before they retract. Long, slender fingers curl into a fist and knock to get his attention.

"Thank you, Michelle," John says absently, immersed in his reading. "Just leave it there, please."

The hands hesitate, pausing to warm themselves over the hot meal. Then they pull back and the rear wall slides shut with a click. John finishes the chapter and sighs contentedly as he places a red ribbon to mark his page. The book is a real cliffhanger. He'll pick it up again after dinner.

With a satisfied yawn, he goes to the bookshelf housing the most recent additions to his video collection. His fingertips drift idly across the titles until they come to *Rocky.* A little somber, but a feel-good flick in the end. He pops it into the VCR for a mealtime viewing and retrieves his dinner.

"Mmm," he murmurs, inhaling. "She's outdone herself this time." He carries the tray to the folding table he has set up in front of the TV. While the opening credits appear through the cracked screen, he digs in, eating a mouthful of noodles.

He pauses, working them around with his tongue. Swallows.

"Salt," he mutters, tossing down his napkin and searching for the shaker. It hasn't been included with his meal. Shaking his head, he goes straight to the phone.

"I need—"

But the familiar, emotionless voice on the other end of the phone interrupts him: "You have what we need."

"What? I—"

"You have what we need."

He swallows. Tension grips him, his body going rigid.

"I don't understand. I just need a little salt." He stares at Sylvester Stallone on the TV. "Hello? Are you still there?" He frowns, gesturing toward the closet. "It's *salt*, for crying out loud. How hard can it be?"

The rear panel of the closet opens wide—far wider than ever before. Three large, muscular men in bodysuits appear at the opening, the black material obscuring their faces. They duck their heads as they enter the room.

"What the—?" John drops the phone, staggers back. "Who the hell are you?"

They move with purpose, without hesitation, dismantling the room and carrying everything back through the open panel in the back of the closet. John's books, his videos, his lamps, his chair, even the drapes on the wall hiding windows that were never there—everything is taken away.

"You can't do this! Get away from that! It's *mine*!" He goes after the man with his chair. A solid blow to the throat knocks John to the carpet where he thrashes around in pain as the men strip the bed and carry it out. They return and start tearing up the shag carpet. John strains to speak, reaching after one of them only to be rewarded with a boot to the face.

John's perspective of the room blossoms crimson, as do the hands he raises to cradle his broken nose. The men strip the room, leaving only bare walls and concrete floor. They rip the phone from its socket, leaving the cord a torn root. The console TV is the last to go, plunging the room into total darkness as they extinguish its light.

"Why are you doing this?" John moans. They answer him with rough hands, gloved fingers that tug and pull at his clothing.

"No! You can't do this to me!"

But the men take it all, and John is left naked on a floor of cold concrete. Their heavy footsteps depart the same way they came in.

John writhes in the darkness, unable to see his own hand in front of his eyes. "No," he whimpers. "You can't. You can't leave me like this. I need—!"

The panel in the back of the closet slides shut with a familiar click.

From the room next door, John hears someone begin to scream and pound against the wall.

JONATHAN BALOG

Jonathan Balog grew up in Maryland and graduated from Washington College in 2005 with a BA in English.

Balog's story "Render Unto Caesar" has appeared in *Independent Ink* magazine, and his story "The Truth" was published in the anthology *So It Goes: A Tribute to Kurt Vonnegut* from Perpetual Motion Machine Publishing. A collection of his short stories, *Inaugural Games,* was released in early 2012.

He lives in Rome, Italy, where he's currently at work on a novel expanding on the haunting events depicted in "The Troll." When he's not doing that, he's usually doing something horrible.

THE TROLL

BY JONATHAN BALOG

The troll lived under the bridge.

The bridge was about fifteen minutes from our house. If you walked to the end of our lane, turned right, crossed the main road, and went all the way up the hill and down the other side into the woods, you'd see it. It was an old, grey stone bridge, the kind that was probably built a hundred years ago, stretching across the river.

I wasn't supposed to go there, even if I was with my friends. My mom said gypsies camped out by the river, and I guess she thought they might kidnap me or something. I don't know what she was worried about. I never saw any gypsies, and if they saw me, they never bothered me.

The first time I met the troll was at the end of summer. School had started the week before, and I was slipping into autumn's long, boring routine. It almost hurt to be outside in the afternoon. Every tree, sidewalk, creek, field and corner store was a reminder that only eight days ago this world had been mine to explore until sundown. Now I had nothing to look forward to for the next four months but bitchy teachers, the dickheads who sat behind me in class, and nights full of algebra and book reports. It was enough to make me pray for a nuclear bomb.

I'm not entirely sure why I went to the bridge that day. Maybe I was just walking, kicking an empty beer can down the street, stewing in misery and didn't realize how far I'd gone. Or maybe I did it on purpose, breaking a minor rule in an act of silent protest against the world that held me prisoner.

Or maybe he called me.

The more I think about it, that's what I really believe.

I stopped halfway across the bridge and rested my chin on the railing. The first leaves were starting to fall, and I watched them land in the water and slowly drift downstream. I picked up some stones and threw them over one by one, listening for the splash a few seconds later.

That's when I heard his voice.

"Who's up there?"

I must have jumped a foot in the air. His voice was loud and angry. It sounded like a wild bull chewing on gravel.

"Come on, who's up there? I can hear you."

"It's, uhh…it's just me," I said, realizing how stupid it sounded as the words came out. I didn't want to give my name, but I was afraid I'd make him angrier if I said nothing at all.

"Well, come on down," he said.

I remember that day like a dream where you see yourself doing things and not only can't stop yourself, but don't see any reason why you should. Our guidance counselor had shown us the same videos you saw. I knew there was no good reason for me to talk to some strange man hanging out under a bridge, far from my parents or anyone else who might hear me if I had to call for help. But for some reason, it didn't occur to me to leave.

I walked back the way I'd come, turned, and hopped down the embankment. There was a pile of dead branches blocking the underside of the bridge from the view of anyone on the path. I put one hand on it and edged my way along the bank. Then I got my first look at the troll's home.

There was a sofa and two arm chairs, the kind that you'd be able to pick up at any Salvation Army. A long bookshelf, stuffed with paperbacks and magazines, lined the width of the bridge. There was a rectangular dinner table with a vase full of daffodils in the center and even a thin brown carpet underfoot. The strangest thing was that despite the fact that it was all outside, and all old and weathered, the whole setup looked as neat and tidy as anyone's living room.

The troll sat in one of the armchairs. He was wearing an old, charcoal-colored pinstripe suit that fit loosely on his tall, lanky frame. His dark red tie hung long and awkwardly past his waist, and his leather shoes were scraped and torn at the toes as if he'd walked across three states in them. On his head he wore a velvet fedora with a walnut-sized hole in the top. The outfit made him look like a cross between an old-fashioned hobo clown and an out-of-work magician.

However, like the cleanliness of his outdoor bachelor pad, his appearance didn't quite gel with reality. He was clean-shaven, and didn't appear to have a speck of dust on his body. Even the locks of black hair that hung down from his hat looked like they'd had a good shampoo in the last twenty-four hours.

"Come on in, Marty. Have a seat," he said. His voice had mellowed, and it was hard to believe the same throat had made the monstrous growl I'd heard a few moments earlier.

I walked over to the other armchair and sat. "Thanks," I said. "How did you know my name was Marty?"

"You'd be surprised how much I know," he said, as he began to roll himself a smoke. "For instance, I know you're not too happy about summer being over, and that you'd probably do just about anything for one more week without school."

"Damn right," I muttered. He offered me the finished cigarette, and I shook my head.

"Well, we might be able to do something about that. We'll talk about it later." He lit up, and rings of smoke twirled and snaked in front of his lizard-green eyes. "So what brings you trip-trapping over my bridge?"

"I..." Not in the least bit sure what I'd been doing in the woods, and with the last twenty minutes starting to feel like a silent home movie of someone else's life, I just shrugged.

"What were you looking for? Everybody's looking for something."

I thought for a moment, and then said, "I guess I was trying to figure out what that something was."

He nodded, his lips stretched in a knowing, close-mouthed grin. "Let me tell you a secret, Marty. Everyone in the world is born into a prison cell. Most of them stay in their cells their whole lives, changing wardens every few years—parents, teachers, bosses, spouses— all serving the same purpose. A select few, however, do manage to break free. The first step towards emancipation is acknowledging the existence of the prison. Of course, it also helps to have a little of this." He held up his right hand, palm forward and fingers spread, then turned it around and showed me the back. He then made a fast duck-and-flip motion with his wrist and held up a shiny silver dollar. He flicked it in my direction, and it landed in my hand.

I looked at the smooth, mint face of the coin. When he'd said "a little of this," I wondered if he'd meant money or magic.

He stood and began to pile branches under a steel pot suspended by a tripod. He then grabbed a magazine from the shelf, tore out a few pages and stuffed them underneath the wood.

"Hungry?" he asked.

"A little, yeah."

He lit the papers with his cigarette and blew on the flames. "Just having beans tonight, if you don't mind."

"No, that's cool."

"Beggars can't be choosers," he said, not unkindly. "I know that better than the rest of 'em."

He grabbed the wooden chair from the dinner table, spun it around and sat down in it backwards less than a foot from me.

I knew I was breaking every rule in the book—going where I wasn't allowed, talking to a stranger, and about to commit the cardinal sin of street safety and eat his food—but I didn't care. It was as if there was a new kind of logic coming from the troll that cancelled out my feelings of guilt and fear.

Something else I noticed as he sat beside me was that he didn't smell like a homeless person. I'd been around bums before and knew about that horrible cologne of piss and body odor that follows them everywhere. Not the troll, though. He had almost no scent at all, only a faint one that reminded me of something I couldn't quite place.

His hand clamped down on my shoulder. It was cold, and the coldness traveled through my veins, all the way to my heart, calming my pulse.

"Now," he said, "let's talk about that school of yours..."

* * *

I couldn't believe how easy it was. The troll's directions were so simple they could have been followed by a fourth-grader. In fact, the most difficult part was tip-toeing across the kitchen floor to the garage at three o'clock in the morning without waking the dog.

Once I had the door closed behind me, I turned on my flashlight. It was a pain in the ass to work in the dark, but I didn't want to risk drawing attention to the garage by flicking on the lights. First I fished three wine bottles out of the recycling bin. Then I carried them over to the riding mower and, using the funneling cup, filled them three-quarters of the way full with gasoline. I've always hated the smell of gasoline—I had to hold my breath to keep from gagging. Finally I took off my t-shirt, cut it into strips with my Swiss Army knife and tightly packed a strip into the mouth of each bottle, with at least half a foot of material hanging loose.

Before I left, I grabbed a heavy black trash bag out of the box near the bins. I cut it in half and used twine to wrap it around my Chuck Taylors, making them look like booties for some over-sized baby. This was another suggestion the troll had given me.

"It's easy to avoid getting caught," he'd said, "if you don't act stupid."

* * *

I was eating breakfast the next morning when we got the news. The phone rang and my mom answered.

"Hello? Yes... What? Oh my God...was anyone hurt?" she asked. "Well, that's good at least. Do they know what happened? Jesus... Yeah sure, I'll do it right now. Thanks for letting me know."

I did my best to look shocked when she told me what had happened. As she dialed the number of the next parent on the phone tree, I smiled into my Mini-Wheats and started planning my day.

The world that morning looked absolutely beautiful. My bonus week of freedom stretched out before me, reflected in every sewer grate, doorway, trashcan and traffic light. During the summer months, the bleak drudgery of the school year fades into an unpleasant memory and you come to take your liberty for granted. But on those odd days off, when the nightmare is still fresh in your mind, you savor every last moment. If I'd been God, I would have made June, July and August entirely out of Saturdays.

My first order of business was to stop by Charlie Weaver's newsstand. Mr. Weaver had a subscription to my four favorite comic books, despite the mature-readers-only warning on each cover. When they arrived on the fifth of the month, he kept them under the counter by the register until I came for them. Each time he made me swear I wouldn't tell my mom or anyone else where I'd bought them. I guess he was afraid he'd get busted for selling obscene material to minors or something.

"Hey Mr. Weaver!" I shouted, the bell on the shop door ringing as I entered.

The stocky, bespectacled man behind the register looked up from his newspaper. "Marty! Bet I know what you're here for."

"Bet you do," I said.

"Your package came in yesterday," he said and pulled up a flat, brown, paper bag which he dropped on the counter. I reached for it, and he pulled it back. "Now if your mom catches you with this—"

"I know, I didn't get it from you."

"Marty, you know what dealers do to snitches?"

"No," I said.

"They slit their mouths open on both ends," he said, tracing an imaginary line away from the corner of his lips with the blunt side of his pen. "So for the rest of their lives they look like a friggin' jack-o'-lantern whenever they smile."

There was a full five seconds of dead silence before we both burst out laughing.

"So can I have it please?"

"Thirteen dollars."

I pulled out a ten and dove into my pocket for some change, then stared disbelievingly at what I'd pulled out. I'd mixed the troll's silver dollar in with the rest of my money. It must have given birth in my pocket because there were now three of them, each identical to the first, shining as if they'd been minted that very day.

"Guess you'll have plenty of time to read these today."

"Huh?" I asked, snapping my head up.

"The school. Saw it on the news this morning," he said. "Bet you're awful disappointed about that."

"Oh…yeah," I said. I handed him three of the large coins. I was expecting him to remark on how odd it was to see a silver dollar at all these days, let alone have someone pay for something with three, but he either didn't notice or didn't care. "They told my mom it's not all that bad. The sprinklers took care of it before it could do any real damage. It just took 'em a while because it was a chemical fire."

"That so? Well, if you find out who did it, buy him a Coke."

As I stepped back out into the escalating summer heat, I pulled one of the comics from its bag. The enraged, skeletal face of some demon or other stared menacingly up at me from the cover. I was about to open it when it was snatched out of my hands.

"Whatcha got here, Marty-boy?" Rick Morris casually flipped through the comic with a condescending smirk. His two idiot co-horts, Pete Brooks and Melvin Bartosh, stood by giggling.

"Give it back, Rick," I said, flatly as I could manage.

"*Give it back, Rick,*" he mocked with an exaggerated pubescent crack in his voice. "What's the matter, little bitch not wanna share his toys?" He handed the comic to Melvin, put an open palm on my chest, and shoved me backwards. It wasn't a hard shove, just strong enough to imply how easily he could beat my ass if he felt like it.

"You know what, I think I'm gonna keep it. Could use some new reading material." Another chorus of moronic chuckling.

No. I was not going to start the year like this, and I sure as hell wasn't going to let that piece of shit steal my stuff. The look of smug superiority in his eyes reflected the years of torment and ridicule I'd suffered at the hands of this jackass.

Every time I'd had the books knocked out of my hands in the hallway, felt a rough smack on the back of my head, been pushed down in the gym showers, or walked home with a bloody nose and a fresh bruise, all were echoed in that stupid laugh. The countless nights that I'd sat in my room with a fury of self-hatred burning in my stomach for not striking back, turning the other cheek, letting him piss all over my dignity, were the black powder that launched my fist into his jaw.

There was a split second when a look of panic passed over Rick's face. All through his life, the meager amount of control he'd been able to wield over others had been balanced on one condition: that everyone smaller was afraid of him. Of course he had no reason to fear I'd actually beat him in a fight. His two obedient lapdogs had his back, and he outweighed me by fifty pounds. But the mere fact that I'd *tried* packed a much harder punch than the one I'd delivered to his face. In that moment he saw his grip on the world weaken before his very eyes.

It only lasted an instant. When the shock wore off, he saw my attack not as an omen of his downfall, but as a minor problem to be corrected. Before I realized I'd lost my chance to make a break for it, I found my back slammed against the brick wall of the newsstand with Rick's rotten breath on my face, each arm held by the other two bullies.

"Ahh, so you wanna play, ya little faggot?"

I knew there was no way I was going to walk away unhurt, so I decided to go for the gold, and I spat in his face.

His mouth hung open as he looked down and deliberately wiped my saliva from his cheek. Pete and Melvin let loose another burst of laughter, with each note pronounced "oh" instead of "ha."

"You? Dead." The first punch hit my gut, two inches away from knocking the wind out of me, and it hurt like hell. I was bracing myself for the next when I heard Mr. Weaver's voice.

"Hey! You little punks leave him alone!"

He was standing at the door ten feet away.

"Or what, old man?"

"Or I'm callin' the cops, that's what, now knock it off!"

A disgusted Rick nodded to the two at my arms, and they released me. I snatched the book out of Melvin's hand and started to make my way down the sidewalk.

"Be seeing you soon, you little pussy," I heard him call, the words firing into my back.

* * *

It had only been a day since my last visit, but already the forest looked like it had made headway into the next three months. It seemed that twice as many leaves were scattered along the unpaved trail, and they swirled around with the dust in the little clouds that I kicked up in front of me. Down below, the river babbled like a head injury.

Going to visit the troll seemed like the most logical thing in the world. I not only felt obliged to tell him how things had gone the night before, but after the incident with Rick, I needed someone to bitch to. I never actually formed this into a conscious thought, but I think I felt that if there was anyone who could make everything all better, it was him.

When I got to the bridge, I skidded down the embankment and

edged my way around the piling. The sight I found in the underpass made my eyelids stutter in disbelief. If I'd thought the woods had changed overnight, it was nothing compared to what had happened to the troll.

He'd grown considerably—either that or his clothes had shrunk. They looked like they'd been custom-tailored for his frame, which was now stout and erect, unlike the awkward slouch he'd carried the day before. What's more, their colors were different. The scarlet tie was now a candy-apple red, and the suit was closer to a pale green than its previous grey. His brown shoes had the shine of a fresh polish. The clothes didn't look like they'd been changed so much as enhanced, the way you can adjust hues in a photo-editing program.

"Marty!" he exclaimed. "I've been expecting you!" He was cooking again. This time he had a clean-looking frying pan over the fire and was broiling steaks. They smelled wonderful.

I sat down in my chair.

As he seasoned the beef with his back to me, he said, "I take it things went well last night, or you wouldn't be here."

"Yeah. Free for the next week."

"That's good," he said, turning around. He had the beef on two plates, and he handed one to me. "But I know there's a big ugly stain on your morning. And I think you know that what happened today is only the beginning. You really pissed Rick off, and from now on he's going to make it worse for you than ever before."

I nodded in resignation as I cut a slice of beef and popped it into my mouth. Every last drop of melancholy dissolved as the juices spilled over my tongue. The meat was lightly seared on the outside, but it practically melted in my mouth, the peppercorns sending off little firecrackers with each bite. I couldn't remember the last time I'd tasted something so good. It must have shown on my face, because he smiled a little and said, "Glad you like it."

I swallowed "Yeah, well, I'll figure out a way of dealing with him. Maybe I'll take a karate class or something."

"It won't be just you who'll suffer," the troll continued, the warmth and humor fleeing from his face. "You really scared him for a second back there. And in front of his friends no less. Now he's going to remind everyone who's in charge every chance he gets. And many on the receiving end won't have the benefit of a karate class."

That hadn't occurred to me. I lowered my eyes. "Well, what was I supposed to do? I mean, he jumped me, I had to defend myself!"

"Of course you did." His voice soft and consoling. "You did what anyone in your situation with an inkling of bravery would have done. But the fact is, in doing so you've started a chain of events that will result in many innocent people being hurt. Maybe worse."

I looked up. "Worse?"

The troll stood and poured water from a pitcher into two wine glasses that had been resting on the table. He handed one to me, then sat back in his own chair.

"Marty, let me tell you about Rick. Rick wasn't born this way. Nobody is. But through an accidental series of familial relationships and harsh encounters, he's developed a fixed world-view of kings and pawns, master and slave, might makes right. Fortunately for him, he has the physique to enforce his view on virtually all of his peers.

"Now, your parents and teachers and guidance counselors would tell you that this is just a phase that he'll outgrow, or one day end up in jail. He won't. He's not stupid, mind you. He's actually quite clever," the troll said, lecturing with all the brevity of a college professor. "Just this morning, when Mr. Weaver shouted at him from the doorway, he immediately calculated what he stood to gain or lose. The instant gratification and certain punishment of clobbering you then versus the delayed pleasure and probable impunity of waiting to catch you later, somewhere no one will hear you scream.

"In high school he'll use the same tactic to force friends of yours to complete his homework and give him test answers. He'll threaten and cheat his way into the university, where he'll employ his methods to force himself on girls too drunk to fight back, or even know they should. After college he'll use it to carefully manipulate his way to the top of his department, cutting down his employees at their most vulnerable points, burning careers to light his cigars. He'll never actually commit murder, but he'll destroy a great number of lives, and long after he's gone his dominoes will continue to fall with his sons, who he'll teach by example."

I barely blinked as he spoke. I saw the course of Rick's life unfolding before my eyes, shaped by the cues of the troll's narration. It was an horrific image, but I didn't feel the least bit disturbed. It was like an anesthetic daze where you feel like you're watching the world through the window of a submarine.

All I could feel was the delicious tang of the beef that I couldn't stop forking into my mouth.

"That is," he said, "unless you want to do something about it."

He snapped his fingers. I looked at the glass in my hand, and saw that the water had been turned to sparkling apple cider.

I smiled and asked him to continue.

* * *

A week and a half later I walked into third period Social Studies, the one class I shared with Rick, and took my seat. I pulled a pencil from my canvas carrier and began drawing on the inside cover of my spiral notebook, ignoring the wall of inane chatter created by the other students. Our teacher, Ms. Reckenburger, started class while I kept on drawing, occasionally glancing at Rick's empty seat, three rows up.

A knock on the door interrupted class, and Mrs. Lion, the school secretary, stuck her head in to ask Ms. Reckenburger to step out into the hallway. They disappeared together. The kids whispered and giggled to each other, while I twirled my pencil and stared at the door.

Ms. Reckenburger came back a few minutes later, her lips pursed and her eyes awkward and embarrassed. She wrung her hands as she slowly made her way to the front of the room.

"Class, I...I have some bad news," she said. "I've just been told that your classmate Rick is in the hospital. Apparently he was walking home from basketball practice last night, and somebody... attacked him."

No one spoke, but I heard a girl near the front draw in a gasp.

"They say it looks like he was beaten with some kind of metal object, like a crowbar."

"Is he OK?" asked a boy to my right.

"He's in critical condition," she responded, looking like the floodgates were about to burst at any moment. "He's in a coma, and they're doing everything they can. Now I don't want to upset any of you, but they're saying that at this point they don't know what's going to happen. He'd lost so much blood that..."

She excused herself and walked-ran to her desk, pulled a tissue from her purse and dabbed at her leaking eyes.

I could feel the shock all around me, every one of my peers processing the concept in their individual ways. And I knew damn well that at least a few of them were thinking, "*Serves the fucker right.*"

"I'm sorry," she said. "Now I want you all to listen to me. I know that some of you didn't always get along with Rick, but I think we can all agree that none of us wanted something like this to happen. I've been asked to tell you that if you know of anyone who might have wanted to hurt Rick, or if you have some information that you think might be important, anything at all, you should come to me or the principal immediately."

I was a little concerned by the fact that they'd figured out the crowbar so easily, but I shrugged inwardly and guessed that it probably wasn't too hard to tell from the marks on his body. Besides, they weren't going to find it now anyway.

As Ms. Reckenburger prattled on, I returned to my drawing. I'd never been much of an artist before, but since school started I'd found I actually wasn't that bad. Admiring the illustration I'd pulled off that morning alone, I was impressed with how well I'd been able to convey the trickling waters of the river, with how realistic my rendition of the ancient crooked oak trees and the old stone bridge looked.

Of course my eye, as well as the eye of anyone else who would ever see it, was perpetually drawn to the hunched figure of the troll, leaning out from under the bridge, waving with one hand and smiling that magic smile.

* * *

People, for the most part, keep their true emotions and motivations under wraps. As the days went by and news of Rick's condition didn't improve, people voiced their token condolences. And many like me who had endured varying levels of torment on his behalf over the years said nothing at all, letting their grim satisfaction pass unseen like dirty water under a bridge.

The removal of Rick's presence had lifted a weighty load. The targets of his scrutiny no longer had to waste their mental energy looking over their shoulders in the hallway, or fretting over his taunts, freeing their minds to focus on their class work. Likewise, the teachers found it that much easier to teach without having to keep one eye on the source of constant disruption. Even his friends seemed to breathe a sigh of relief, as if they'd only been playing along with his crap for fear of ending up on the receiving end of his antics.

I thought about the troll and what a blessing he'd been in my life. I thought about the gift of sight he'd given me, showing me what I'd always been capable of but what I had never known—the slight touch of courage to seize control of my world. More than anything, I thought of how much more he'd be able to give my friends, and not just my friends but every other kid in the city, all the untapped potential and dormant fantasies he could awaken with just a few words.

* * *

Our visits multiplied and grew longer. I spent several afternoons a week under the bridge, listening attentively to his wisdom and riddles. His insight resonated in my ears, and his subtle magic tricks glimmered in my mind. Sometimes hours would pass like minutes, and I'd emerge from the secret underfoot cave to find that the sun had long since set. I took his advice to heart like the earnest young student I was, always reporting back the next day. And with each nocturnal task I carried out, each mission of anarchy designed by my secret mentor, his body and apparel grew sharper and brighter, more visceral, more real.

Neither guilt nor fear kept me from sleep. The former me would have lain awake for hours each night, wracked by shame and paranoia for the so-called crimes I was now committing. But with my new outlook, I was protected by a force-field of logic. Even the most perceptive detective in the world would be thrown off by the sheer randomness of my actions.

No doubt the old folks in town were shaking their heads and remarking on how things weren't how they used to be, but none would ever suspect that these acts of arson, theft, online hijacking, vandalism and assault were all the work of the same person, let alone a twelve-year-old with no criminal record.

* * *

The other night, after my guiltless mind swam into the ether of the dream world, I found myself in the midst of a crowd, surrounded by flashing colored lights and tinny music.

It was the July Fireman's Carnival. All around, people were sifting powdered sugar onto funnel cakes, popping balloons with darts, demolishing milk bottle pyramids with softballs. I watched a guy built like a football player slam a mallet down on a high striker, earning a victorious chime when the ball hit the bell, while dozens of kids harnessed into swings swooped over my head.

What made this dream so much more vivid than any I'd had

before—and I noticed this even while it was happening—was that I could actually *smell* the carnival. The aroma of popcorn, malt vinegar, cotton candy and oiled machinery mingled with the midsummer sweat of hundreds of fair-goers and permeated the air.

I meandered through the crowd, and as I rounded a corner by the Tilt-A-Whirl, I noticed a small group of kids gathered around a tall man. The kids were younger than me, probably in the fourth grade, which made the man seem that much more ridiculously large. He looked like a long-legged Uncle Sam impersonator walking around on stilts on Independence Day. But his suit wasn't red, white and blue. It was painted in outrageously clashing shades of neon green, cherry red and day-glow yellow. Charcoal grey stripes ran up his freakishly long legs, and his waistcoat fastened at the collar with an over-sized purple bow-tie. On his head was a black tophat.

I knew it was the troll before he even turned his face in my direction. He grinned at me and gave a conspiratorial wink before turning back to his task at hand.

The troll was giving balloons to the kids. In his right hand he held a huge colorful bunch, which hung eerily still in the air, unaffected by the breeze. One by one he handed them out to the children, who waited patiently, not making a sound. After receiving their balloons, each turned and disappeared into the crowd.

As I watched, I understood what was happening. It was that baseless dream-logic where you simply *know* something without being told. The balloons were filled with poisonous gas. Each contained enough toxin to kill everyone within a twenty-foot radius if popped.

Of course the troll knew it, and I was his accomplice because I knew it too. What's more, I found that I was perfectly fine with it. As the act unfolded before my eyes, I felt with every fiber of my being that all was precisely as it should be. Perhaps even the kids themselves knew what was going on, or at least to the extent their young minds could grasp.

Then, the scenery changed. The lights went out, the sounds

were muted and I was no longer in the carnival. I was in the woods, walking along the unpaved road with the bridge less than a stone's throw ahead. When I reached it I hopped off the path and made my way underneath. There was a fire in the hearth as usual, and it illuminated the troll's abode in a flickering half-light. He was sitting with legs folded on the edge of the bank, his back to me. He was still wearing the vibrant costume, but the spry animation he'd displayed at the fair was gone.

Without his tophat, tufts of his short black hair stuck out in all directions. Protruding from his head, like the claw-handed arms of an ancient forest god, were two antlers.

As I approached him, the fear that had lain dormant for so long returned—my emotional thermostat cranked from zero to full throttle.

Suddenly I wanted it to stop. I wanted no more of this, and I wanted to get as far away from the troll as I possibly could. Yet, unable to control my own legs, I continued on.

I didn't call out.

I expected him to turn around at the sound of my footsteps. But he didn't move.

I stood behind him, mesmerized by the horrific beauty of the antlers on his head.

As my hand came to rest on his shoulder, he turned around. And that's when I saw it. His true face.

I knew then what he really was. And so, I also knew what I was.

The revelation came with all the calm reason that had accompanied my understanding of the poison balloons. It was nothing but what it should be, and now that I knew, there was nothing left to fear.

* * *

The next night I left the house at one in the morning. This time I walked out the front door. I had too much to carry to worry about sneaking out through a window or over the backyard fence. Besides, by the time the sun came up it wouldn't matter if anyone had seen me or not.

I remember the sound of the crickets that night. I couldn't recall hearing them on any of my previous expeditions. But that night their maddening chirping resonated through the trees and across the roads, as if trying to wake the neighborhood with their warning.

The sound of my footsteps thumped from the weight of the heavy duffle bag. I stuck to the roads, since I didn't know any other way to get there. Once in a while I'd have to duck behind a dumpster or into an alley to avoid being seen by the headlights of a passing car. But, for the most part, I was alone in the night.

It was a long walk, and I had plenty of time to think on my way. I thought briefly about my parents and wished I'd given my mom another kiss before I tucked them into bed. It hadn't been easy, not by a long shot, but I knew I was doing them a favor compared to what was coming for everyone else.

When I finally arrived it was a quarter past two. I looked up at the towering grey monument—a cold, solid and round aquifer on four long legs. It was the speaker through which I'd amplify my disgust, the facility for the distribution of justice. I pulled the bolt cutters from my bag and let myself in through the fence.

The most difficult part was getting to the ladder itself. They're usually left about ten feet out of reach to prevent anyone from doing what I was doing. I hurled my grappling hook three times before it snagged hold of the bottom rung. I then wriggled my way up the rope, the canvas bag hanging like an anchor from my shoulders. Once I reached the ladder I began the real climb. From then on it was easy going. The ladder was enclosed by a tube of bars so I never had to worry about falling backwards. I just had to focus on maintaining my strength and not looking down.

I felt the strain of each rung in my biceps and shoulders.

My breath grew heavy, but I struggled on.

After I had climbed higher than the roofs of the surrounding houses, I looked out over the checkerboard of traffic lights that made up my town—my wretched little briar patch of poison thorns all cutting into one another from every direction

That's when I felt the spotlight on me.

They'd seen me.

The awful realization that I was caught swelled in my gut.

Below, I heard voices shouting for me to freeze, accompanied by the distinct wail of a police siren, but I didn't look down. Instead I began to double-time up the ladder. I figured I may as well try to make a run for it and, who knew, maybe I could even pull off the operation before they caught me. I'd made it up another dozen rungs before my grabbing hands fumbled over each other. I lost my handhold, followed soon after by my footing.

I remember falling.

Then I remember nothing.

* * *

I awoke in a hospital bed. God knows how long I'd been out, but it felt like ages.

Soon after, my vision cleared and the white blur sharpened into the outlines of the ICU. The nurse on duty left the room and came back shortly with a policeman.

He asked if I knew where I was, to which I replied that I didn't.

He explained that I'd been caught trying to climb the water tower in the middle of the night and had fallen, but had luckily been saved when my bag, which had still been looped around my shoulder, snagged on a bar.

I'd suffered a massive contusion on my head, and the strap had broken three of my ribs. I also had a nasty bruise that ran diagonally across my chest like that caused by a seatbelt during a car crash.

He then told me I was under arrest, and as soon as I'd recovered I was to stand trial for the murder of my parents and the attempted poisoning of the town's water supply.

I tried to rub my temple and found that my right hand was cuffed to the bed.

A few days later, I met with a public defender. Since there was no way I was getting out of it, I decided to tell him everything—about burning the school, attacking Rick who had recently died and everything else. I recounted it all, step by step, taking care not to omit a single detail, no matter how trivial. I might have failed at poisoning the drinking water of every last person in town, but my God, when this story went public, I was going to make damn sure their minds were forever poisoned with fear.

Though I wasn't entirely sure why at the time, I even told him about the troll. It seemed a lot easier to just tell the truth than try to make up an explanation about where I had gotten my ideas. Besides, I had a feeling it was exactly what he would have wanted.

Later, with my preliminary hearing a few days away, my lawyer told me that he was going to use the "troll" story as the basis for an insanity plea. I told him I couldn't care less. He explained that from where I was standing, I had the option of maximum security prison, by way of juvenile hall, or an institute for the criminally insane, and between the two it would be in my best interest to shoot for the latter.

In bemused curiosity, I asked how he planned on explaining how I learned the chemical recipe for what I'd been about to pour into the tower, the cocktail that would have had every man, woman and child in town bleeding from every orifice in their body by noon. He looked at me without speaking for a bit, then said that I must have found it on the Internet somewhere.

He was afraid of me. I was happy about that.

* * *

Sometimes I wonder why the troll let me go. I assume he had his reasons. Maybe I'd served his purpose to the best of my abilities. Maybe he's gone back underground to wait for someone else—someone older and meatier—to come trip-trapping over his bridge.

I'm not offended.

According to my lawyer the police have been to the woods, and they found nobody under the bridge. Nor was there any evidence that anyone had ever been living there.

I figured as much, but it doesn't matter. I know he was there, and I know he'll be back to set me free when the time's right.

I know this by the dreams I have each night after the sedatives kick in, where I see the troll standing in the doorway, unmasked and speaking without words, and by the balloons I find tied to my bedpost in the middle of the night that are always gone the next morning.

BRIAN FATAH STEELE

During the last ten years, Brian Fatah Steele has written a number of both short- and long-format horror fiction pieces. Much of his work is currently being published by the indie co-op Dark Red Press.

Steele is the author of the novels *In Bleed Country* and the collection *Further Than Fate*. His work has appeared in several popular e-magazines and online journals. Steele's story "Wet Heavens" will be appearing in *Blood Type: An Anthology Of Vampire SciFi*, the net proceeds of which will benefit The Cystic Fibrosis Trust.

Surviving on a diet consisting primarily of coffee and cigarettes, Steele lives in Ohio with a few cats who are probably plotting his doom.

He still hopes to one day become a super villain.

DELICATE SPACES

BY BRIAN FATAH STEELE

While it is best to act according to reason,
that manner of thought has little power in the face
of the unreasonable. One has little hope of ascribing logic
to certain human experiences like love or fear,
and can only define them as subjective.
We like to think madness is something objective,
something agreed upon by the collective consciousness,
but reality often tends to disagree.

* * *

The glass doors swung open, and Dietrich nodded at The Traveling Couple. He found he often named people in his head when out doing research, some quirk he had picked up. Taking another drag off his cigarette, he found it incredibly easy to build an entirely fictional life for them. It took only a few moments, but The Traveling Couple soon had a backstory and a plot. All by the time they reached their car.

His back still hurt, and the bench outside the Rayburn Hotel was still soaked from an early morning rain. The hammered wrought iron of the bench matched the building's trim, the structure itself a dark brown stone affair with maroon shutters affixed in that faux-colonial fashion. It wasn't the nicest place Dietrich had stayed in, but its turn-of-the-century charm sold him. The perky concierge with a sprinkling of freckles definitely hadn't hurt.

The doors swung open again, and Aldridge gave him a gesture of greeting. "I wondered where you had wandered off to."

"My habit called."

"Understood," replied Aldridge, pulling out his own pack.

Dr. Alvin Aldridge was another random researcher at the Rayburn Hotel, one in a long string during the past two months. An anthropologist by trade, he spent most of his time as a professional skeptic. Surprisingly, he and Dietrich had gotten along despite the author's more optimistic leanings. Dietrich suspected this was because he held to no particular dogma and still kept a relatively scientific mind. Dietrich also suspected why the good doctor couldn't stand Sean Bell.

"Bell's in there blathering on with that young woman at the front desk about the difference between spirits, ghosts and poltergeists," said Aldridge.

"I'm sure you found that a rousing discussion."

Aldridge snorted. "I've never met a man so equal parts intelligent and imbecile."

* * *

Patricia enjoyed her job as the Rayburn Hotel concierge, but at that moment she wished she could be anywhere else in the world. Standing like a statue on the third floor of the East Wing hall with clean linens in her hands, her jaw trembled and her eyes darted about. The corridor should have a peach color, the doors fumed oak. Instead, the walls had taken on a hue most associated with vomit, the doors now only black voids. Everything had become *lesser*, except for those aspects that didn't fit and hadn't been there before. The whispers were back, echoing out of those dark maws and leeching any hint of vibrancy.

It was like the hum of insects, nondescript except for the occasional crack of a consonant. No real word, no message, just bleak nothings whispered in your ear. But the sounds caressed you, made you feel dirty. It was honey oozing over broken shards of glass, sweet poison distilled into audio form. They hinted at perversions, promised the most exquisite violations. It wasn't anything that could be articulated, nothing so definite, but more of an understanding on some deep, primal level. Body, mind, soul, it was irrelevant. It was as though one's being would be torn asunder in ways unimaginable, and the whispers begged for it. Whispered bits of black that told Patricia she wanted to be claimed and made anew.

Teeth clenched to stop them from clacking, Patricia struggled to turn her gaze away from the corridor and into an adjacent doorway. The whispers tickled the back of her neck like a serial killer's breath. The spots of darkness that once led to rooms seemed never-ending, the shadows there now tangible. The sounds continued unabated, as though they were examining her, judging her. The hallway grew paler, and the off-rhythm sharpness became louder.

The hand lightly touching her arm made her scream and fling the clean sheets into the air.

"Whoa," said Bell. "I didn't mean to scare you."

Patricia grabbed his arm, unashamed of the blossoming tears. "You didn't hear it?"

"Hear what?"

"The whispers. They were filling the hallway."

Bell grew agitated. "What, just now? Like, right before I touched you?"

Patricia could only nod.

She had been with the hotel for three years and had loved her job, for the most part. Only in the last few months, since the closing of the Rayburn Lodge on the other end of town, had things gotten weird. Quality jobs were hard to come by in the area, and Patricia didn't really want to tell her next employer she had been scared off by ghosts.

However, the situation was getting out of hand. Due to the economy, Travis Rayburn had closed the smaller, twenty-four-room lodge to concentrate on the fifty-two-room hotel. Most of the lodge furniture had been sold at auction or put into storage, while some had been moved to the hotel. The one item most of the ghost hunting types were interested in was the tapestry.

While Patricia hated the thing, it and the surge of unexplained sightings in the hotel had prompted Rayburn to push a marketing gimmick to help his weakening financial situation. Two weeks before Halloween, he had issued a press release stating that any paranormal activity group, physic, medium, skeptic or scientist who wanted a crack at the phenomenon could stay free one night in the hotel. As expected, many stayed for a few more. Two months later, people like Sean Bell were still showing up, and the matter had, if anything, grown worse.

Bell awkwardly tried to help her gather up the pile of linens. "Um, do you want me to stay up here with you?"

"No," said Patricia, shoving the hastily folded sheets into a small closet. "I'm heading back down. But thank you, Mr. Bell."

She could feel Bell's gaze on her as they walked down the stairs, a mixture of concern, excitement and desire coming off of him in waves. She had always considered herself empathic and figured that was why she had witnessed more paranormal experiences in the hotel than any of the other staff members. Billingham, the general manager, sure didn't admit to hearing anything, but she had noticed recently that he now avoided the sun porch as well as the back hallway.

So did she.

* * *

"Dude, Patricia heard the whispers."

Aldridge sighed and lowered his newspaper. "Did she now?"

"She about jumped out of her skin," said Bell, ignoring Aldridge in favor of Dietrich. "She was really creeped out."

Dietrich leaned back into the loveseat, not entirely thrilled with his role of mediator. "Did you have any recording equipment up there?"

Dejected, Bell mumbled something incoherent.

"What?"

"No. I thought I should stay in the back hallway last night. So everything is set up there."

The back hallway was a space only thirty-two feet long and twelve feet wide. The majority of examination and speculation into the incidents at the Rayburn Hotel centered there. A path between the lounge and a storage room that led to the sun porch, there was nothing particularly unusual about the hallway itself. It was the two main items *in* the hallway that garnered so much attention.

The Rayburn Hotel had been built in 1902, and the decorative mirror was installed in 1938. Still in perfect condition, the mirror was comprised of twenty, two-foot-square panels arranged in a rectangular fashion—wider than it was tall. The mirrors had a very slight frosting on them and a splattered patina of gold paint that matched its ornate frame. While you'd be hard-pressed to examine your hair or makeup in the mirror, you could stand back and see your outfit in it. Or appreciate it as a gaudy piece of art. Rumors had circulated since the 1960's of people glimpsing strange movements within the mirror.

Now, directly opposing it on the other wall, hung the tapestry. Vaguely arabesque in design, it was an abstract pattern that Travis Rayburn himself had purchased in 1974 specifically for the lodge. As one of the few things he had been nostalgic about during the decommissioning of his other estate, it was brought here and placed in the only location it would fit. That had been almost eight months ago.

Popular theory held that the mirror reflected things that weren't quite there, and that if you looked at the tapestry through the mirror, images would emerge from its weave. Some claimed to see a group of figures standing in the tapestry. Others stated they had witnessed movement. A few had described what they saw as a landscape, a single large tower to one side amongst a city of similar ones. Along that line of thought, a number of individuals spoke of a forest of dead trees swaying in the wind. In a singular occurrence, a college-aged woman had taken one look at the tapestry, proclaimed "It's an army," and checked out of the hotel immediately. Regardless, almost everyone agreed the back hallway was filled with negative energy. This included the esteemed Dr. Aldridge, but he suggested the reason for this was simply due to the ugly décor.

"Does anyone need anything?" Patricia asked, stepping into the lounge.

"Bell tells us you heard whispers. Is that true?" Aldridge asked.

The concierge barely kept herself from shooting the sound technician a withering look. "I think I heard something, yes."

Dietrich narrowed his eyes. "You okay?"

Patricia pushed a smile onto her face. "Yes, I'll be fine."

"Billingham okayed my experiment with ultra-low frequency generators. I'll probably be switching them on in about an hour," said Bell.

Patricia nodded and turned to leave when Dietrich called out her name.

"Let me know if you need anything, okay?"

This time she graced him with a genuine smile. "Thank you, Gabe."

She walked from the room, and Bell spun on Dietrich. "Dude, why are you *Gabe* and I'm *Mr. Bell?*"

"You're seriously going to ask that?" asked Aldridge, coughing back a laugh.

* * *

The voices were back. And they *were* voices, Turgenev was sure of that now. He laid his book down in his lap and peered about the sun porch. The first time he had heard the noises, he believed them to be coming from the old windows. It had sounded like the panes of glass had been grinding within their wooden frames. Today, he could pick out something more distinct, the subtle reverberation of words. The voices were more melodic than German, but more guttural than any of the romance languages.

An Asian dialect? Farsi, perhaps? He speculated.

Geoffrey Turgenev was a self-educated man, well traveled and better read, but he had never acquired any linguistic skills. He knew a little Latin, and therefore a smattering of French and Italian, but even that was more in print than in the spoken word.

The whispers scratched at the windows, off sync with the light raindrops pelting them from the outside. There was something else too, something about the rain as the clouds darkened the room.

Entranced, Turgenev watched as the rain splatters themselves became more akin to splashes of ink. As black rivulets ran down the windows, the sun porch sank into a deeper gloom. The shadows cast by the wicker furniture thickened, grew bulbous and began a faint undulation. All around him, the darkness seemed to become organic, providing a sensation that pulsed and quivered. The sound of the shadows, combined with the whispers and rain, grew into a numbing cacophony.

Then, it was silent. The thundercloud passed overhead and the rain abated ever-so slightly. The shadows became barely noticeable in the dreary afternoon. Clicking his tongue and returning to his book, Turgenev decided to speak to that young author later in the day.

* * *

"ULF is considered between three hundred hertz and three kilohertz, but I'm thinking—"

"Sean, man, you're talking to a guy who barely passed basic Earth Science in high school."

Bell gaped up at Dietrich from behind a monitor, clearly exasperated. "It's just that I know my field."

"I never said you didn't."

"Dr. Aldridge thinks I'm an idiot."

"Dr. Aldridge thinks everybody is an idiot," replied Dietrich.

Bell grumbled. "He likes you well enough."

Dietrich decided to switch conversation topics. "Did you give anymore thought to what I told you last night?"

"Actually, yeah," said Bell, rising to fiddle with the monitor's settings. "Who gave you this idea again?"

"Jonathan Dukestein. He's another author I vaguely know. He's also the one who told me to check this place out."

"That's a pretty heavy theory," said Bell. "It's not the hotel, or the stuff in the back hallway, it's the *space between* the mirror and the tapestry. Wild."

Dietrich idly examined Bell's nest of wires. "He has some pretty out-there ideas. Things like there are certain spots where reality is 'looser,' and that's why humans perceive all types of events and feelings at specific locations. Or that we can imprint our will on places where the universe is malleable."

"I know some sociology professors who would argue that," said Aldridge as he walked past.

"He also questions who are we to claim any knowledge of the universe in one that accepts the Heisenberg Uncertainty Principle and Schrodinger's Cat Paradox as fact?"

"Clever!" Aldridge responded as he walked through the front door, waving his pack of cigarettes.

"I'm going to join him for a smoke. You need me for anything?" Dietrich asked.

"Nope, I'm good."

Bell started flipping switches as Dietrich left. Gabe seemed cool enough, but the sound tech felt like an oddball around those other two. He thought taking vacation time from the studio for this excursion was going to be awesome, that he was going to meet some like-minded people investigating the unknown. So far the entire trip had been a letdown. Throwing the last switch, he turned to wander back into the lounge and stopped short.

Staring into the mirror with the machinery running behind him, he simply said, "Shit."

* * *

"I'm leaving tomorrow," Aldridge announced as Dietrich handed the professor back his lighter.

"I figured as much."

"There's nothing here, nothing even to debunk. It's all contagious hysteria brought on by marketing and an old building."

Dietrich stepped closer to the building, out of the rain. Aldridge did have a point. While there was something undeniably creepy about the back hallway, he hadn't experienced anything worth mentioning in his books. His latest offering of *The Haunted Rust Belt* now looked to only mention the Rayburn Hotel in passing.

"I don't know, I might stay an extra day to help out Bell."

Aldridge gave him a look. "You're staying an extra day to get our young Patricia into your suite."

"Okay, maybe that as well."

They both chuckled and puffed away.

Regardless of anything else, Dietrich liked the cynical old professor. He had met enough people like Bell in his travels, and Aldridge's staunch skepticism had been refreshing.

He was about to ask Aldridge about his class schedule when a scream came from inside the hotel. Both men flung their half-smoked cigarettes and rushed back through the doors. Dietrich saw Patricia in the lobby with her hand outstretched, as if warding off a blow.

"What's the…" he began before following her line of sight and then screaming himself.

The older gentleman that Dietrich had named in his head as The Distinguished Ex-Pat was stumbling out of the back hallway, away from a liquid darkness that bubbled and flopped around on the floor. The darkness had already consumed half of Bell's body. The old man fell back against the frame of the lounge doors, his head whipping back and forth between Bell's prone body and the tapestry.

"What is that?" screeched Aldridge, starting forward.

"Be careful!" the old man yelled back. "It's coming out of the tapestry. Look! Look in the mirror!"

Dietrich, Aldridge and Patricia nervously shuffled over to obtain an angle that allowed them to peer into the mirror. Dietrich muttered the name *Billingham* to the concierge, but she just shook her head. A few more steps and the reflection revealed itself.

"What am I looking at?" asked Aldridge quietly as the sounds of whispers began to grow around them.

The abstract tapestry had taken on a much more realistic quality. A figure on the left side of the weave appeared to be female, attired in some type of ceremonial garb. Behind her was another figure, but its sex was indeterminate. What looked like a sea of people on their knees dotted the landscape. On the right side of the tapestry, and featured prominently, was a massive creature arching over its supplicant. A biomechanical monstrosity without visible legs, the length of its arms exaggerated to unnatural proportions as was its lower jaw. Something peered out beneath its robes, something all too similar to a male organ. The beings in the tapestry were wading in the living ink that had now spilled out into the back hallway.

Patricia sobbed. "Mr. Turgenev, please get away from there!"

The older man made his way toward them, assisted in part by Dietrich. "I tried to help him," he said of Bell, "but he was stuck as though he were in either quicksand or mud."

The whispers in the hallway were now a litany of foreign sounds. An alien prayer or an infernal incantation, the voices rose from the darkness and bit those who listened. The image in the mirror had only moved a miniscule amount in the minute they had been standing there. Bell had not moved at all, already dead by the time they had staggered into this nightmare.

"We have to shut off the machine," said Dietrich. "Stop the noise Bell was making. That's got to be what caused this."

"No," said Aldridge shaking. "No, that can't be it. This can't be real."

Patricia backed towards the front doors. "We need to call for help."

Suddenly, the liquid darkness splashed farther into the lobby. Patricia screamed, fleeing back to the others.

Aldridge continued to run his hands through his hair and deny what he was seeing. "No, it has to be a trick, something Bell is doing to play with us," he said, stomping forward.

"Aldridge, wait!" Dietrich yelled after him.

Aldridge stormed up to Bell's machines, driven by his own devout skepticism. The black flood rolled back, allowing him to proceed. He started hammering buttons and flipping switches. The turn of the last dial brought the tapestry to life.

Dietrich and Patricia screamed, watching as Aldridge turned to the scene unfolding in the tapestry.

The revered creature—an amalgamation of beast, man and machine that towered over its subjects—had taken its acolyte's head in its hands and lifted her to a standing position. Its jaw, unhinged like a snake, had gently taken hold of the woman's face, her look blissful. The jaws began to grind, crunching and chewing away her features. As her face was slowly devoured, a torturous device rose erect from the robes. Its genitalia—the size of a small tree—was a nightmare of flesh and blades that began to savagely eviscerate her torso, its climax a baptism of the liquid darkness. The serene mask of joy never left her face, even as the ink infected her whole body. In moments that felt like a millennium, the creature began to turn. A shift, a flux, and the abomination in the tapestry regarded the delicate space in the hotel as if now aware of it.

It was only a handful of seconds before Aldridge met the gaze of the searing embers that were the monstrous priest's eyes. It was at that moment when he knew insanity.

With a final shriek, Patricia brought the base of a lamp down onto Bell's monitor and the scene disappeared, returning the hallway to normal.

The mirror was again just a mirror, the tapestry once again a tapestry, and Bell lay dead in the middle of the corridor. Vacant, glassy eyes stared up at them. Aldridge slumped to the floor as Dietrich ripped the tapestry from the wall.

* * *

They hadn't yet notified the police. Instead, Dietrich, Patricia and Turgenev surrounded the dumpster as they burned the tapestry inside. Dietrich had every intention of finding a hammer and attacking each panel of the mirror—Billingham and Travis Rayburn be damned. Bell was dead and Aldridge was in shock.

Turgenev broke the silence.

"I was in Texas once. Saw the ground bleed. Not water, not oil, actual blood like a wound on flesh. I was going to come see you earlier to tell you that I heard voices and saw something on the sun porch. Doesn't much matter now."

"We're okay now, right?" asked Patricia, hugging herself. "It's over?"

Dietrich didn't say anything.

"It wasn't the tapestry," said Turgenev. "Of course, burning it helps. It just became a door, the mirror a window maybe. Those things, this place, Bell's gadgets... I've seen a lot, dear. The whole world is haunted."

"Looser spots, delicate places," mumbled Dietrich.

"What?" asked Turgenev.

"Nothing."

A second scream came from inside the Rayburn Hotel.

They found the people Dietrich had named The Traveling Couple standing terrified over two bodies. Bell was still lying against his machines, but at some point Aldridge had the same idea about that hammer. Halfway through breaking them, he had decided to start using the glass shards on his wrists instead.

"What happened here?" demanded the husband.

"Turns out the whole world is haunted," replied Dietrich.

SEAN LOGAN

Sean Logan's superbly crafted fiction has appeared in more than thirty publications. His work can be found in *Black Static, One Buck Horror, Once Upon an Apocalypse* and *Eulogies II: Tales from the Cellar*.

Logan's story "Pushers" will be published in Volume 4 of *Postscripts to Darkness* magazine in October 2013.

He lives in northern California and enjoys reading, skateboarding, bad movies and good tequila.

RAINING STONES

BY SEAN LOGAN

The body was the same as the last one—split from throat to groin, skin pulled back with holes along the ragged edges from where it had been nailed to the living room coffee table. The rib cage was fractured along the sternum and spread wide, viscera exposed and glistening in the dull yellow light of the torchiere floor lamp.

It was just like the body that was found one week ago, and Lonnie Leigh didn't know what to think about that. He'd try to get one of the cops to comment for tomorrow's article, but SFPD wouldn't be putting anything on the record tonight.

"Thanks," Lonnie said.

Officer Lau zipped up the black cadaver bag. "My pleasure. You seen Nate yet? He's looking for you."

Lonnie took some notes on the state of the drab, musty apartment—the red handprint on the entryway wall, the blood sprayed across the mustard yellow couch, the sticky carpet beneath the coffee table where the blood had pooled.

He went to the kitchen and found Inspector Nate Lyles sitting at an old Formica table cycling through the pictures on the Department's cheap digital camera. Nate glared up at him. He wasn't tall but his arms were as big around as Lonnie's legs. His bald head and hard look were enough to make most lanky white boys like Lonnie break into a sweat.

Lonnie didn't fall for it. He knew Nate too well. But Nate didn't know everything about Lonnie. Not yet.

Nate passed him the camera.

Lonnie clicked through the crime scene photos and stopped on a close-up shot of the victim's face. He hadn't thought to look at it before, when the kid's insides were spread out in front of him like a butcher's display case. The kid was in his late twenties, not much younger than Lonnie himself, with the same straight black hair. His head lolled to the side, eyes closed, mouth half-open.

"You remember last week?" Nate asked. "We were at an apartment a little bit like this one here?"

"Yeah."

"You remember that apartment had a body in it that looked a whole lot like the one we found nailed to that coffee table?"

"Sure."

"Well, I remember you asking me to make sure to call you if we saw another one like that. I thought it was a little weird at the time, but I didn't say anything, figured you had your reasons. But here we are, a week later, with another body. So what I want to know is why you thought there might be another one?"

Lonnie set the camera back onto the table. "Just a crazy hunch."

"Is there something you want to tell me, Lonnie?"

Lonnie started looking through the kitchen cupboards, calmly taking his time because he knew it would piss Nate off.

"It reminded me of something from a long time ago," Lonnie said. He picked up a mason jar, looked it over, put it back, found a couple of shot glasses. "A guy named Dan MacAndrews killed six people the same way—sliced right down the middle. You were probably still in St. Louis, just a teenager at the time, but it was pretty big around here. They called him the Bayside Stalker. But he didn't do it. He was shot down twenty years ago."

"Yeah, we know," Nate said. "One of the other inspectors made the connection. But what aren't you telling me? I know you, man. I can tell you're holding back. What is it?"

Lonnie found a bottle of tequila above the refrigerator. Now he was getting somewhere.

"It's personal."

"When we got two people killed, there's no such thing as personal."

Lonnie took a deep breath and shook his head. He knew it would go here eventually.

"All right, you want to know why I'm interested in this? The reason I didn't say anything?" Lonnie shut the kitchen door and sat across from Nate. He poured Nate a shot of tequila and one for himself. "How long have we been friends?"

"I don't know," Nate said. "Ten years? Since you started the homicide beat at the *Chronicle*."

"Well, after all that time there's still something you don't know about me."

"What's that?"

"My name."

"Get the fuck outta here."

"My name's not Lonnie Leigh. It's Lonnie MacAndrews, and twenty years ago I watched my father get shot to death."

Nate stared a minute, trying to read him. "No shit?"

Lonnie raised his glass. "No shit."

"Son of a bitch," Nate said, and they both drained their glasses.

* * *

It was after 4:00 a.m. by the time things started winding down. The apartment was still filled with tired cops, joking and laughing, bagging evidence.

"So you find anything good?" Lonnie asked.

"Maybe, but you can't use it yet."

Lonnie flipped his notebook shut and slid it into the pocket of his peacoat.

Nate pulled a baggie from a cardboard box. Inside was a silver chain with a small pendant—a cross with a circle in the center, bisecting each arm like a Celtic cross, but with the word 'Yun' inside of the circle.

"We found it in the middle of the entryway, so we think it must have fallen off tonight. The kid we found on the coffee table, he was already wearing a gold chain. So unless he was wearing both gold and silver chains we don't think it came off him."

"Yeah, but what does it mean?"

Nate got a tattered paperback off the kitchen counter, *Unrecognized Religions of North America*, the binding held together with duct tape. "Lopez from GTF brought this over to help us identify it." He opened the book to a marked page. "Okay, here it is. 'Yunism. Founded in England in nineteen forty-three by Stephen Yun, formerly of China.'" Nate scanned the page. "I guess it's a combination of eastern and western philosophies. They believe in reincarnation and believe that Yun is what the Buddhists call a Bodhisattva, which is an enlightened being that chooses not to pass into nirvana but dies and gets reborn so that he can teach others how to become enlightened. But it looks like he didn't just think he was *a* Bodhisattva, he thought he was *the* Bodhisattva, that he's been here since the beginning of mankind teaching people the meaning of life, and in his former incarnations he was Prince Siddhartha and Jesus Christ.

"This book's about ten years old, but it says here that he's still alive. But then again, one way or another, I suppose he would be, right? Says he lives on a commune in Marin, but there's a church here in San Francisco, a big gothic building downtown, used to be a Catholic church. Two big gargoyles on the roof."

"Gargoyles?" Lonnie asked. He felt like he'd been punched in the chest.

"Yeah. It's over—"

"In the Bayview, just off Westhaven. I know. I used to go there when I was a kid."

* * *

From the passenger seat, Lonnie stared up at the gargoyles perched over the arched doorway of the church, keeping watch with bulging eyes. Their giant, bat-like wings were wrapped tightly around their bodies, pointed ears up and alert, curved beaks open, talons curled over the edge of their platforms, gripping the concrete.

He had woken to sweat-soaked sheets as a child, after dreams of the gargoyles swooping down from their perches to tear him apart.

Lonnie got out of the car.

"You gonna meet me for a drink later?" Nate asked.

"Yeah," Lonnie said absently. "I'll see you later."

Nate drove away while Lonnie tried to remember something about this place, but his memories were so vague that he'd wondered, as an adult, if they were just dreams. Now, standing in front of the church was like having a dream materialize in front of him.

It was a nice piece of architecture, with Romanesque and Gothic motifs, but Lonnie guessed that most people had never paid it much attention. The church was in the middle of a narrow one-way street, facing the back of a factory, and bookended by warehouses.

He remembered having been here with his father, but that's all. And he seemed to remember waiting outside while his father had gone in. Maybe he'd know that more clearly if he could get his feet to move so he could go inside.

Lonnie walked up to the tall, arched doorway. He pushed and found it unlocked. It was heavy and swung slowly open into a dark room. The stained-glass windows were boarded. The light from the doorway cut across mounds of rubble piled on the floor — soiled clothing; rusty shopping carts; a ripped, cushionless couch. The air smelled wet and moldy. Lonnie would have figured the church had been abandoned if it weren't for a long-haired man hunched in the far corner, in the flickering yellow light of a half-dozen candles.

Walking towards the man, Lonnie stepped carefully among the broken bottles that littered the floor. The wedge of sunlight coming in from the open doorway narrowed and vanished as the door swung closed behind him.

There were still pews here, but some were overturned. Lonnie walked down the aisle between them. He heard a faint rustling and sensed movement. It was coming from all around him.

People sleeping, maybe, but it was too dark to see.

The man in the candlelight hadn't moved. He was kneeling before the symbols of several religions—a crucifix, a statue of the Buddha, a menorah, a prayer wheel, rosary beads.

Trying to ignore the noises coming from the shifting shadows, Lonnie walked up behind the man. When he stepped into the candlelight, the man reluctantly turned around. He wore thick glasses and his bulging eyes darted nervously between Lonnie and the floor. He flashed a quick, wide smile. His teeth were large and spaced apart. His gums looked bruised. He was wearing loose black pants and a black robe, a silver Chinese character over the breast. The robe was open, exposing his sunken, scarred chest.

"Hello," he mumbled. "Can I help you?"

"Hi, my name's Lonnie." Lonnie stuck out his hand. The man shook it, but as he reached out, he curled his face into his left shoulder, away from Lonnie's gaze. His grip was like a wet paper towel.

The man didn't say anything.

"What's your name?" Lonnie asked, as if speaking to a child.

"I'm Adrian."

"Well, I was hoping I could ask you a few questions."

"About what?" Adrian was already starting to close up, slouching his shoulders, bowing his head and staring at the floor.

"About your religion and the sort of people that come here," Lonnie said, tip-toeing in before the guy closed up completely.

"People call it Yunism," Adrian said.

"Yeah, after Stephen Yun, right?"

Adrian looked up, surprised. "You know Stephen Yun?"

"I've heard his name. Is he still alive?"

"He just died eighteen weeks ago. What do you know about us?" Adrian's shoulders were still hunched, but he was looking at Lonnie now.

"I know about Stephen Yun. He used to be the Buddha, used to be Jesus, that's about it."

Adrian's bulging eyes were fixed on his. "You've lived other lives too, you know."

"Yeah, and so have you, I guess. Who else have you been?"

"I've always been me. I've gone by other names and been in other bodies, but I've always been me, as I always will be. Just as you have always been you, and the Lord Yun has always been the Savior, and the Devil has always been the Devil. New souls are incarnating all the time, but some of us have been here since the beginning. The earth is starting to flood over with new souls. Did you know the world's going to end soon?" He asked this cautiously, but as if he was offering good news.

Lonnie smiled. "No, I didn't know that."

"Did you see the Two Beasts on your way in?"

"The gargoyles on the roof?"

"Those are the Two Beasts of the Great Cleansing. There are too many souls in the world. The Two Beasts will be reborn soon to cleanse the earth and send the souls back."

"Back where?"

"Into the Hells. They'll dive down from a black sky with their beaks and their talons and tear the hearts from the wicked."

Clinking glass behind him. Lonnie spun around. A bottle rolled to a stop in one of the front pews. A dark shape reached down to pick it up. Lonnie assumed it was a hand attached to an arm attached to a human body, but all he saw was a shadow coming out of the shadows to grab a half-empty bottle of malt liquor.

Lonnie felt a coldness crawling up his back, and he wanted out of the church. He'd had enough prophecy and darkness. He muttered, "Thanks," as he backed away, but Adrian kept talking.

"It's going to be soon, the Great Cleansing. Your holy books are interpretations of interpretations, but Lord Yun is the source."

By now, Lonnie's eyes had adjusted to the dark, and he could make out shapes curled up on the pews and sprawled out on the floor, writhing in alcohol nightmares. Some of them sat up as he walked past.

"Only those with pure hearts will be spared. The rest will have their beating hearts torn from their bodies while they scream."

Lonnie walked quickly, people sitting up in their pews, dark shapes staring, the door miles away. He slipped on something wet, fell, his hands landing in broken glass, a jagged piece stabbing his right palm. He scrambled to his feet and kept walking, pulling the glass from his hand.

"The righteous will reclaim the earth, but the evil..."

Some of the dark figures beside Lonnie began to stand.

"...will be devoured."

Reaching the door, Lonnie jerked it open just enough to squeeze through, pulling it shut behind him. He could still feel the darkness of the church clinging to him like mud, but the sun was slowly burning it away.

He stepped away from the door, feeling like a dozen shadow-hands might come bursting through to drag him back inside.

* * *

Lonnie walked to O'Malley's and stopped for a drink on the way. When he arrived, Nate was just sitting down with a beer.

"Man," Nate said, "you're even later than I was."

Lonnie took the seat next to him. "Where've you been?"

"I've been waiting for the blood tests to come back. Found something interesting too."

"What's that?"

"The blood wasn't all human," Nate said. "Almost all the blood belonged to Nordberg, the kid on the table, but the lab found a small trace of chicken blood."

"No shit?"

"No shit. And there was no chicken, or any other kind of meat, in the house. Nordberg had tomato soup for dinner."

"So what the fuck, Nate? You think the guy was killed by a chicken?"

Nate laughed. "Naw, I'm thinking that maybe this was something religious, some voodoo, human sacrifice type of shit, you know? Maybe this guy isn't a copycat of your old man. Maybe he's just got the same religious practices. Has any of this sparked any memories for you? Anything at all?"

"No, but that's what I'm hoping. I don't really remember my childhood. My first ten, fifteen years—it's like it didn't exist. I'm just hoping that if I can learn something about whoever's killing these people, maybe it'll help me remember something about my father."

"Yeah, then again, you remember something about your father, maybe you can help me learn something about the killer."

The bartender came over. He was a sporty, muscled German named Brock. If there was ever an O'Malley, he hadn't been around in a while. Brock was wearing his lopsided grin, showcasing a wall of straight, white teeth.

"Mister Leigh," he said, extending a meaty hand. "Good to see you."

Lonnie nodded and forced the lower third of his face into an unconvincing smile. He knew it didn't show any pleasure, but he was pretty sure it didn't look sarcastic. Unless he'd been mistaken all these years, it was the smile of a joyless man making an effort to be cordial, and somehow that seemed to please people even more than if he were bubbling over with warmth and cheer. He knew what his face looked like to others—long, pale and thin, surrounded by a mop of limp, black hair—and there was something about his expression of continual distaste that made people feel good when he showed the slightest emotion to the contrary.

Lonnie shook Brock's hand. "Could I get a shot? Tequila. Something from your bottom shelf, comes in a plastic jug."

Brock poured him a generous shot and went dutifully back to the other end of the bar.

Nate drained half his beer and stood. "I'm going home. I'm on again tonight. You need a ride?"

Lonnie tossed back his shot and chased it with the rest of Nate's beer. "I could use a ride."

It was nearly as dark and drab outside as it had been in the bar, even though it was still only three in the afternoon. A smiling kid with a scraggly beard and a baggy, tie-dyed shirt asked Lonnie for change. His right eye was looking up at Lonnie and the other was aimed down and to the left.

Lonnie didn't give him any money. He had a policy of reserving his spare change for people over forty.

"Thanks anyway!" the kid said with an overenthusiastic grin.

"So, you think your dad's the reason you never found your religion?" Nate asked.

"Maybe, but I hadn't even thought about my father's religion in nearly two decades. But maybe that's the problem. Maybe it's getting to me subconsciously. I should probably go to a shrink and get this shit sorted out."

They passed a woman sitting cross-legged on the sidewalk with a scratchy, gray blanket across her lap. Her long, graying hair was pulled away from her smiling face, half of which was tightly wrapped in the warped, pale flesh of a healed burn, her smile a bit too wide on the right side of her mouth.

Lonnie tossed his change on her blanket.

"Bless you," she said, beaming.

"Actually," Lonnie continued, "I think the reason I never got involved in religion is because, at least in the Christianity I was taught, we know how it all ends: God wins."

"Don't tell me you've got a problem with *that*."

There was yelling across the street. Someone was carrying a sign. Someone protesting something. Lonnie ignored him.

"No," he said, "it makes sense to me that if the final act of this play has already been written, then everything leading up to it has already been written as well. Which means that every move I make and every thought I think has been preordained."

The person across the street seemed to be following them. He was yelling, but Lonnie couldn't understand him.

"So if I have no will of my own," Lonnie said, "then why should I put any effort into being good? Why should I put any effort into anything?"

Nate's lip curled, like he'd just noticed the urine smell on the street. "So you can get into Heaven," he said.

"Well, if I have no free will, then whether I get into Heaven or not has been decided for me."

"Okay," Nate said, "if any of that shit's true then I guess I was just 'preordained' to be a motherfucker that gives a shit."

They continued on without talking. Nate didn't seem to notice the man across the street, but he was getting more belligerent, yelling an indecipherable phrase over and over and shaking his sign. Lonnie was trying not to make eye contact with the man, giving him an excuse to cross the street and rant in their faces, but he couldn't ignore him.

Lonnie looked and was disturbed to see that the man was dressed like a priest, wearing a long black robe and white collar. But the man wasn't a priest. His robe was tattered at the bottom, and over it he wore a puffy, blue ski jacket that was too small. He had long, knotted hair and Lonnie could tell, even from a distance, that there was something wrong with his face. The features seemed too large and badly formed.

They reached Nate's car. Nate got in and opened the passenger door. More homeless people lined the street ahead of them. They watched Lonnie get in the car, all wearing wide grins.

The man dressed as a priest ran out into the street and followed, shaking his sign at them as they drove off.

In the side view mirror, Lonnie could see the sign was blank.

* * *

Lonnie found himself in a courtyard, surrounded by concrete walls. An oppressive black sky hovered overhead. He was facing a stairway that dropped into the earth. He stepped down into the darkness and allowed himself to be swallowed up by the shadows.

He couldn't see the stairs in front of him, but he sensed that they descended for miles. As he continued downward, the walls beside him disappeared. He felt like he was in a vast, empty space. There were no handrails, and Lonnie knew that if he slipped over the edge, he'd fall through miles of darkness.

The void around him felt infinite, filled with black, stagnant air. But somewhere a phone was ringing. It was very close, right next to him. He reached out cautiously, leaning only slightly so he didn't slip and fall off the side.

The phone rang again. He slid his foot to the edge and reached out, sure that he was almost touching it. He leaned just a bit further, and the stairs shifted beneath him. He swung his arms, trying to regain his balance, but he was too far forward. He scrambled and slipped, falling into nothingness.

The phone rang again.

Lonnie woke. He sat up, and his head was like an unbalanced tray in a drunk waiter's hands.

He picked up the phone. "Hm?"

"Lonnie, it's Nate."

"Man, I love it that you work nights. What the hell time is it?"

"It's eight in the morning. You should be getting your ass out of bed anyway."

Lonnie saw slivers of light between the blinds. It felt like the middle of the night. "What do you got?"

"I've had the Gang Task Force looking into this Yunism. Lopez was able to dig up some of their literature—some photocopied fliers and shit like that. One thing he found was called *The Book of Prophecies*. Says a lot about the rebirth of Stephen Yun, and a lot of shit about the 'Two Beasts of the Great Cleansing.' At the end it says that the Devil is a man walking the earth and that he won't be sent to Hell until this Great Cleansing, which is supposed to be some sort of apocalypse. So when he thinks it's about to happen, he tries to make amends by offering the wicked to the Two Beasts. It doesn't get any more specific than that, but there's a crude drawing of an evil-looking man standing over a body that's been split up the middle."

"So what does it mean?"

"We talked to the shrink about it. He thinks we got a guy who feels guilty, maybe he did some bad shit in the past and he wants to make amends. The shrink said something about bi-polar disorder. Anyway, this guy thinks he's the Devil. And he's also a Yunist. So what we're going to do is check out which of these Yunists have criminal backgrounds or histories of mental illness, which'll probably be half of them 'cause I understand most are just bums off the street."

"So can I use this?"

"No. You can't use any of it."

"Then why the hell did you call me at eight in the morning?"

"Because I wanted to tell you not to go down to the church again. I don't want you down there fucking up our investigation. But I'll tell you what—you meet me at O'Malley's tonight, I'll bring you up to speed."

* * *

Lonnie stared at the gargoyles. He imagined them gliding down on giant, bat-like wings to dig into his flesh with their curved beaks.

His water bottle was filled with tequila. He was going to have to get drunk if he expected to go back into the church. He didn't see any cops around. Nate would be furious if he knew what Lonnie was doing, but he needed to be here. He had information. For now, that information was stored away in the back of his mind. He needed to keep reaching for it, going to places that might knock memories loose, going to places where the killer might be.

Lonnie took a long drink. And with one last look around, he walked to the front of the church, past the winged sentries, and shoved the door open.

Just as before, it was dark inside, aside from candlelight burning in the far corner. This time, however, there were dozens of people surrounding the yellow glow. And there was sound—a murmur of disorganized chanting, people speaking rhythmically but not in unison. There must have been thirty people or more surrounding the candlelight, the closest ones well lit, the rest fading into the darkness. Those Lonnie could see were staring down at something that was out of his field of vision.

The worshippers looked like a collection of the city's most unfortunate creatures—their mouths filled with yellow, crooked teeth; their filthy hair knotted and greasy; their faces made asymmetrical with scarred and malformed features. But they were all smiling—wide, sickly-sweet smiles. Whatever it was that was at the center of the circle made these horrible creatures very happy.

A memory flashed in Lonnie's mind, quickly, like a glimpse of a photograph. It was this same church, but not so dark or dirty. A congregation gathered in the pews, turning around to look at him as he entered. And he had the feeling of being unwelcome.

Another image flashed, almost the same as the first, but in a different church—smaller, wooden walls, a lower ceiling, fewer people—and the same unwelcome feeling.

He tried to build complete memories around these images but nothing more came to him.

The voice of the crowd was hypnotizing. They were chanting at an even pitch, but overlapping, creating a sea of rhythmic speech that he couldn't understand.

He walked toward the crowd as the door swung closed behind

him. He didn't know what he was going to do, who he'd talk to or what he was going to say, but he knew that if he wanted answers, this was where he had to get them.

He walked slowly, hoping to ease into the crowd unnoticed.

Clanking glass. He kicked a malt liquor bottle. The crowd turned, and the chanting stopped. Their smiles remained, but their eyes had changed. They now appeared upset and suspicious, maybe hostile, but it didn't show on their lips.

Another image flashed in his mind of a similar scene, but in yet another church, if it was a church at all. It was a dark, damp room underground. A crowd was staring. They were walking toward him. A hand grabbed his arm. A large hand. His father's hand. It dragged him backward, away from the crowd.

Again, he couldn't fill in the details.

As in his memory, the crowd of worshippers approached, some of the unhappy, smiling faces backlit by candlelight, the rest in darkness.

Lonnie backed up toward the door, his heart pounding so hard he was beginning to see spots dancing in the periphery of his vision.

The crowd walked toward him, smiling and silent.

He backed into the door, felt the handle and pulled. The sunlight that spilled in fell on the approaching crowd, on the figures that had previously been hidden in shadow. Their faces were even more horrible than the rest—a man whose smeared features looked as if they'd been pressed under glass, a woman with a puckered scar bisecting her face as if it was collapsing in on itself, another man with an empty cavern where his left eye should be and the right eye a ghostly white.

Lonnie slipped through the door, leaving the crowd squinting at the daylight. He slammed it shut behind him and ran from the church. He jogged two miles up 3rd Street before he stopped and knelt, panting, his lungs burning and his black hair stuck wet to his forehead.

He took a long drink from his water bottle and started walking, not sure where he was going.

He took the pieces of what he knew about the killer and tried to put them together—the religion, his father, the chicken blood, the church in the Bayview, and the churches from his memory. The pieces didn't fit. He hoped Nate would have something to fill in the blanks for him.

Lonnie changed his course and headed for O'Malley's. The walk would take more than an hour, but he wasn't due to meet Nate for another three. He sipped at his tequila as he went. He hated the taste of cheap tequila, but at this point his mouth was numb to it.

* * *

Lonnie was swaying on his feet when he entered O'Malley's, tired from the walk and drunk to near blindness. He toddled unsteadily up to the bar and ordered a shot.

The last thing he needed was another drink, but that didn't stop him.

"How you doin', Mister Leigh?"

"Fine thank you, sir," Lonnie said. Evidently the bartender knew him, but Lonnie couldn't discipline his eyes to focus on the man.

Lonnie went to a booth at the back and sank into the red, cushioned seat. He stared at his drink with slack eyes, his head swirling with half-formed thoughts.

Three other reporters from the *Chronicle* came into the bar and ordered drinks. They spotted Lonnie and sauntered over to say hello. He forced his face into a smile and shook their hands, barely looking up from the table. The fact that he didn't want company didn't escape them, so they slapped him on the back and rolled off to a table at the front of the bar, all laughs and witty banter. Lonnie couldn't give a shit about them. That's why he rarely came here, because half the writers from the paper did. He had their respect, if not their friendship, and that's all he wanted. They could keep their friendship. Their friendship wouldn't help him find the killer.

Lonnie drained his shot glass and was refilling it under the table with the tequila from his water bottle when Nate marched in, saw Lonnie, and made a beeline for his booth. He started yelling before he even sat down.

"One of my guys saw you coming out of the church today," he said. "I thought I told you not to go in there, and I could have sworn you heard me, and I'm pretty goddamn certain you said you wouldn't. So is my memory starting to fail me, or did you change your mind and decide to interfere with my investigation?"

Sitting so close, Lonnie wasn't able to see Nate clearly, and watching the blurry image of the man yell at him almost made him laugh. He controlled himself and spoke, trying to form his words clearly.

"You're not losing your memory," he said, "but that's not what's important right now. I need to know if you've found anything out."

The blurry Nate leaned back in his chair and looked at Lonnie with an expression Lonnie assumed to be a mixture of bewilderment and anger. "What the fuck you mean, 'That's not important right now?' Do you know what you did, you drunk son of a bitch?"

Lonnie felt like getting a rise out of Nate. He knew he was being juvenile, but diplomacy was never one of his virtues when he was this deep in the bag. "Yeah I know what I fucking did," he said. "I went out and tried to find a fucking killer since you're sitting on your ass waiting for someone else to get killed."

Nate pointed at Lonnie. "If I see you near that church again I'll have you arrested." He got to his feet and started back for the door.

Lonnie couldn't let him leave yet, he didn't get what he had come for—his information. "Hey, tell me what you guys found out today."

He ran up to Nate and shoved him hard from behind. Nate tripped onto one knee, got up pissed as hell and grabbed Lonnie by the collar, shoving his shirt up under his chin. Lonnie was laughing now, unable to stop himself.

"Listen, you drunk piece of shit, you're losing it." He gave Lonnie a little shove and let go of his shirt.

"I need to know. You gotta tell me what you guys found today."

Nate stared at him for so long that Lonnie's eyelids grew heavy. "All right," he said, finally. "I'll tell you what we found, but only because this is your first fuck-up and because you've never printed anything I told you not to. When we went in the church we picked up a few loose items of clothing we found on the floor. One thing we found was a scarf. We tested it and found traces of chicken blood and chicken fat. That's all we got. Don't print that, and I meant what I said about having you arrested if I see you near that church again."

Lonnie squeezed Nate's shoulder. "Thanks man, you're a good friend." Lonnie staggered toward the door.

"Where you going?"

"I'm going to the church," he said, busting out laughing.

Nate wasn't laughing. "You son of a bitch."

"Yeah, fuck you too, Nate," Lonnie yelled, walking backward toward the front door, his head a blind, dizzy mess. He turned to the booth where his co-workers sat staring at him. "And fuck you too, you fucking hacks." And to the bartender: "And fuck you too, you anonymous fuck." He found the front door. "Fuck you all," he said to the bar, "and to all a good night."

Lonnie slammed the door shut behind him, leaving a room full of severed ties. It felt good. It felt like suicide. He tried to think of more friends he could tell to fuck off, but he couldn't think of any. A million contacts but no friends. Nate was the only one.

Lonnie staggered up the street, stumbling left when the sidewalk slanted left, and stumbling right when it tilted back. It tilted a little too far and knocked him off into the gutter. He smacked his head on the rough asphalt. He didn't try to get up. He felt a warm, tingling blackness spilling over him. He was glad he was on a side street—there weren't many cars. And he was glad there was no water running down the gutter. It wasn't a bad place to black out.

* * *

Lonnie was surrounded by concrete walls facing a stairway that dropped into the earth. He stepped into the darkness.

Blind. A long, narrow stairway with no handrails. Miles of stagnant air and empty space.

But it wasn't entirely empty. Something was down there with him. He couldn't see it or hear it but he could feel it, a stir of the air. Something was there, floating through the murk, like a squid through water, but slower. Very slowly. Easing toward him.

Lonnie continued downward, focusing on the miles of narrow steps in front of him. But he couldn't ignore the presence that loomed nearby. He could feel it coming closer.

Down. More narrow stone steps. But what was this? Was the black air taking shape?

The presence was coming into view, and the suggestion of form turned Lonnie's heart cold. Long, thin tendrils. Sickle-shaped curves. It was above him, the size of a building. Spreading. It was spreading its wings.

There was now color in the darkness. It was red, oozing through the black like blood seeping through clothing. Two long tendrils whipping like cat tails the size of pine trees. It loomed over him, like a storm cloud falling from the sky. Red wings, twin tails, and cold, icy-black eyes.

Lonnie's heart collapsed. It shriveled in his chest as the demon hovered over him. It filled his vision. Sharp talons reaching...

* * *

Lonnie opened his eyes, screamed, scrambled backward on the sidewalk. He looked around, panting, his heart thudding.

He was on a San Francisco street. It was night. He didn't know how he'd gotten there. His head ached. Memories of the bar came back and he winced.

He couldn't remember ever being this low. But, no, he could... A memory came back to him from his childhood. It was after his father had lost his job down on the piers. He was out of work for months, and during that time there was no heat, no electricity and no new clothes. For food they went to the meatpacking plant and paid a quarter for a bag of giblets for stew. Lonnie remembered walking for three miles twice a week carrying home those bags of guts.

A light switched on in his mind. He remembered that once while he was waiting for his father to buy the giblets, he went into the alley around back, by the dumpsters. The smell was horrible. Homeless men were sleeping under a vent blowing warm air.

Lonnie saw a squat, hairy man hunched against a dumpster, sitting in a pool of blood. He thought the man was hurt, maybe even dead. But then he saw that the blood wasn't coming from the man, but instead from the dumpster itself. It was trash from the meatpacking plant that was leaking onto the ground. It wasn't human blood, it was chicken blood.

And Lonnie also remembered that the plant was just behind the church in the Bayview.

* * *

After more than twenty years, the smell behind the Westhaven Meat Packing Company hadn't changed—it still smelled of wet asphalt, urine and rotting meat. It was a cold, overcast night. Three men were huddled under blankets near the vent, which pumped the same warm, wet air.

The alley separated the meatpacking plant from the empty warehouse adjacent to the church. The area was dark, but lit faintly in yellow by a distant streetlamp.

Lonnie sat against the dumpster, trying to get comfortable, careful not to sit in the blood. In his condition he didn't think he'd have any trouble blending in. He sipped at his water bottle, trying to make his headache go away. The tequila tasted like toxic waste.

Time passed. His headache faded and swaying drunkenness returned. The vent blew warm air. His companions slept. After a while

Lonnie began to doze, but he couldn't close his eyes without seeing a giant, red demon floating through black, stagnant air.

Lonnie was finally starting to fall asleep when he heard footsteps in the alley. He opened his eyes and saw a short, skinny man walking toward him. Lonnie stayed where he was, feigning sleep.

The man was carrying a black, plastic trash bag. He tossed the bag into the dumpster and walked across the alley to urinate at the back entrance to the warehouse. While his back was turned, Lonnie slowly got to his feet. Careful not to make any noise, he fished the bag from the wet, foul-smelling trash. He ripped through the plastic, and what he saw sent an icy numbness up his back and down through the tips of his fingers. Gloves, a washrag, a hunting knife, a pair of pruning shears—all smeared with blood.

Lonnie heard a zipper closing behind him. He turned and saw the killer just as the killer saw him. He was just a kid, a young man with scraggly hair on his chin and upper lip. He had long, curly brown hair that was pressed down with a baseball cap. He had big brown eyes, wide with fear, staring at Lonnie, who knew who he was.

The kid sprinted off and Lonnie ran after him, carrying the evidence. He hadn't counted on chasing him, but he hadn't thought this out, hadn't known what to expect. He couldn't go find a phone and call Nate. If Lonnie lost him now he might never find him again.

The boy ran up the alley to the back of the church, into a courtyard surrounded by the tall concrete walls of the warehouses. Lonnie's lungs were already burning, but he was faster than the boy, and when he was close enough he dove, grabbing him around the waist. The two of them tumbled to the cement, Lonnie's knuckles scraping under the boy as they slid to a stop, the contents of the plastic bag scattering around them.

The kid rolled over, knocking Lonnie off of him. He was small but terribly strong. He got his hands around Lonnie's throat and squeezed, pressing his thumbs into Lonnie's esophagus.

Lonnie gasped for breath, but no air came through. His chest hitched, he panicked, tried to scramble, but his arms were pinned under the boy's knees. His chest convulsed. He felt a tingling in his head, bright specks of light were popping in front of his eyes. Then suddenly he could breathe again. He sucked in air and coughed. He saw the boy had the knife and was pulling it open. Lonnie lunged for him, knocked the boy over, grabbed the pruning shears, swung around, and hit him with them. They stuck in his neck.

The boy stood and backed away, his eyes wide and panicked. He pulled the shears from his neck, and blood pulsed out in a thick stream. He pressed his hand to the wound, and blood flowed between his fingers. He looked woozy, his eyes drooping, walking unsteadily. Finally he tripped and fell, blood pooling around him in the alley.

Lonnie stood, numb and dazed, backing away from the young man he'd just killed. With his head spinning, he saw something that caught his attention. It was important, but he didn't know why. It was a stairway at the back of the church that led down into the ground.

Vague memories returned. He'd come here as a child, he knew that. With his father. His father had begged to be let in. Someone on the other side of a door had said no.

"*Please,*" his father had pleaded, "*I've changed my ways.*"

Lonnie walked to the stairway.

It was a dark night, and he couldn't see past the first few steps, but he stepped down into the shadows. He expected to run into a door, but the stairs kept going. Lonnie was fully immersed in darkness, ten feet down, fifteen, twenty.

Finally he came to a cold steel door. He pushed, and it swung open easily. Inside was a narrow, stone hallway only six feet tall, and he could see the flickering of candlelight from around a distant corner. He walked forward, unafraid, his mind empty and his body numb. If there was any sense of logic or reason inside him, it was buried away somewhere that it couldn't do any harm.

He walked, slightly hunched, down the cold, damp passageway. He turned a corner and came to a room filled with people, aglow in the light from dozens of candles. The people were the same horrible creatures he'd seen that morning at the church, jagged shadows dancing across the broken surface of their warped flesh and aberrated features. But Lonnie was no longer afraid.

Adrian, the man in the robe that he had met previously, stepped from the crowd. He too was smiling, showing his yellow teeth. "We're glad to see you, Lonnie. We knew you'd be coming tonight. We've known for a long time. It's a happy night for us." He took Lonnie's hand in both of his. "It's the first night of the Great Cleansing."

Lonnie looked around at the room. It seemed to be the basement of the church—plain and square; cement floor, walls and ceiling. There was an exceptionally wide stairway leading up into the church proper. The hatch door was open, and Lonnie could see through to the front of the building, the doorway and its boarded windows. Candles and dirty, smiling people lined the walls. There were two large oak tables at either end of the room. One table was empty and on the other was a peaceful infant wrapped in blankets.

Adrian saw Lonnie looking at the baby. "Do you know who that is?" he asked.

Lonnie shook his head, numbly.

"It's our Savior. Before He died and was reborn, back when He was known as Stephen Yun, He told us the Great Cleansing would begin tonight. Do you know why?"

Lonnie shook his head again.

"Because it begins when the Devil is killed by his son, and He made it known that tonight you'd kill your father."

"But I didn't," Lonnie mumbled. "I killed a boy."

"That boy was born on August twenty-third, nineteen ninety-four. Does that date sound familiar to you?"

"It was the day my father died."

"That boy you killed was the Devil. He has walked the earth since the beginning of humanity. And you have *always* been his son."

Adrian led Lonnie to the empty table at the end of the room.

The crowd began their disorganized chanting.

Adrian helped Lonnie onto the table and had him remove his shirt. Lonnie didn't question him. His only thought was way in the back of his mind. He wondered if any move he'd ever made in his life had been his own.

There was a deep rumble, and the whole church shook.

"Do you hear that?" Adrian asked. "The Two Beasts are coming." The chanting grew louder. The misshapen faces smiled.

Adrian's smile turned sad. He looked at Lonnie, and there was compassion in his distended eyes. "The Great Cleansing will have to begin with the Devil's son," he said. "And we have to prepare the offering." He pulled a long, curved knife from a bag on his belt.

The crowd was wide-eyed and smiling, lost in their mosaic of words.

Another tremor passed through the church. Lonnie lay back on the table and closed his eyes. As he felt the cold sting of the knife slicing his chest, he heard the concrete cracking above the front of the church, the sound of stones raining down on the sidewalk, and the beating of giant, bat-like wings.

JOHN F.D. TAFF

Having been writing dark speculative fiction for twenty-five years, John F.D. Taff has had more than seventy stories published by *Cemetery Dance, Deathrealm, One Buck Horror* and *Big Pulp*.

Taff's work has also been featured in anthologies that include *Hot Blood: Fear the Fever, Hot Blood: Seeds of Fear, Shock Rock II, Box of Delights, Best New Vampire Tales* and *Horror for Good*. Over the years, six of his short stories have been selected as honorable mentions by Ellen Datlow in her *Year's Best Horror* anthologies.

Upcoming stories will be appearing in *Horror Library V, Edge of Sundown, Shades of Blue & Grey, Postscripts to Darkness* and Grey Matter Press' soon-to-be-released anthology *Ominous Realities*.

Taff's latest collection of short stories, *Little Deaths*, was published by Books of the Dead Press (Toronto) last year, has been fantastically well reviewed and made it to the Bram Stoker Reading List with several recommendations. His latest novel, *The Bell Witch*, was also released by Books of the Dead.

SHOW ME

BY JOHN F.D. TAFF

Steve watched Dr. Geoffrey Wranger end as an exclamation, a smoky tail erupting from a fiery point.

Wranger's screams echoed among the buildings surrounding the university's quadrangle, halting the flow of conversation among students moving between classes. He collapsed near a stone bench at the edge of the Victorian rose garden—a gift from the Class of '23. A thick, sooty line marked his path, the air above him shimmering with heat.

A charred hand clawed convulsively as students ran to provide assistance. They stepped away from the heat as much as from the hand that fell to the ground, scrabbling at the concrete.

When Wranger looked up, he did so with eyelids soldered shut over empty holes. Blood oozed from the ruin of his face. His skin looked very much like a hot dog left too long on the grill.

By the time EMTs arrived, several of the rose bushes nearest where Wranger lay dying had burst into sputtering, rose-scented flame.

"He showed...*me*," Steve heard him moan, a wisp of smoke curling from the professor's scorched mouth like an escaping soul.

As Steve turned, he saw Joe Middleton standing nearby, his hands thrust deep into his pockets.

* * *

"Burned his eyes out with a Bunsen burner," Rachel said, breathless as she squeezed in beside Steve at lunch the next afternoon.

"Cool!" Brant nodded, his long hair swaying with each bob of his head. "Who'd you hear that from?"

"Sarah," she answered, cutting her salad into increasingly smaller pieces until it resembled nothing so much as confetti scraped up after a St. Patrick's Day parade. "She was in the lab when the alarms went off. Wranger flew out of the room on fire, ran screaming down the hall."

She waved her fork between bites to punctuate certain words.

"That's not all. Wranger made a pass at Joe Middleton."

Shock silenced the table.

"Joe?" bellowed Brant. His voice echoed across the crowded cafeteria. "He hit on *Joe?*"

"Yep. A guy outside Wranger's office heard him propositioning Middleton."

"Propositioning?" Steve asked as the others talked around them. "How?"

"All the guy heard Wranger say was 'Show me.'"

Steve didn't breathe for a minute, remembering Wranger's last words.

He thought about Joe Middleton standing in the crowd that day, trying to recall the expression on his face. Something inside made him shiver so violently that he kicked one of the table legs, upsetting some drinks and bringing a few annoyed looks his way.

Joseph Middleton was a junior from somewhere in Ohio. He had the kind of looks that made everyone a little jittery to be around him; guys because they were jealous—but would never admit it— and girls because they could barely conceal their desire.

Even with his looks, though, Joe was a social dud. Shy, and something of a loner, he never really made friends, never showed up at parties or went to football games or even meetings of the chess club.

Everyone had seen him with girls at one time or another. But it seemed that most of the girls he'd dated later dropped out, moved away or just lost touch.

While Joe had been at the university for almost two years, no one really knew that much about him. Except, of course, for the gossip about his supposed sexual endowment. No one was quite sure where the rumor had come from. It couldn't be traced to a particular event or person. It seemed to have simply come along with him when he enrolled, and he weathered it as well as could be expected.

The funny thing about the stories, it was never quite clear whether Joe was really, really big; really, really small; or possessed some deformity.

* * *

"Come here," Rachel hissed, staring out the window of Steve's dorm a day or so later. She had peeled back a bit of the blinds and was looking out onto the parking lot one story below.

"What?" Steve whispered, closing the door. He'd just come back from the shower, one towel wrapped around his waist, another around his neck, a shaving kit in hand. He padded across the room, rested his chin on Rachel's cool, smooth shoulder.

"Look." She pointed outside.

Betsy, a mutual friend of theirs, was outside in the parking lot between two cars. Standing nearby was Joe Middleton.

Steve and Rachel watched in silence as Joe and Betsy talked, embraced, kissed.

Or, more properly, Betsy embraced *him*, kissed *him*.

The expressionless look on Joe's face didn't change. He may as well have been licking stamps.

A few more words were traded, and then Betsy climbed into her car, closed the door and pulled away.

Joe remained, a small, indefinite wave poised on his hand. He watched Betsy's car wind down the hill away from the dorms, then he turned and slowly walked across the quad.

"She slept with him. I know it!" Rachel said, letting the blinds snap back into place and flopping onto the bed.

"I didn't even know she *liked* him," Steve said, rummaging through a pillowcase stuffed with clean laundry and grabbing a pair of underwear. He dropped the towel to slip into them.

"Hmm?" she asked, and he realized she was staring. He blushed. "Oh! I...uhh...thought you knew."

"I don't know," he said, quickly pulling on a t-shirt. Rachel's frank look threw him for a loop.

"You dope," Rachel said, snuggling down into the bed, still giving him *that* look as he thrust his legs into jeans. "She likes him, but she's afraid of all the shit she'd take if everyone knew. Keep it quiet, okay?"

"Hey, you know me," Steve said. "*No speak a de englaze.*"

He finished lacing his sneakers and felt her gaze.

"Is something wrong?" he asked, lifting his head.

"You know, you could stay here this morning," she said, smiling. "I'd make it worth your while."

Suddenly, Rachel—the girl who'd been his friend for years, his off-and-on lover for years—embarrassed him. The look she now gave him was different, somehow deeper.

"Love to, Rach," he said, gathering his books like a shield. "But I've got a helluva exam on Milton this morning."

"Sure," she said, pulling the covers around her. "I'll be waiting. No classes today."

* * *

On his way back from the library later that afternoon, Steve saw Betsy. She was once again in the parking lot, this time carrying a huge box of stuff to her little Corolla.

"Here, let me help, Bets," Steve said, rushing over and pulling the box from her.

Her eyes were empty, hollow.

"Thanks," she said with all the emotion and inflection someone might use to read the ingredients from the back of a soup can.

Steve hefted the box into the open hatchback, noticing clothes, books, a lamp and a television already inside.

"Bets, what's going on? Are you leaving school?"

She looked at him, but there was no emotion in her face. Her gaze was so uncomfortable Steve found himself wishing she would look away.

"Yeah, it's time for me to go."

"What's wrong, Betsy?" Steve wanted to reach out to her. To embrace her. To shake her. But her cold gaze stopped him.

"I saw," she said, her voice as limp as raw fish.

"Did Joe hurt you or something?"

"No. No."

"He showed it to you? Him...*it*. His...*you know*."

Her gaze floated over the nearby parked cars, the surrounding trees and up into the sky. She nodded imperceptibly.

"Jesus, Bets! What did you see?"

She turned slowly, looked him right in the eyes and smiled. But her smile was empty, joyless. "You don't understand. I didn't see him...*that*. I saw *me*. It was me all along. So needy, so... I have to go."

She pushed past him, opened the car door and climbed in.

"Betsy, wait!" He yelled. "What was it? Tell me, goddammit!"

She put the car into gear, pulled away, the open hatchback flapping as she drove over the speed bumps.

* * *

That night, he and Rachel shared a bottle of cheap wine she'd bought. They talked about Betsy's departure from school, what she'd told Steve.

I saw me. It was me all along. So needy...

They couldn't decide what she'd meant, what Joe had done to her, showed her. But Steve noticed that their discussion had taken on an oddly elliptical tack, as if they weren't actually talking about what Steve thought they were talking about.

Ultimately, Rachel became less interested in deciphering Betsy and more interested in making out with Steve. With the wine fogging their brains, they settled onto her bed, kissed. Slowly, they removed each other's clothing, settling into the rhythm they had grown to know well.

But everything had changed, at least for Steve. He was up for sex—when wasn't he?—but this time it seemed different, filled with some potent subtext, a meaning that he seemed unable or unwilling to process.

While before her hands were urgent, demanding, they were now slow, caressing. Her kisses were still deep, but now they lingered, as if she wanted to draw into her his every breath.

When he entered her, she shuddered, breathing deeply. She released her breath in one long exhalation and kept breathing out and out, into his mouth, until Steve felt as though he was filled with her.

She was giving herself to him, he realized, breath by breath.

He found himself holding his own.

Afterward, they lay spooning in the cramped bed.

"I love you, Steve."

There was no response.

"What's wrong?" she asked.

A million things to say ran through his head at that moment, but Steve couldn't manage to get one of them out. The truth slipped out instead.

"I'm getting the feeling...you want to be more than friends," he admitted, not looking at her.

"Is there something wrong with that?"

"We tried that once, and it didn't work, Rach."

"That was a long time ago."

He still didn't meet her gaze. "I don't want to lose you as a friend."

There was a long silence. Steve heard only her breathing. He listened to it change, hitch in her chest.

"Lose a friend, gain a lover," she finally said.

"Or maybe lose a friend and lose a lover. Lose it all."

"I need to take that chance."

"I...love you, Rachel. I really do," he said, wincing at how unconvincing the words sounded as they came out of his mouth.

He cupped her head in the crook of his elbow, held her as she cried softly, fell asleep holding her.

When he woke, his arm was full of pins and needles. Thinking Rachel was still asleep, he slowly pulled it from beneath her.

She was already awake.

"I'm going to ask Joe to show me."

"You're going to...what?" Steve sputtered, raising up on one elbow. "*Why*?"

"I want to see it."

"Are you trying to make me jealous?" he yelled.

"Friends don't get jealous! *Right*?" Rachel jumped up and grabbed her clothes.

"Rach, wait," he pleaded, realizing the conversation was spinning out of control. "Something's wrong with Joe. I don't want..."

"What? You don't want me to see another guy's dick?"

Now completely dressed, she stared at him for several seconds as he searched for something to say but couldn't.

"Oh, go fuck yourself," she cursed, springing for the door and running away down the hall.

* * *

A couple weeks after their argument about Joe, Rachel's laconic roommate Sarah called Steve, concerned about Rachel's behavior. When he arrived at Rachel's dorm, Sarah met him outside their closed door.

"Steve, she's been like this for a week," Sarah explained. "I wasn't going to bother you, but she's getting worse. She won't eat or sleep. She won't even take a shower. Now she's hiding underneath her desk."

"Hiding? Why?"

"I'm not sure. But I know she had a date with Joe Middleton."

Steve felt the temperature in the hallway drop twenty degrees.

"Stay here," he told Sarah, then pushed past her into the room.

The smell hit him immediately. It was like an animal's—musky, thick and overpowering. The room was black, but the light from the hallway reflected red in her eyes. She was gaunt and shaking, huddled beneath the desk.

"Rachel? We're all...kind of worried about you."

"Worried?" Her voice was weak, like a child's. "About me?"

He crouched, steadying himself on the desk.

"Did Joe do something to you?"

"He didn't *do* anything. He showed me. *Me.* I saw...saw how much I'd been throwing away on you, how much of me I was... letting fall into a hole where nothing was ever returned. How I've become OK with that."

She was oddly detached, oddly matter-of-fact, as if having been confronted by something so simple it should have been self-evident.

"Did you see it?" Steve managed to croak, still not understanding, unable to get away from Joe and his mysterious genitalia.

Rachel laughed. It was low and rumbling and not quite right.

"Big deal," she said, giggling. "I could have seen it anytime I wanted. I was just too stupid. And I've thrown so much away... there's just not a lot of me left anymore. That's what I saw..."

"Why don't you come out now?" Steve asked, trying to coax her out from under the desk.

"No. I don't think so."

Part of him wanted to yank her out. The other part, though, seemed infected by her martyr-like culpability for some imagined shortcoming or character flaw.

Because of this, the smell in the room, and the fear gnawing at his gut, Steve did the only thing he could. He backed out of the room on his knees.

In the hallway, Sarah's face was a question mark.

He looked at her, moved his mouth but nothing came out.

Then he walked away.

* * *

The next time Steve saw Rachel she was in a casket.

Pills, likely purchased from one of the nameless shadows that lurk on campus dealing pharmaceuticals to the desperate.

Wearing a hastily found and pressed black suit, Steve stood in a long line of mourners—most of them young—who filed past the brushed pinkish-bronze casket at the front of the chapel. A gauzy material draped over the opening blurred the rigid lines on Rachel's face. A fine powder of makeup glistened on her cheeks, lending a hopeless daub of color.

Faces passed by him, full of grief and pity. Yes…pity for him. Why? Because they thought he knew Rachel best, knew her more than anyone else now packed into this hot, small, tastefully appointed room that smelled of old roses and something neutral, blank. Steve stood among them like an island, stood and realized that he didn't know her at all…had *never* really allowed himself to know her.

That realization caused something inside him to stir; some emotion that had been lurking around the edges of his consciousness for some time, pacing like a caged animal.

This was not something he wanted to confront right here, right now.

He had walked away the last time he'd seen her, crouched under her desk.

This time, he ran.

* * *

After a week or so of grieving alone, Steve pulled himself together, threw some clean clothes over his unclean body, yanked open the door and stepped outside of his dorm room for the first time since Rachel's funeral.

The semester was now over. Most of the other students had gone home for the summer. A few remained, tossing a Frisbee back and forth as he ran across the wide swath of the quad. They paid him no attention.

Walking into the adjoining dormitory, he slammed open the front door. It banged against the wall behind him. Dashing up the stairs, he heard nothing but the slap of his rubber soles on the steps and the rush of his blood in his ears.

At the end of the corridor he slid to a stop at a door marked with the name "J. Middleton."

Steve didn't knock, just threw the door open.

Joe sat still on the bed, his back straight, his hands folded in his lap.

Somehow, Steve thought, Joe didn't seem particularly surprised to see him.

Joe stood, his hands fell, met at his fly. There was the rasp of the metal teeth of his zipper, the whisper of fabric on skin. Joe wore plain, white boxers—a guy's underwear. His hand slipped beneath the waistband, pulled it away from his hips, down. He crouched a bit as he let the underwear fall to his ankles.

Surprise made Steve take a step backward.

It was...*gone. Gone...* Not that someone had cut it off or that he'd been born without one. *It just wasn't there. Never had been.*

Between Joe's legs his flesh was as smooth and unadorned as a young girl's Ken doll, just a sweep of pink plastic skin.

"What do you see?" Joe asked.

"Nothing," Steve croaked.

A combination of regret and sorrow washed over Joe's face.

"Everyone sees something different," he explained. "People see *who* they are. *What* they are. But you...you're just like me."

"You're lying," Steve panted, closing his eyes and averting his gaze from Joe's naked groin. "What the hell are you?"

Joe didn't have time to respond. With all reason gone, all sanity having slipped away, Steve lunged at the half-naked man.

In no position to brace for the attack, Joe made no effort to avoid Steve's hands.

They rolled to the floor, Steve punching him over and over. When he felt Joe's cold, naked skin, he became more enraged, fueled with even more revulsion than from the sight of Joe's featureless groin or what Joe suggested it might have meant.

One of Steve's hands felt for Joe's throat. The other hand groped above his head for something, anything. He found it. It was hard and heavy and flat in his hand.

Joe's thick chemistry text.

The sight of that book made Steve think of Dr. Wranger, his eyes gone, skin melting.

He thought of Betsy, confused and running.

He thought of Rachel, cowering under her desk, as devoid of life then as she was after she'd killed herself.

And finally, he thought of himself...what he'd seen when Joe had lowered his pants.

Nothing.

He was nothing...felt nothing.

He showed...me, Wranger had said.

Steve suddenly knew what the professor had meant; what Betsy and Rachel had meant.

But what Joe had shown him was a lie, because now he felt *anger.*

He brought the book down hard onto Joe's skull.

Again and again, he brought the edge of the textbook down on his head.

Joe's body bucked, his feet kicked. After a few minutes, the book made wet, meaty slaps as something fundamental inside Joe's skull gave way.

Steve stopped to wipe away the blood that had splashed in his eye. His hand came back red. He dropped the book, its pages quickly soaking up the spreading blood that pooled on the floor.

When Steve looked again, Joe lay sprawled on the floor, his legs spread open.

Now, a perfectly normal, perfectly average, perfectly dead penis drooped between his splayed legs.

Steve gasped, his insides growing cold. Pulling himself up, leaving bloody handprints, he staggered to the bathroom to vomit. Afterwards, he washed his hands until they hurt, lurched to the urinal to relieve himself.

His hands fished uselessly with his fly, his brain at first unwilling to accept the message his fingers were trying to convey

Hurriedly, he pushed his pants and underwear to the floor.

Bare and smooth.

But you...you're just like me.

Steve laughed. He laughed until it hurt, until he could laugh no more. Then he slumped to the ground, pressed his cheek to the floor and wept.

* * *

They make it look so hard in the movies.

The earth was loose and wet—it had not yet had time to settle, compact.

When the bronze-pink metal winked through its earthen veil, he locked his fingers under the lip of the casket's lid, pulled.

Rachel was still beautiful. The blue light from the moon highlighted her even bluer skin. Steve held her for a long time, whispered into her ear, caressed her lacquered hair. Swallowing, he stroked one shaking hand down her form, down to the hem of the plain white dress her parents had picked out for her.

She wore no pantyhose, but the mortician, in a fit of propriety, had dressed her in a pair of underwear. It was actually pretty hard, even given all his experience, to remove her panties. He trembled as his hand moved up and over the cold curve of her thighs, between her legs.

Stopping, shocked, he retraced the movements of his hand.

It was her…just her, as she'd always been.

He let her body slump gently back into her coffin, pushed himself away to lean against the grave's damp wall.

Steve was not a man who cried, but there was nothing left.

* * *

The police found him crumpled in the open grave, Rachel's half-dressed body sprawled beside him. It took him a long time to convince them that he had done nothing more to Rachel than dig her up.

He just needed to *see*.

They had, of course, already found Joe.

They locked Steve up, had him talk to a lot of doctors. But he told them nothing.

Nothing.

They told him he would be there for a long time. If not forever.

Steve had heard a lot about prisons, how the inmates treated young men like him.

He'd only been there a few days, but already he felt their eyes on him. *Show me*, their eyes said.

It won't take them long to discover that I have nothing to offer them but themselves.

I think they'll leave me alone.

CHARLES AUSTIN MUIR

If you're looking for evocative fiction with an exceptionally dark point of view, then you must be reading the work of Charles Austin Muir.

As a youth, Muir chronicled his own fan-fiction adventures of *Conan the Barbarian* and *John Carter of Mars*. Now he creates his own worlds and writes about automatons, sexual vampire orchids and otherworldly tumors.

Muir has contributed to numerous popular magazines and anthologies. His darkly introspective work has been featured in *Morpheus Tales*; *Mutation Nation: Tales of Genetic Mishaps*; *Monsters, and Madness*; *Whispers of Wickedness* and *Hell Comes to Hollywood,* a collection which was nominated for a Bram Stoker Award.

He lives in Portland, Oregon, with his wife and three pugs.

THANATOS PARK

BY CHARLES AUSTIN MUIR

I first met Nakamura in the gym beneath my apartment. Our conversations tended to run heavier than the weights we hoisted.

Prejudiced by his simian frame, I expected little more than poorly executed bench presses and tiresome discussions about college football. But he was well-versed in such disparate topics as UFOs, Alfred Hitchcock and Charles Baudelaire. He thundered his pontifications over the rusted, prehistoric machines that clanked and groaned about us to the agonizing tempos of old and middle-aged men attempting to maintain their youth.

When Nakamura discovered my living arrangements—the toilet having even less guts in it than my Honda—he offered to rent out his basement to me for an embarrassingly low price.

I accepted.

My own neighborhood was dreadful enough, but a few miles south—down Nakamura's way—spread the eeriest exhibition of urban decline I had yet seen. While the buildings met a banal expectation of inner city decay, a furtive energy buzzed through the deserted streets, subtly agitated by our cars as I followed Nakamura to my new home. It was as though we drove through a slum burial ground where the souls of its residents watched greedily from the blasted tenements, trash-choked alleys and gutted vehicles all around us. Like blackened signposts, the passing scenery receded in my rearview mirror. My unease persisted even as we turned onto Nakamura's tree-lined side street.

At first I attributed this fanciful impression to my tendency to escape into metaphysics whenever I encountered new levels of poverty as I found myself moving further and further from the suburbs and the cozy bungalow I once kept. But my anxiety wasn't unfounded, as Nakamura told me the district was a condemned stretch of housing known as "The Crawl."

The nickname referred to the manner in which people were typically seen leaving—mostly drug addicts and gunshot victims who dragged themselves into some alley or field to die. Children didn't play in The Crawl, and no one went there after dark if they had any sense. Except for the automobile Nakamura heard cruising the streets after midnight, as smooth and business-like as a hearse.

Despite our proximity to the place, I quickly warmed to my new surroundings. The rent was cheap, and Nakamura was decent company. His rugged presence made me feel, at least, less unsafe. The plumbing alone had been incentive enough for me to relocate.

His street was quiet and fairly well-kept, his neighbors stony and withdrawn. This allowed me to review my lesson plans and grade papers with little distraction, save Nakamura's television droning through the ceiling on the days he had off from his job as a night watchman. It was on such an occasion that he showed me Thanatos Park.

* * *

That night, Nakamura had a lingering head cold that he blamed on hay fever made worse by the cheap beer he drank. I was, as they say, "in recovery." To ease his distrust of my abstinence I shared with him my dreary tale of visiting once too often at what Poe referred to as "the palace of the fiend, Gin." I even came clean about my affair with a student.

Her apartment had been similar to Nakamura's house in its disapproval of unadorned or unused space. When the affair became public, I moved in with her, though I soon grew to abhor her obsession with clutter. It wasn't filthy, but rather too busy. It was as though, through the floor-to-ceiling photo collages and heaped clothes and magazines, she sought to wall up an insect-like world buzzing beyond the visible, behind the empty space.

Nakamura's own clutter was of a different order. He was obsessed with debris. He had turned his living space into an art exhibit, a collection of artifacts recovered from The Crawl. Broken television sets. Bicycle fenders. Rebar. Most of these elements he had converted into storage or decorative use.

"I felt like a zombie," I said, wrapping up my confession. "Dragging myself through these motions to satisfy a hunger. Like I was animated by this want alone. All my strength gathered around the need to be drunk and fondled by a woman half my age. It was the gym that saved me. Reactivating my body, putting it through more constructive motions."

"Motions," Nakamura said through his blocked nasal passages. He slurped his beer. "You go through the motions at a gym because someone tells you it's good for your body. You go through the motions of teaching because someone tells you it's necessary to promote greater awareness of the world around us. Motions... Nightly, I make the rounds of an industrial complex because someone tells me it's vital for our technological future. We're the instruments of institutions, Bane, acting only to ensure their survival. I keep these things..." he said, sweeping his arm around the living room, "...to remind myself of that every day. All these leftovers of *motions*, programmed human activity, the bread crumbs scattered by zombies crawling toward their death." He belched.

"That's a neat metaphor," I said, "if somewhat mixed. Are you planning to use it in one of your stories?" Nakamura had been published in some small magazines that he refused to show me.

He looked at me then with dead eyes—eyes like tinted glass.

"I'll show you something," he said.

We shrugged on our coats and headed into the street. His thick-set shape, hulking in an oversized flannel, outpaced me as he guided us through a maze of traffic islands, side streets and plots of dead grass. In the shadows I spied the outlines of bent signposts and over-turned swing sets. The night air tasted metallic.

With a pang of trepidation I looked back the way we had come, knowing I could not have found my way home. I was completely dependent on Nakamura. I assumed a false sense of bravado as I trailed him, imagining us as urban explorers testing our wits against a notorious death trap. Because after what he had said about it, and what I had sensed about it from my car, we were returning to The Crawl after dark—on foot.

We came to another field, larger than those before. The grass was nearly knee-high, and I cringed at what I might disturb with each step. Vacant buildings bordered us on all sides, the plywood mouth-pieces of condemned housing projects grinning in the streetlight. At the far end, Nakamura came to a telephone pole and stopped.

"I call this place 'Thanatos Park,'" he said, indicating our sur-roundings with a tilt of his beer can. "I used to cut across here when I worked at another site. This was before the area became known as The Crawl. At the time, a few folks still lived here. Anyway, this is where I found the body." He tilted his beer can again, pointing up-wards.

"On the telephone pole?"

"Yep. Boy in his teens, I'd guess. He'd climbed a third of the way up. He wasn't moving. I kept calling to him. I wondered how he held onto the pole like that. He either had incredibly strong legs or he was wearing something like lineman's shoes.

"I had a bad feeling, like I'd come upon something I wasn't sup-posed to. It was getting dark. No one was around. I didn't know what to do. Finally, I called the cops. It seemed like I waited forever, watching that boy's gangly body hugging the pole. With his com-plexion, filthy sweatshirt and dark jeans he was wearing he was almost invisible, blending in with the pole."

I looked up at the pole, conjuring up my own version of what Nakamura had seen.

"Then he moved," he said, "sort of shivered. I heard loose change clinking around in his pockets. Then—and I saw this as sure as I see you right now—something burst through his sweatshirt and out the back of his head."

The look on my face must have betrayed my skepticism.

"I swear it, Bane," Nakamura said. "Stalks grew out of his skull and all the way down his spine. They were about three feet long. At the end of each stalk were these scaly globes. They looked a bit like spores."

"Spores?"

He nodded.

"I thought about sticking around, but I couldn't imagine what the cops would think. I couldn't afford to be implicated in whatever the hell was going on. Plus I was late for work. I started to walk away, but then I heard cars coming and ran behind a dumpster. A column of black SUV's pulled up to the telephone pole and a bunch of guys got out wearing dark suits and—" He frowned. "Masks."

"Masks? What kind of masks?"

"Like...Halloween masks. Mummy masks, maybe. Or a very old man. God, I wished I could have gotten it on video. But all I could do was watch. They covered the area in stealth mode, talking to each other with hand gestures, like a commando unit. I'm amazed they didn't catch me. Then they took the body down."

I was hanging on every word. "And?"

"I got a glimpse of the kid's face in the streetlight. He had these mandibles. Like teeth growing out of teeth. That's the truth," he insisted.

"Well, go on," I prompted him.

Standing in the field on the dead-end street, walled in by crumbling tenements, I found myself beginning to accept Nakamura's surreal story.

Shadows scored his cheeks in the streetlight, making him look old and tired. He crumpled his beer can but didn't toss it.

"My dad told me a similar story about something that happened to him as a teenager," he explained. "I'd forgotten about it until that night. He'd worked as a mortician's assistant in a hellhole much like this. Sometime after midnight, this gang member buzzes the door. Dad answers it. The guy drags in a body. He's says it's his grandfather. It has the same stalks growing out of its head and back. The same mandibles. Bits of wood sticking in its teeth. Dad said he'd never seen anything like it, so he calls the police. Only, instead of the police, a dozen strange guys show up. They were wearing dark suits and the same old-man masks."

"What about the gangbanger?"

"Took off. As soon as dad got on the phone. Even left his car behind. Anyway, one of the men tells dad to leave the premises and stay away 'til the next day. He doesn't question him, but when he comes back the next morning the body's gone."

"And you say this happened how long ago?"

"Years and years. But listen... Last week it hit me—what connects the two incidents. I was reading about this fungus that preys on carpenter ants. They live in a forest way up in the trees. The fungus takes over their brains and makes them crawl down close to the bottom. The infected ant clamps its mandibles into a leaf," Nakamura clawed his fist, "and dies. But the fungus continues to grow. It bursts out of the dead ant and releases spores onto the ground that infect other ants. It's wiped out whole colonies."

"And you think this fungus has found its way—?" I hesitated, looking up at the telephone pole again. I knew how absurd it sounded. "You think it can infect human hosts?"

"I think *the government* has developed a way to imitate the fungus," Nakamura growled, breathing beer in my face. "It's the ultimate mind control—getting the host to destroy itself while continuing to serve the parasite. And what is the government, if not a parasite?" He asked, conspiratorially. "Imagine you had the power to send zombie soldiers into the field to turn the enemy into zombie slaves. Or infect a civilian population..."

This unwelcome thought was cut short by a scream from one of the tenements.

Moments later, someone ran out of the gangway between the buildings. He or she—it was hard to tell through the baggy clothing and the hand clutching at their face—dashed blindly through the field, vanishing down a side street.

Nakamura looked at me with wide eyes, chucked the beer can and rushed across the street into the darkness of the gangway. Ferns brushed me as I hurried after him.

Likely it was due to Nakamura's tale, but I felt as though I were floating in the dark toward unseen jaws. *Mandibles?* I thought of giant ants clinging to the exterior walls of the buildings around us, frozen in a fungus-driven death grip.

A flashlight beam swung into my eyes. It revealed a hole through which the screamer had exited the building, the middle boards broken off. Dust motes swirled about Nakamura's sweaty moon face.

"Hurry. I think I heard something," he said before disappearing into the building with the flashlight.

His footfalls receded.

My breathing pounded in my ears. My heart hammered in my chest.

Motion.

I had to stay in motion.

It must have been my sense of bravado kicking in again, but an adolescent thrill, a delirious sense of mischief, coursed through me as I ducked past the remaining boards and stumbled into the building. It felt like the night had exploded into some fantastic swashbuckling adventure. Then, breathing in the choking dust and straightening to full height, I peered into the shadows and recovered at least a partial sense of sanity. We were not rogues who had stumbled upon some supernatural terror, I realized, but fools breaking every law of self-preservation.

I batted at cobwebs and things stirring within the cobwebs. Cement dust rasped beneath my feet. It was chilly and smelled of rotted wood. I sneezed several times. Overlapping each sneeze, it seemed, was the whisper of something dragging itself along the floor somewhere above. In the darkness, I kicked something aside— it might have been a dead cat—and headed for a landing whose outline I could see in the lesser gloom next to a window in which night hung like smoke.

From the landing, I heard Nakamura shouting. There was a crash. It was followed by a scream. I raced up the last set of stairs and saw his beam of light playing across the ceiling at the end of a long corridor. But there was no Nakamura.

"Don't come any closer," he said, from somewhere below.

The floor had collapsed.

Eight feet beneath me, Nakamura lay propped on his elbows in a pile of plaster bits and smashed wood. The flashlight beam lanced through the haze of dust his impact had kicked up. Caked with the powdery substance, he looked like a macabre street performer made up to resemble some industrial ghost.

It was then that cold logic washed away the last of my assumed bravado. Even if nothing hostile lay in wait for us, the building itself seemed dangerous enough.

Still, despite the alarms sounding in my head, I said, "I thought I heard something."

He sniffed. "What?"

"Are you okay?"

"I'm fine." He kicked one foot up from the debris as if to prove his intactness. "What did it sound like?"

"I'm not sure."

"Take this." The flashlight sailed up toward me. On the third try its weight, warm with Nakamura's heat, sank into my palm.

"You have to go see what it is," Nakamura said.

"But it might be nothing."

"And it might be *everything*."

I opened my mouth, but his look froze my words.

I went.

I felt like a child leaving his parents' side. The darkness swallowed all but the flashlight's beam, pressing against me like a hundred layers of musty clothes. I moved cautiously, testing my weight with each step.

The tenement seemed like its own dark universe then, without stars or sound, other than my own breathing and Nakamura's coughing fading behind me. At the landing, I turned and mounted the stairs to the third floor, moving toward a higher window. The lesser darkness upstairs revealed the paleness of skies toxic with city light. Toward that light I climbed, my hand tracking the rail, around another turn, up another flight and onto level floor. The flashlight picked out doorknobs on both sides of a long hallway. Tiptoeing along, I saw a door ajar.

I crouched low and entered. I was in a living room. The window had been boarded up from the inside, but a section appeared to be missing or had never been completed. Night smells drifted in through a hole in the broken glass, dark odors of gasoline and things burning. I played my light over the outlines of furniture—an ancient Barcalounger, a TV tray, a bookshelf. The belongings of some long-deceased shut-in, I supposed. The detritus of successive occupants—beer bottles, hamburger wrappings, soiled garments—littered the floor.

From the next room I heard a succession of taps.

Fearing unseen assailants, I duck-walked through the doorway.

I had never known how silent a kitchen could be without even a refrigerator's ever-present hum. Still crouched on my heels, I worked my way past the table, avoiding rat droppings. I don't know why I was crouching; the flashlight would give me away. But I couldn't bring myself to face the dark unaided—until my light gave out.

My breathing pounded in my ears. For a moment I lived only in its jagged rhythm and the limitless space of the darkness. Then, like a voice insinuating itself into a dream, I heard a rustling. It grew louder.

Then the tapping again.

Like the tortured souls for which the vicinity was named, I crawled toward the doorway into the hall. Three strides later—which I measured on hands and knees—I found myself at the threshold of a small bedroom. I made it out by the dim light streaming through a window somewhere out of view.

Finding the nerve to climb to my feet, I inched my head around the doorjamb. Inside were two windows, separated by an oddly shaped mullion. Milky streetlight sheeted their spider-cracked panes.

I rammed the heel of my hand into the butt of the flashlight, hoping to jog it into functioning. No luck. But as my vision adjusted, I began to comprehend what I was staring at.

Obscuring most of the mullion was a silhouette. A human shape. It clung to the dividing structure and to the glass on either side like a gecko freeze-framed on a wall. Its arms and legs splayed, face inward. It, or I should say he, as the body had a thin but masculine build, wore denim jeans and a flannel shirt. One shoelace was undone.

Then I heard a noise like the groan of a tree branch bending to its breaking point. And that is what the growths resembled. Branches. Silhouetted in the cloudy light, three antenna-like extensions sprouted from the figure's spine.

I stood motionless.

As a child I had once accidentally slammed the car door on my aunt's thumb and stared stupidly at the white digit protruding from the door seam. So I gaped now, uncomprehending.

Only the scream roused me to action.

I scrambled out of the room, banging my knee against the kitchen table, upsetting the TV tray, tripping over a ragged nap in the living room carpet. Guided by Nakamura's hoarse cries, I pelted down the corridor, the stairs, then along the second-floor corridor to the hole through which he was now cursing.

"Nothing," he snapped, as I shouted for a status report, "just a rat. You'd think I'd be used to them. What happened? Did you find anything?"

"No," I lied.

Nakamura grunted, disentangling himself from the mound of debris.

I tried the flashlight again, more out of a compulsion to keep my hands busy than the hope that it would magically recharge. But it lit, as conveniently as any light device in any thriller I'd ever read. I raised it in warning and dropped it through the hole into his waiting hands.

If Nakamura had suspected I was lying he didn't show it. Moving onto more pressing matters, he arranged that we would shout to each other at ten second intervals traveling in the direction of our access point in as parallel a fashion as possible, given the building's straightforward layout. Compared to my third-floor adventure, our escape was anticlimactic.

As I felt my way down the corridor, I tensed for the sound of a tree branch cracking. It resounded in my mind all too clearly, along with the rustling that I had heard. That noise, like a malignant whisper, had conjured an image of something on its belly dragging itself across the floor in pained, concentrated movements.

Not something, but someone.

* * *

Now and then an event looms too large for summary, for interpretation. Mundane or extraordinary, it defeats the mind's search to unravel it back to a starting point. Such was my experience on the tenement's third floor. I couldn't stop thinking about it, yet I found myself incapable of speaking of it. My inability to articulate it developed into avoidance, my increasing dread into a form of denial by imperceptible degrees, until I realized I had built a wall of silence so palpably dense around the subject that I could no longer tear it down, even had I wished to do so.

Besides that, Nakamura had immersed himself in his own private world. He seemed to have resigned himself to a condition of suffering that was, at its core, as quiet as his bodily noises were loud. Through the floor that separated us, his sneezes sounded like gunshots, his coughing fits like some blind-drunk youth puking his guts out.

Glancing at the ceiling, listening to his muffled curses from the room above, I felt stifled and helpless, reminded of how relations between us had changed since our foray into the abandoned building. He had grown incommunicative and stony like his neighbors, while I, for my part, avoided him like a sulking adolescent. This was not out of aversion, but instead because I disliked the warring impulses I felt in his presence. Inside, I struggled between confessing to him what I thought I had seen and rejecting it as a confused impression influenced by his story.

The general effect of our mutual reticence was a gradual estrangement that neither of us alluded to in our few encounters. Familiar with solitude, we adapted easily to our spheres of aloneness, as contiguous as they were in Nakamura's cramped, oppressive house.

Adding to the isolation was the change in his daily habits. He began to miss work. And he quit the gym. I would hear his weights clanging upstairs, punctuated at intervals by convulsive fits of sneezing and coughing. He exercised at odd hours of the night, so that I slept uneasily. I dreamed often of tree limbs snapping and unseen sufferers screaming. Sometimes the quiet would wake me as well. Keen and concentrated, I could feel him lying awake among the shadows of his discarded furnishings, preparing himself for the sneak attack on his computer where, when an idea struck, he would pound on the keys until morning.

We still met occasionally for drinks—him a beer, soda for me. I would sit in his salvaged armchair, a loaded barbell racked in uprights staring me in the face. Perhaps we were less like estranged friends than brothers well adjusted to coexisting in close quarters.

We settled into conversation easily, even as it became clear that whatever had happened to us in the tenement had widened the divergence in our thinking.

Nakamura's devotion to conspiracy theories grew more idiosyncratic and intense. While my discomfort degraded into a snobbish, calculating pretense of interest only to see how foolish he could sound if I let him expound his ideas long enough.

As for the secret I carried away from that tenement room, I dismissed whatever suspicions or insights his ranting might have stirred in me. This became easier as Nakamura too had distanced himself from that night, alluding to it only in his occasional groan of protest at the aches and pains produced by his fall.

Toward the end though, we abandoned all communication. The sleeplessness caused by his erratic behavior was beginning to wear on me. And worse, I would come home from school to find my belongings subtly rearranged. He seemed especially interested in my students' papers. I didn't confront him about it. I saw a time-bomb look in his eyes and a new economy in his movements. It was as though he were conserving energy for some ultimate expenditure of the strength he had built up with his weights.

In our final conversation he discoursed at length on the men in dark suits and old-man masks, alleging they were the ones we sometimes heard at night, cruising quietly and slowly through The Crawl. Their rounds, he claimed, were part of a surveillance detail focused on his activities.

* * *

I was grading exams one night when I thought I heard a door slam above me. This was followed by three closely spaced thuds that induced a sour feeling in my stomach. I had heard those sounds before, when one of my students had fainted in class. Flashing on the incident, and realizing there was no door upstairs from where the noises had come, I rose from my desk and began pacing, tracking the rhythm and course of new movement above me. It was identical to what I had heard upon breaking into the tenement—the sound of a body dragging itself across the floor.

With a stab in my chest, I realized that Nakamura had likely delivered on the expenditure of strength for which he'd been training—the slightest contraction of his forefinger on the trigger of his gun.

As I mounted the steps to his kitchen, an almost superstitious panic seized me. It was as though, beyond that peeling, red-painted door at the head of the stairs, I knew I would not find my friend, but a nightmarish creature. A thing that had once been a man crawling on its belly, its life draining second by second, split open by horrible stalks…

My hand trembled upon the knob.

Then came another noise—another shot. Not a shot, I realized, but the front door being kicked open. The clatter of heavy shoes thundered across the living room floor, martial and business-like. And, like Nakamura in his account of what he had seen on the pole in Thanatos Park, I froze in my hiding spot, listening to the intruders.

Their operation was swift and efficient. Without a word the body was wheeled out, furniture straightened, mops poking and scraping in the area where I had heard Nakamura's gunshot. All the while I stood at the top of the stairs, immobile, my neck itching with sweat, cowardly.

What could I have done? What might have been done to me had I revealed myself?

My heart slammed in my chest each time the trespassers entered the kitchen. I had only the pencil clutched in my fingers to wield against them should they discover me. But at last their footsteps ceased, and I heard what sounded like a block-long caravan of vehicles start their engines and drive away.

A quick look through Nakamura's house showed no signs of

any recent activity. The living room contained only the faintest whiff of cleaning products.

I thought to fetch my phone, but how do you report a suicide when there is no body? Again, like Nakamura, perhaps even influenced by his story, I feared I might be implicated in what I had witnessed. I then lowered myself to a new level of cowardice. I stuffed my belongings into my duffel bag and suitcase and, relying on the taciturn neighbors, walked out the front door for the last time.

I blended in, surely, with my hood pulled up and a brown bag in my free hand, bulging with a bottle of Nakamura's cheap beer.

* * *

The events in the tenement and in Nakamura's house still haunt me like an embarrassing nightmare. Whenever I think of them I feel as I did as a child in my parents' bed, crying over a dream where Martians abducted my kindergarten teacher, flushed with guilt and shame for having dreamt it. Of course, I need only think of the gunshot—or the unopened bottle of antidepressants I found in his medicine cabinet before his death—to remind myself that I was not the author of Nakamura's pathetic end.

Still, I now kill these thoughts and the dreams that come with them with frequent visits to the palace of the fiend, Gin. Because when I try to reconcile what I believed I saw in that tenement room with what I heard through the ceiling the night Nakamura took his life, I want to cut myself. I want to hack off the invisible tissue that binds me like a victim to my thoughts, giving me maddening, hateful visions.

Nakamura believed the government was conducting biological experiments in low-income areas. In The Crawl, no one would notice people dying like brainwashed ants. He saw the government itself as a fungus, controlling our bodies, our minds, forcing us to crawl through every aspect of our lives toward final, mandated death. Nakamura died convinced that it had discovered a way to manufacture a synthetic, human-targeted version of the fungus; that the New World Order was to emerge from the chemically-driven industrialization of zombies.

In one of our last conversations, I decided to test him. Playing devil's advocate, I asked him: What if the government isn't covering up its own hideous experiments but is instead trying to *contain* the spread of the fungus? What if there is a deeper malignancy at work? What if we're all puppets—or zombies, as he put it—our every action the manipulation of a cosmic fungus god who decides the fate of every living thing, directing our life paths toward our final destination, that being the underside of a leaf where we dig our teeth in and die?

Nakamura chuckled. He discounted this image as a fiction of people who would rather romanticize their suffering than escape from it. He argued that it was easier for people to blame their woes on an all-encompassing, unconquerable menace than to give the evils of the world a face like their own.

I had only wanted to rattle his dogmatic chains. But, judging by his glazed eyes and hollow tone, I could tell I had committed a grave error. It wasn't my idea of an "all-encompassing, unconquerable menace" he objected to, but my heresy in suggesting the government was not our greatest threat.

From then on, he rarely took me in his confidence. It was only when his anxieties reached a fevered pitch that he entertained my company.

In truth, I wasn't sure how much I believed of what I had said to him. But I was, and am, convinced that what I had seen in the tenement hinted at forces vastly darker than what I believed any human agency could devise.

As I said before, whenever I encounter a new level of poverty I tend to escape into metaphysics. It's no different today. I now live in a squalid apartment not far from Nakamura's house. I'm like the ant making its way down the tree, traveling through a route of desolate places toward the bottom of my life. Of course, I don't deny my part in the events that have hastened my journey; but after my experiences with Nakamura, I wonder.

As I gaze out my window at the boarded-up tenements, vacant storefronts and sidewalks sparkling with shattered glass, I wonder if, no matter where you are or how you live, you are always, in your heart, crawling toward Thanatos Park.

Declarations of Copyright

MORE FROM
GREY MATTER PRESS

greymatterpress.com

A COLLECTION OF MODERN HORROR

DARK
VISIONS 2

VOLUME TWO

EDITED BY
ANTHONY RIVERA AND SHARON LAWSON

DARK VISIONS
A Collection of Modern Horror - Volume Two

Dark Visions: A Collection of Modern Horror - Volume Two begins where the collection you have just read ends. *Dark Visions - Volume Two* continues the terrifying psychological journey with an all-new selection of exceptional tales of darkness written by some of the most talented authors working in the fields of horror, speculative fiction and fantasy today.

Unable to contain all the visions of dread and mayhem to a single volume, *Dark Visions - Volume Two* will be available from your favorite booksellers in the FALL of 2013 in both paperback and digital formats.

Prepare to continue the ride with *Dark Visions: A Collection of Modern Horror - Volume Two*...

FEATURING:

David Blixt

John C. Foster

JC Hemphill

Jane Brooks

Peter Whitley

Edward Morris

Trent Zelazny

Carol Holland March

David Murphy

Chad McKee

C.M. Saunders

J. Daniel Stone

David Siddall

Rhesa Sealy

Kenneth Whitfield

A.A. Garrison

DARKVISIONSANTHOLOGY.com

GREY MATTER PRESS

greymatterpress.com

SPLATTER

REAWAKENING THE SPLATTERPUNK REVOLUTION

LANDS

COLLECTED AND EDITED BY

ANTHONY RIVERA and SHARON LAWSON

SPLATTERLANDS
Reawakening the Splatterpunk Revolution

Almost three decades ago, a literary movement forever changed the landscape of the horror entertainment industry. Grey Matter Press breathes new life into that revolution as we reawaken the true essence of Splatterpunk with the release of *Splatterlands*.

Splatterlands: Reawakening the Splatterpunk Revolution is a collection of personal, intelligent and subversive horror with a point. This illustrated volume of dark fiction honors the truly revolutionary efforts of some of the most brilliant writers of all time with an all-new collection of visceral, disturbing and thought-provoking work from a diverse group of modern minds.

Exploring concepts that include serial murder, betrayal, religious fanaticism, physical abuse, societal corruption, greed, mental instability, sexual assault and more, *Splatterlands* delivers on the promise of the original Splatterpunk movement with this collection of honest, intelligent and hyper-intensive horror.

FEATURING:

Ray Garton	Michele Garber
Michael Laimo	A.A. Garrison
Paul M. Collrin	Jack Maddox
Eric Del Carlo	Allen Griffin
James S. Dorr	Christine Morgan
Gregory L. Norris	Chad Stroup

J. Michael Major

Illustrations by Carrion House

SPLATTERLANDS.com

GREY MATTER PRESS

greymatterpress.com

Made in the USA
Middletown, DE
06 June 2016